# post civ

## books by Julianne Harvey

*Jamesy Harper's Big Break*

*Winter to Spring: Thoughts on Pain and Transformation*

*It's On You: Taking Responsibility for Your Choices*

*Authentic = Happy: A Guide to Dismantling Your Disguise*

*B The Wonder Bear*

# post civ

## Julianne Harvey

Ruby
Finch
BOOKS
intuitive courage

Cover design by Dani Compton
Cover images by Justin Schultz
Book design by Gage Rodelander
eBook design by Jan Westendorp/katodesignandphoto.ca
Author photo by William Harvey

Epigraph quote by Anthony Oliveira reprinted by permission.

Published by Ruby Finch Books, Vancouver, BC, Canada

www.rubyfinchbooks.com

ISBNs 978-0-9877978-4-1 (paperback)
and 978-0-9877978-5-8 (eBook)

*For Ava and William,*
*the future is yours*

*What is power? A beautiful flower, whose earth is soaked in blood.*
*- Anthony Oliveira*

**Content Warning:** Climate Crisis, Tsunami, Death, Racism, Misogyny, Xenophobia, Injuries, Weapons, Murder, Grief, Depression, Disassociation, Emotional Trauma

**Discussed but not Shown:** Civil War, Physical Violence, Sexual Assault, Tornado, Domestic Abuse, Suicide, Forest Fires, Pandemics, Drought, Protests

# one

## MIN

Min thought she could see the outline of trees in the distance, swaying in the coastal breeze, but she knew that was impossible. Only her mind playing tricks on her. She had stopped eating three or four days ago, and Min couldn't remember the last time she drank from her rusty rain bucket. She still had canned food, and some water from the last storm, but she simply could not be bothered anymore. Somewhere in her logical scientist brain, Min realized she could be hallucinating. Was this how Chul had felt when he died in the freezing cold? Did he imagine something like healthy green trees, deep in his memory, and see them as real?

Water sloshed onto the damaged wood of the raft, sounding like knocks against the rubber tires underneath her. She lay on her back, under the torn blue tarp, watching the fraying yellow rope sway with the ocean current. The sun was so hot. There was so much water, and nothing else to look at. When Min closed her eyes, she could pretend she wasn't alone. Or marooned. Daeshim was here, his body solid against hers, smelling like the spicy aftershave he splashed onto his face after a shower. She could almost feel his long fingers entwined in her black hair. His voice, reminding her, "It will be okay. We'll make it through this."

But they hadn't made it through. Dae had done everything

right, gowning and masking and following every medical protocol to treat his patients, and he still died in one of the endless pandemic waves. Min used to sleep in Dae's scrubs, refusing to wash them, until eventually his scent disappeared. Chul had tried to help Min through that disorienting time, saying, "Dad would want us to be safe. We have to keep moving." At fourteen, Chul was an unstoppable force. Taller than Min, and so much braver. He convinced her that the long prairie drought meant no crops, and with winter coming that equalled no food. Min was the climate specialist, and she should've made those decisions, but with Daeshim gone she had been paralyzed in place. Chul had found them rides out of Regina while there was still gas to be scrounged. But when the power grid went down in western Alberta and it got so cold so fast, one morning Chul didn't wake up.

Min's throat was bone dry. Swallowing took concentration. She turned her head, opening her eyes to see her metal pail with enough rainwater to have a drink, but she was ready to let go. Turning on her side, Min ran her hand over the rough planks of wood. The kind family who had brought her to the coast had built this raft. It was designed to save them all, but one by one Min lost them too. Images of the destruction from the last year ran through her mind: Calgary's downtown buildings flattened like cardboard in the super tornado; police stations ablaze in every big city, the cops hung or decapitated; all those goddamn clean-cut Men of God on Legislative Building steps in tailored three-piece suits hoisting assault rifles, the maple leaf flag in tatters under their shiny black lace-up shoes; Min's favourite coffee shop shuttered because Enderpal and Roman were gay, the notice nailed to the door citing a breach of True Canadian Values; and the day the internet went dark, and there was no way to collaborate in order to fight back. Everyone said if they could just make it across the western provinces to Vancouver, they could survive. There would be water, something those on the prairies could only imagine. Water meant the possibility of healthy trees, shelter from the punishing heat, and fish to eat.

For Chul, water meant life. He talked about it constantly. But now Min was alone, surrounded by nothing but water, and couldn't even recall why they once believed water would save them. Now she dreamed of land. And being cold instead of sweating. Wearing flannel pajamas, feeling a blanket up against your face. The comfort implied in being safe, in knowing you could keep your loved ones alive and with you.

Min's eyes closed again. Dae was here, and Chul. Not fourteen, but four, with his sticky hand warm in hers. A grin on his chubby face. He waited at the front window for her to come home from yet another lecture at the university, warning of a disaster that no one cared about. The audience didn't believe it would ever matter that the temperature of the planet was rising. The alarm bells had been ringing for decades, and no one had listened. Min and her climate colleagues had wasted their careers. It all came true, yet somehow, she was the only one left, alone on this rickety homemade raft. Still trying to survive.

"Min." Daeshim's voice was loud in her ear. She blinked, seeing her careful, dwindling supplies lined up against the wooden lip of the raft, coloured with a blue tint from the flapping tarp above. "You made it."

She shook her head, pushing up to a sitting position. Min rose and fell on the waves. She raised her hand to shield her eyes. The sun lit the space in front of her like a stage. After days, weeks, maybe even a month of ocean: sun, rain, day then night, with nothing else but solitude and aimless drifting, now Min saw a beach. Stones, logs, dark wet sand, seaweed green and tangled. Trees—tall, dignified, standing like soldiers with leafy green branches. So many trees that Min laughed out loud, then clapped her hand over her mouth as though she might be scolded for making too much noise. She was shaking, trembling in spite of the heat, at the sight before her. Trees, all around the beach and leading up into the air, reminding her of a child's picture book. Such green, the colour of hope, breaking up the endless blue of the waves. Min could not remember the last time she saw a forest that wasn't decimated by fire, people, or pestilence. She had to be dreaming.

Min smiled at Dae, who sat next to Chul on the raft. They both nodded at her, as if to say, "You're on the right track. You can do this."

She knew it would disappear, like the mirage it had to be, but just in case, Min untied the battered oar and started rowing toward the promise of land.

# two

---

## IRIS

When Iris saw what looked like a beach bonfire, she experienced a sense of shock in her nervous system, as though she'd been plugged in to an electrical outlet. She sniffed the air, her head tilted back in the inky darkness, trying to figure out how fire could be feasible in the middle of the Pacific Ocean. Mingling with the ever-present tangy brine of saltwater, Iris swore she could smell a hint of smoke.

She was on the deck of her client's boat, drinking his fine scotch, when she glimpsed flames in the distance, smoke curling up toward the clouds. It had rained most of the day, so Iris had stayed below deck, reading a battered historical novel on the brown leather sofa. When the sky cleared, she came out for some fresh air. Iris believed in certainty. Now, she was only interested in what she could count on. Everything else was a fool's errand.

Sipping the alcohol, enjoying the burn in her throat, Iris closed her eyes. She visualized the useless motor below her, unable to function without gas. Iris summoned her dead client in her mind, strolling around her minimalist office like he owned the place, pontificating about how much he loved this boat and how guilty he felt about its exorbitant price tag in the uncertain economic times they lived in. As a therapist, Iris liked some clients and hated others. Gregory Stone fell into the latter category. When all flood preparations failed in Vancouver, the icy water washing away whole city streets in a heartbeat, Iris felt grateful that good ol' Greg had spent so many sessions talking about his beloved pleasure craft boat. She knew where he moored it and where he kept his spare keys, and it was the only reason she was alive now when so many were not.

She opened her eyes. The flames were closer now, moving up and down with the rhythmic motion of the waves. Her breathing became ragged. Iris ran a hand through her hair. "I am calm, I am safe, I am here," she said out loud. "No one can hurt me." Her boat inched closer to the fire, which appeared to be on land. She hadn't seen land in so long. In the distance, by the dancing firelight, Iris could make out the form of a person. Standing still. Not shifting constantly like Iris was doing on the water. She finished her drink and placed the cut glass tumbler in a cupholder.

She ran down the four stairs to the cabin below, opening the cabinet by her bed to retrieve her handgun. Holding it gave her instant courage. Iris walked back up the stairs and to the edge of the boat deck. Oh my God, she had come upon land. Actual, real, not-in-her-imagination rocks, trees, dirt. How was this not underwater like everything else on the West Coast?

And there was a person. Iris peered as hard as she could, but couldn't see more than a vague outline in the dark.

"Hello!" Iris called, her voice cracking in fear. She gripped the gun by her side. "Is someone there?"

The figure rushed from the fire into the water. Arms waved above their head. "Yes! I'm here!" Iris gasped. Her knees turned to water at the voice. It was feminine.

She made sure the safety was on, then tucked the gun into the waistband of her shorts. Iris dropped the anchor, then climbed down the rear ladder and waded closer to the woman in the water, backlit by the fire behind her on the beach. She was Asian, middle-aged, rail thin.

Iris followed the woman onto the pebbly sand. For a moment, Iris swayed back and forth, unable to move. Her head felt strange, like she might be drunk. It was difficult to focus her eyes.

"Take your time," the woman said, approaching Iris with caution. "I felt like I was still moving for ages when I got here. It's disorienting." She smiled, and in the dim light Iris could see she was late forties or early fifties, about a decade older than Iris. But this woman looked kind and non-threatening, which was really what mattered to Iris.

"I'm Min," the woman said, sticking out her hand to shake. Iris reached out, without even thinking about it, and felt the warmth of Min's hand in hers.

"Iris." Her name sounded strange in her ears, after being unused for so long. Min was the first to pull her hand away, gesturing toward the fire. Iris's steps were unsteady, but the process of moving with earth under her feet felt luxurious. Both women approached the flames. Iris felt fear rise up through her body. She had thought she would never experience fire again.

Min sat down on a scratchy log, with a raggedy blanket stretched over it. "You have a beautiful boat. Better than what I had to travel in, that's for sure." She pointed to a rudimentary wooden raft pulled up on the shore, tied to a nearby tree.

Iris couldn't fathom the treacherous journey she'd just made in something so open to the elements. She looked at Min with newfound respect. "You are brave."

Min stared into the flames. "I don't know about that."

She wanted to ask how long Min had been here, and if she were alone, but all of a sudden, with no warning,

Iris was back in her house. She felt the cold knife against her throat, smelled the man's rancid garlicky breath as he forced his rough whiskers against her face, heard the angry voices calling her a rich whore. Iris had tried so hard to forget how rigid her body went. How tightly she was held down, forced to watch as they ripped her Monet from the living room wall and pissed on the lilac flowers. She could smell the white leather sofa burning. The flames flickered, the smoke rose into the air and Iris couldn't breathe. Her legs failed. She heard Min call her name.

When she woke, her head was in Min's lap. They were on the beach, a few feet away from the fire. Iris could feel the cold steel of the gun against her belly. It was dark, but far above them Iris could make out a few stars. She focused on those. Min stroked her forehead, like Iris was a beloved child with a fever, speaking words in a language that Iris couldn't understand or interpret. Iris let Min's soft voice wash over her. She forced her attention to Min's hands, the soothing sensation of being tended to. Breathing in and out, Iris stared at the sky. *I am calm, I am safe, I am here.*

*No one can hurt me.*

# three

## JASPER

Jasper was outside, tinkering with the broken propeller of the stolen float plane, when he first heard the laugh. Turning his head from side to side, he tried to figure out what that sound could be. He'd heard lots of strange noises on his long journey from Fort McMurray to wherever the hell he was now in the Pacific Ocean off the coast of what used to be southern British Columbia, but that sounded like a woman, not a sea creature. It was raining, more of a mist than actual drops, and Jasper had to hang on tight to the slippery metal to avoid falling. His right leg ached, and his lower back felt tight the way it did before it seized up and laid him out flat. Straight ahead, he thought he saw what almost looked like a glass windshield, glinting like a lover's wink as his plane rose and fell with the waves. Peering harder into the mist, he could've sworn he saw land, rising up like a ghost behind whatever was reflecting off the surface of the water.

Jasper waited, running through potential scenarios in his mind. He had learned over the course of his fifty-four years not to rush into anything. Take stock, analyze, see where you might be useful but not pushy. That was Jasper's philosophy.

His plane kept shifting and moving as he floated in the current. Jasper heard it again: a woman's voice. Speaking words he couldn't decipher over the rain, and then a short barking laugh. He felt an answering response bubble up inside of his chest, bursting up and out of his mouth, flooding his chest with warmth and optimism.

Jasper waved. Putting all his weight on his good leg and hanging onto the plane with one arm, he swung the other hand in a wide arc. "Hello!" he called. "I can hear someone laughing!"

Cold water splashed up over his legs. He crawled higher up onto the plane, shielding his eyes against the sun breaking through the clouds. Two women stood (stood!) on a rocky beach not far from where he was floating. It appeared to be a medium-sized island, with actual trees ascending on an angle toward the sky. It was hard to tell how big it was, after so long on the water, but Jasper guessed a person couldn't walk the circumference of the place in a single day. That meant lots of space to explore, and maybe animals to hunt. The chance to rebuild some of what he'd lost. Jasper had no idea how this place was possible, when he hadn't come upon anywhere remotely livable to this point. A wooden raft was tied up near the shore, and a fancy cabin cruiser boat floated nearby in the cove. The tall thin dark-haired woman waved back, while a shorter, compact blonde woman beside her stood with her arms crossed over her chest.

When he drew closer, Jasper slid down to stand on one of the floats, wincing at the hot shard of pain in his injured leg. He leaned into the plane to pull out some rope from under the seat. Then he stepped carefully into the water, astonished when he felt his left foot connect with the slippery rocks. He laughed again, trying to get his footing along the shore, while struggling to hold one of the front float bumpers as well as the coil of rope.

The thin Asian woman waded in near Jasper, the water lapping at their legs. "Should we tie you to our tree?" she asked.

"That would be great." His voice sounded hoarse. He tied one end of the rope around the front strut, feeling uncertain and shy.

The white woman spoke, her voice sharp and loud. "Min. We don't know anything about him."

Jasper turned to look at her. She made no move to help, standing back a few feet near the remnants of a fire on the shore. "I can't lose my plane," he said. "I have no wish to harm anyone." The plane bucked and rolled with the waves. Jasper struggled to hold onto it, as he couldn't put much weight on his useless right leg.

"We're not going to send him away, Iris. Come help me tie up this plane and then we'll find out who he is." Jasper tried to smile at the tall woman, who spoke softly, but with authority. The suspicious lady, presumably Iris, stepped forward, reaching out her hand to take the rope. Both women worked to tie their end to the tree.

Jasper said, "Thank you. I couldn't believe it when I heard someone laugh. I thought I had to be dreaming."

"I know the feeling," said the friendly lady. "I was the first to arrive here and I thought the trees looked like a picture in a book." She smiled again. "I'm Min. And this is Iris."

Jasper nodded to both of them. He was finding it challenging to let go of the plane. Everything he'd managed to scrounge or steal to survive was inside of it.

"Do you want to double-check our knots?" Min asked. "We've been here a few days now, but what we've tied up has stayed put."

She seemed to know what he was thinking. Jasper had forgotten what that kind of kinship was like with another person. He had trouble forcing the words out of his throat, which suddenly tightened up on him. "I'm sure it will hold. Thank you."

Iris walked back onto the shore, followed by Min. Jasper came after them, limping through the quiet waves, slowing down to notice the sensation of taking each step. The salt water burned the jagged cuts down his right leg, making Jasper wince. How many days had he gone home after twelve hours of construction work, muscles screaming in pain, longing to retire so he could rest? And now that there had been nothing to construct or do, he found himself longing for those hard, stressful days. At least he knew what he was working for back then. Ginny and the kids were still there, the condo filled with their voices and their mess.

When he got near the women on the beach, he stopped, stretching out his stiff back, intentionally leaving some distance between them. "My name's Jasper. I'm from Fort McMurray, Alberta. Do you know where we are? Is this Vancouver?"

Iris shook her head. "No. I'm from Vancouver, before it flooded. We must be somewhere near Vancouver Island, west of the mainland. And maybe north too, which might explain why this island isn't underwater like everything else."

Jasper looked around, trying to reconcile this uninhabited space with the beautiful capital city of Victoria on Vancouver Island, where he and Ginny had spent their honeymoon thirty years ago. It had been such a vibrant place. They'd stayed at a beautiful white clapboard B&B, had high tea at a stately old hotel downtown with ivy creeping up its stone face, and visited a stunning garden with what seemed like millions of flowers in fragrant bloom. It was one of the happiest weeks of Jasper's life.

Min said, "Of course it's impossible to tell exactly where we are, without any technology or maps. I came all the way from Regina, and you from northern Alberta. It's a long way to travel, to end up in the middle of the ocean."

Jasper nodded again. He shifted from side to side, avoiding his bad leg, trying to figure out what should happen next. Were they just going to live together here? Would Iris, who frowned at him throughout this brief discussion, even allow him to stay? Now that he was here, on dry ground, Jasper didn't want to think about getting back into his plane to float aimlessly until his supplies ran out. He would have to leave eventually, of course, to keep searching for Ginny and his girls, but he wanted some time to recover. To make sense of what couldn't begin to be understood.

"Have you both been sleeping on the beach?" he asked. Other than the fire, a pot, an axe, and a few other tools, he couldn't see a shelter.

"No. We've stayed in Iris's boat since she arrived."

"But that wouldn't be appropriate for you," said Iris. She had a real edge to her voice. Jasper wondered what had happened to both of them. They must be curious about what he'd gone through to get here. He knew immediately that he had to get Iris on his side, or nothing about this would work.

"I can stay in my float plane," Jasper said, in the subdued voice he used for his white bosses at work, and the police when they hassled him in Fort Mac. Ginny used to call it his 'nice Indian' tone. He smiled, hoping to disarm Iris. "I'm a construction worker by trade. If we can gather up enough tools, I can build us somewhere to stay on the beach. But I won't do anything that makes you feel uncomfortable. We've all seen enough violence and hatred to last a lifetime. I'll wait to hear what you'd like me to do, and I'll respect whatever it is you ask from me."

He shuffled away from them, back toward his plane. Jasper turned, looking at this miraculous island, giving Min and Iris space to huddle together and discuss his proposal. Jasper spent a lot of his life waiting for others to feel comfortable around him. Even now, at the end of civilization itself, he was trying to please a white woman who looked at him with wary caution like there was no way he could be trustworthy. Jasper was tall and sturdy, but he knew how to curl in on himself to seem smaller and more insignificant.

Both women walked to Jasper. Her face stony, Iris said, "You can stay, in your plane, but we need you to keep your distance from us and never come up behind me when I don't know you're there."

Min added, with a lot more warmth, "And we'd love for you to help us build a shelter. Welcome, Jasper."

"Thank you." He had unexpected tears in his eyes. He felt like a schoolboy getting a rap on the knuckles from the strict teacher, but if there was one thing Jasper knew how to do, it was to bide his time and wait.

"I'll keep my distance and I promise you don't have to be afraid of me."

# four

## MIN

Iris, Jasper, and Min had been together now for a few weeks. Time tended to blur at the edges, making it hard to define and remember, but Min had completed one menstrual cycle since she'd arrived, which was a clear tracking device. Once again, Min wondered when her goddamn menopause would finally start. Soon Iris would likely sync up to Min's cycle, the way the female coworkers in the lab used to bleed in unison. At least here she had moss to use as a pad. When Min thought about the IUD she had before the Modesty Act made women's contraception illegal, she wanted to weep. Of all the things that had been lost, perhaps not getting a period every month was minor by comparison, but on a practical level it represented so much more to Min.

"Good morning," Iris said. She closed the door to her tiny bedroom, stepping down into the kitchen of the boat, where Min was lying on the leather sofa.

"Hi," Min answered. "How did you sleep?"

"Quite well, thank you." Iris had her clipboard in hand. Every morning, she completed a full circuit of her boat, checking and double-checking her supplies. Min and Jasper had pooled theirs, but Iris refused to part with anything she owned. In a detached intellectual manner, Min could understand and appreciate Iris's fear, but since Iris had significantly more than Jasper and Min, her refusal to share anything was irritating.

Min sat up, folding her blanket and stowing it away. Iris liked the cabin of her boat to be pristine and orderly. She opened the luxury blinds, seeing Jasper at the edge of the trees, beavering away on their shelter even though sunrise was only moments ago. The day was clear, the humidity making everything damp and soggy. Min ran her fingers through her hair, noticing how dry her scalp felt. Iris's blonde hair shone in the early morning light, but then again, she hoarded bottles of expensive shampoo that Min would love to use. Even once. She watched Iris open pale wooden cupboards to count cans, boxes, and jars, jotting down notes on her paper with a blue pen.

"I'll go see if Jasper needs a hand," said Min.

Iris gestured with her hand, intent on her inventory. Min grabbed her sandals and held them under her arm as she went down the back ladder into the water. They all agreed it was probably mid-July, with the hottest temperature any of them had ever felt before in Canada. She tried to ignore the sweat trickling down her back, staining her ragged red tank top.

Min waded through the cool waves and walked onto the sand. She slipped her shoes on and approached Jasper.

With a shy smile, Jasper said, "Hello there. Have you had breakfast?"

She shook her head. He pointed to a couple of halibut on a short wooden table he'd built from skinned logs by their fire area. "When I finish this, I can fry us up a feast."

"I don't know what we'd do without you, Jasper." Min meant it. Iris continued to treat him with caution, but Min felt nothing but gratitude for his presence. He reassured them at night when the coyotes howled somewhere above them in the trees, and the handful of times they'd ventured up into the forest, Jasper seemed more confident than both women among the trees and brush. His wounded leg caused him a lot of pain, but Min found it touching that Jasper tried to hide this from the women. Iris was afraid of everything. Fear wasn't really Min's issue. On her raft, she had accepted that death was near. She felt ready, with no energy left to try to stay alive. Even now, with a couple of weeks of living with two other people, Min couldn't summon energy for anything that required courage or even interest.

Jasper seemed to sense that Min was tethered quite tenuously to survival. He never pushed. Min found Jasper more restful than Iris, so she found excuses to spend time with him. Iris liked to be alone, and never wanted to be in the same space as Jasper without Min present, so it worked out on all sides. Not one of them had talked much about their harrowing experiences that led them here. It was too early somehow. In the evenings, as the twilight thickened and the birds sang, when they sat around the campfire, the energy between them lagged, as though it couldn't handle the weight. Each of them went deep inside their own memories, thinking of those they loved and lost. Dae and Chul were close to Min in those moments, her throat tight with unshed tears.

Now, Jasper watched her. After looking out to sea, trying to visualize or imagine a horizon that failed to materialize, Min met Jasper's dark brown eyes. "Would you like to see how the shelter is coming along?" he asked. "I worked on it last night after you and Iris went to bed."

"Sure," Min said. "Do you need some help?"

He shook his head. "Not right now. I managed to get your blue tarp in place as a roof, but I'm weaving in more evergreen boughs to fill in the gaps."

They walked up the beach, with Jasper's plane and Min's deconstructed raft behind them, tied to a small copse of trees near the shore. After a lot of discussion, with Iris becoming quite heated and opinionated, they had determined that the best place for a shelter would be just at the edge of the trees. The firs, cedars, maples, and pines made an excellent canopy against the punishing sun, but they didn't want to go too far back into the woods because when it rained, it was hard to dry out the wood. They worried that the few tarps they had would become waterlogged and mouldy if the sun couldn't reach them. Min knew Jasper longed for the tarps in Iris's boat, but Iris flatly refused to give any of them up.

"Oh, Jasper, this is incredible." Min saw how carefully he had sanded the wood he had cut and skinned, fitting it together at the ends to make what looked like log cabin walls. The roof was not yet finished, but the sun pierced through the worn sections of Min's tarp, making a familiar blue haze inside the shelter that reminded her of the long days alone on the raft. "You've worked so hard."

He shifted his weight off his bad leg, limping over to sit down on the wooden structure. Min came to perch beside him. "It's good to be useful again. To do what I know how to do."

A comfortable silence fell between them. Across the beach and over the water, the sound of Iris's cabin door closing, and then locking, meant she would be coming to join them.

# five

## JASPER

His pulse quickened at the sight of Iris's blonde hair as she strode up the sand, still damp from high tide. God knows, Jasper had tried to make peace with Iris, giving her a wide berth so she would feel comfortable. He had seen firsthand what men had done to women before and during the collapse. The misogyny and entitlement over women's bodies was like something from a horror film. First were the Modesty Act and the Father First laws, causing women to flood the streets in protest. Jasper's ex-wife Ginny was in the thick of it, as she never backed down from a challenge, and he had worried constantly about her and their three grown daughters. The images of the riot squad trying to settle the crowds still haunted Jasper when he tried to fall asleep. He never thought he'd see a time where he felt sorry for police officers, but the broken bodies of the cops, hung up in the streets like marionettes, had been the turning point for Jasper. When the police forces were gone, and the Men of God imposed martial law when they took over the local and federal governments by force, he fled Fort McMurray. Jasper longed for news of Ginny and his girls, but they remained lost to him.

Iris moved like she was made of stone—a jigsaw puzzle ready to shatter into a thousand pieces but for the sheer force of will keeping her in one piece. Jasper sensed Min stiffen beside him on the shelter. They were both bracing themselves. Whenever he felt that familiar flicker of rage in his belly about Iris, Jasper reminded himself that she'd probably been through hell, like he had. A separate hell, but no one had escaped the former world without profound suffering. His compassion was running out, trickling away like the last of the water in the rain bucket. Jasper worried about snapping and Iris forcing him to leave. When the shelter was built, he was going to spend more time exploring the island. He'd find his own space here if he had to.

As Iris approached, Min and Jasper both came to their feet. "This is really coming together," said Iris by way of a greeting. Jasper smiled.

Min said, "We'll be able to try sleeping in it soon."

"Not me. I told you it doesn't seem like a good idea. Men and women should stay apart, after everything that's happened. Safety is our first priority. Plus, there's animals, and all kinds of other nightmares out here." Iris shuddered. "Why is it so big when there's only two of you?"

"If the three of us found this place, other people might, too." Jasper made sure his voice was gentle, but it took a concerted effort. "I'm trying to build for the future."

Iris made a snorting noise.

Min intervened, saying, "Jasper caught us a couple of fish. Do you want to keep me company while I clean them and fry them?"

Jasper gave Min a grateful glance. When Iris wasn't around, he and Min had long meandering conversations about what a future could possibly look like here. Something fair and hopeful and not fucked up with money and politics and power and hierarchies. Come to think of it, Jasper was the one who did most of the talking, but Min was a skilled listener. She would nod, encouraging him to continue, letting the words roll off her without fighting them the way Iris would. Jasper knew Min was a climate scientist before everything went to shit, but he had trouble imagining what that must have been like for her. To sound the alarm, and give your life to proposing solutions for an upcoming extinction that people robustly ignored. No wonder the woman had all but given up.

Min picked up one of the knives, rusting along the blade from the humidity, and moved with Iris toward the table of fish, steaming in the sun.

Jasper refused to accept that a better future was out of their grasp. Why would the three of them still be alive, happening by chance upon this miraculous liveable island, if they couldn't at least try to fix what had so badly gone wrong?

# six

## IRIS

ris sat in the new shelter, leaning against the back wall. She was supported by silk pillows from her boat, her clipboard on her lap. Min was beside her. Jasper sat outside the shelter he had built, on a stump he had cut so it had a short back, reminding Iris of the white leather bar stools at her kitchen island back home. Don't think about it, she reminded herself. Stay here and now. Focus. She breathed in and out, trying not to remember how she began most of her therapy sessions with rounds of intentional breathing to calm her anxious clients down. Jasper and Min both watched her, waiting for the meeting to start.

Iris pulled her clipboard close, peering at it in the evening light. The wind blew gently, rustling the leaves of the maple trees behind the shelter, but Iris enjoyed the feeling of being protected by the illusion of being inside. "Okay," Iris said, "now that the shelter is almost finished, let's discuss the next priorities. I say we need better washroom facilities."

Min shook her head. "Our privy is fine. Jasper raised it already, so it's off the ground, instead of the holes we were digging and then covering up before he got here."

"But with animals around, we need walls on it. Like a building. It feels too exposed to the elements."

"You don't even use it, Iris," added Jasper. "Don't you usually go in your yacht?"

The word "yacht" got under Iris's skin. She'd been on some yachts in her time, the kind with full-time staff, a dozen cabin bedrooms, and chandeliers in the mahogany dining room. Her cabin cruiser was nowhere near as grand. With the rioting after the MOG nutjobs took over the government, and then the subsequent economic collapse, she never would've made it out alive if she'd been in a proper yacht. Iris took another long, deep breath, determined not to storm out or fight. Too many of their early committee meetings had ended this way.

"I do prefer the toilet in my boat. That's true. But I've been collecting waste and burying it as you asked me to." Before Jasper arrived, Iris handled her toilet like she did when she was at sea: by dumping it in the ocean. Out of sight, out of mind. But now, the three of them often bathed and cooled down in the bay where the boat was anchored, so Iris was asked (not so politely) to change her unsanitary practices for the good of the group. Iris despised having to think about others. Wasn't that the point of living through the end of the world? To not have to consider what others need from you anymore and simply make sure you had what you required to survive another day?

Jasper asked, "What do you think we should build next, Min?"

"I'd love more of a cooking area," Min said. "Something where we protect the fire and the few pots we have. And maybe a place to sit down, so it feels like we are eating at a table instead of hunched over our food while sitting on logs." Iris thought this suggestion a total waste of time, as she ate everything in her boat. She set the table properly, even if she only opened a can of beans or SpaghettiOs, but it was much more civilized than eating out on the beach. Iris preferred to dine alone, which up to this point Min and

Jasper had accepted.

"As Min seems happy with the john so far, and Iris hardly uses it, I think I'll focus on the cooking and dining needs next." Jasper looked around at both women as he spoke, but Iris didn't meet his glance. "I want to do more than fish, even though that's working well so far. I want to go farther up the mountain, to see what I can find. If anyone wants to join me, you are welcome."

Iris wrote some notes on her clipboard, knowing that Min and Jasper wouldn't expect her to go tramping around in the woods. It was too dangerous. She had enough supplies for now without having to resort to that.

"Min, would you like to sleep on the boat with me a little longer? Or are you ready to try a night in the shelter?" asked Iris.

"Jasper has been sleeping in the shelter for a few nights and he says it's quite comfortable with a blanket and pillow. I'll try it whenever he's ready for me."

Jasper grinned, showing his crooked teeth. "Any time. That's what it was built for. I've got one curtain hanging up, but it's an old raggedy sheet with some holes showing through. If Iris could spare any bedding for privacy curtains, I'd be grateful."

Iris lifted a sheet of paper on her clipboard to study her inventory list. "I might have an extra bath towel, but I'm sorry, I can't spare a sheet."

"Anything would help." Jasper's voice had a slight edge to it. Iris knew how both of them felt about her inventory list and her careful supply management. She understood shifts in energy very well. Iris was trained in childhood to manage her alcoholic parents, and she chose a career as a therapist because it was obvious to her what people thought and didn't say. For Iris, human energy was a code that she knew how to break.

She simply couldn't give anything away to these two people. Iris drew a solid boundary around herself and wouldn't let anyone cross it. This was the only way she could manage here, without carrying her gun around every day, like she'd done for Jasper's first week. It made Min and Jasper upset, even just the sight of it in her hand or the waistband of her shorts. When Jasper didn't attack her, she stored it in the boat. But the gun was never far from her thoughts.

# seven

## CLAUDINE

Once again, Claudine dreamed of her keyboard. She could hear the rhythm of her fingers flying across the smooth keys. When she slept, Claudine's mind swam with lines of code and algorithms. By profession, she was a high school information technology teacher, a job that became irrelevant when those asshole MOGs shut down the internet to stop the underground dissidents from targeting the power grids and banks. Claudine had only been teaching for four fucking months when the screens went dark. She was still furious about this, more than a year later, when True Canadian Values had cratered everything, not just the internet. But Claudine missed cyberspace the most. The freedom of it. The ability to disappear, out of your physical body and into another dimension.

The consistent sound of the rain on the flat roof of her aluminum fishing boat brought her back into reality. The web, with its infinite possibilities and connections, faded from Claudine's mind. She opened her eyes, taking a moment to orient herself to the bobbing of the waves. Her desk, her laptop, her confused and frightened teenaged students disappeared, leaving Claudine alone again on this wreck of a boat. Any day now it would be her twenty-fourth birthday. She tried not to think about her parents and her younger brother, Patrick, standing around her coconut cream birthday cake last year, singing bravely as though chaos weren't already unfolding, threatening the security they had so blindly taken for granted.

She sat up, noticing that her air mattress needed to be patched again. Stretching her muscles like a cat, Claudine came slowly to her feet. She stepped out of the shelter onto the deck, enjoying the warm summer drizzle. It felt good on her skin. If Claudine closed her eyes, she could pretend she was in her blue-tiled shower at home in Kelowna. Mom would be in the kitchen, singing old Roy Orbison tunes as she cooked dinner. Patrick, sprawled on the couch playing video games, trash talking on his headset to his brain-dead friends. Dad, at the university in his poli-sci department office, crammed floor-to-ceiling with books. No white supremacy groups targeting the Black, Indigenous, and Asian professors, under the Men of God's new nationalism campaign. Once they were in power, and the old police force was decimated and out of the way, the bullshit MOGs took over the internet to force-feed the nation propaganda about white Canadians being the ones to trust. The holders of Truth and Values. From there, it didn't take long to generate fear for anyone who didn't happen to possess True Canadian status. And fear turned quickly into hate. Claudine wouldn't have been able to graduate with her teaching degree if she'd been any younger, as Black students were banned from the university after her senior year. It was all such a ridiculous waste.

Claudine despised having so much time to think. She longed for the distraction of her computer. She pined for the relative safety of her online relationships, behind her smudgy screen, where she had the option to hide her true identity and skin colour when necessary. At least there she could fight back. She could find others brave enough to sneak in through the back doors and wreak havoc on the MOGs. Until those fucking bastards hit the kill switch and destroyed any hope Claudine and her online friends had to communicate with each other and make secret plans.

Opening her eyes, she realized she was weeping. Claudine allowed the storm to pass through her, not bothering to stop it, letting her shoulders shake until the tears were spent. Her body rose and fell on the old boat with the movement of the waves, so familiar after all these months that she barely registered the sensation. When they fled Kelowna for the coast, one suitcase of meagre clothes and supplies between all four of them, a cousin let them hide on this boat. It was supposed to be temporary, until the American military or the Europeans came in to restore a sense of order to Canada, but no outside help ever came. And now Claudine was the only one left from her family.

The rain was slowing down. Soon the sun would be back, in full force, and her clothes would dry quickly. She thought about fishing again for dinner, but she wasn't hungry enough to bother. Claudine drank from one of her rain buckets, plotting again to rebuild the internet. If she could survive this long, out at sea with no other person or land in sight, surely it must mean something. She'd wait until the evil burned itself out on rage and hate and destruction, and then Claudine would start over. With safeguards in place against the white supremacists and the religious nuts and the men with guns who decided they were the ones in charge. Claudine had nothing but time to think up ideas for fixing the technology that had been hijacked and exploited.

Out of nowhere, she thought she heard a plane, but that was not possible. Claudine tipped her head up, looking into the sky for the source of the sound. There it was again—not a jet but the pfft-pfft-pfft of helicopter blades. She peered into the sky, not really expecting to see anything, when from under the cover of the rainclouds a graffitied chopper emerged, flying at a strange angle, falling alarmingly toward the water. Claudine felt like she was watching a movie scene in slow motion. Liquid dripped from the helicopter at a steady pace before it hit the surface with a loud bang. In the distance, the hulking machine disappeared from view. Had she imagined it? No, Claudine could smell gasoline, causing a piercing sense of déjà vu and memory, from the before world.

If someone still had fuel, so long after the collapse, that might mean fresh supplies. It might also mean a rich person, which for Claudine likely spelled trouble, but she had to see if there was anything she could salvage from this helicopter wreck. Quickly, she fashioned her homemade yellow sail to the top of her boat, and set off in the direction of the crash.

# eight

## AINSLEY

When the helicopter fell out of the sky, Ainsley felt relieved. *Finally* was the thought that flashed through her mind. The urge to survive was strong, primal even, but Ainsley had been getting through these long, awful days by wrapping herself in a kind of protective gauze against the coldness of reality. The last thing she remembered with any clarity was Thomas's own golf clubs, being swung over and over into his head and body. She heard the dull thud sound every night in her dreams. His blood had looked so bright against their living room carpet and furniture. After that, everything became muted, grey, and slow.

She knew she was going to die, her stomach roiling like this was a ride at the fair, but Ainsley welcomed the inevitable. Before succumbing to the virus, Ainsley's friend Janna had set this escape up for her, and it was already a miracle that Ainsley and the pilot had made it out of Seattle with only a few bullet holes shot into the side of the chopper. They had leaked fuel for around an hour, looking for a safe place to land that continued to elude them. Far more serious were the pilot's injuries. Ainsley guessed he finally passed out, which is why they were plummeting into the ocean.

For some reason, the tall elderly priest from her childhood flashed through her mind. Catholicism had been left behind, like so much of herself, when she married Thomas. His faith had been the evangelical church that had caused immeasurable damage to the stable fabric of society, but if she wanted Thomas, she had to embrace his religion. But not here, in Ainsley's final moments. This belonged solely to her, and she wanted the God of absolution and forgiveness from when she was a girl. Ainsley hoped he'd understand her defection and accept her now.

She braced for impact.

The water was icy, slamming hard into her body, pinpricks of pain on her pale Irish skin. She was plunged into darkness. Disoriented, she gasped for air and felt her chest fill with water. Fumbling with her seatbelt, Ainsley realized the chopper was upside down. She kicked her arms and legs, pushing at the glass of the windows but not expecting anything to open. She felt surprisingly peaceful, even though her lungs were screaming for air.

After a while, she noticed wind on her face. Coughing, Ainsley expelled water from her mouth and nose, while attempting to force her eyes open. The smell of gas and salt water was overpowering. Ainsley could not see the helicopter or the pilot. An orange lifejacket floated nearby. She swam over to it, putting her arms through the holes and zipping it up. Shivering, Ainsley wondered what would happen next. Why would the pilot get shot instead of her? The helicopter had gone down in the Pacific, miles from land or any other person, and somehow, Ainsley was still breathing. None of this made any sense. She lay on her back, looking up into the cloudy sky, noticing that her head was pounding. Ainsley hoped the cold would get her before a shark did.

She waited, floating aimlessly. Ainsley would not think about Thomas, or her two beautiful children. She wouldn't think about her friend Janna, gasping for breath by the end, and her last sacrificial act to get Ainsley out of Seattle. She refused to remember the fine layer of ash over the city when Yellowstone blew, and how many refugees poured into their Washington cities, adding to the unrest and civil war already brewing under the surface. Ainsley needed the gauze of her foggy mind. It helped her not to scream or claw at her skin until she bled.

Instead, she turned her imagination to Galway in Ireland, where she had lived until she turned fifteen, when her parents decided to emigrate to America. She'd been in Seattle for twenty years, but in times of stress, she traveled back to Galway in her mind. Galway was vibrant and green, a study in contrasts between pastoral farmland and azure blue of the water. Ainsley saw the cheerful paint colours of the rowhouses by the bay. She could smell the vinegar from the chip shop and hear the cheeky gulls screech as they dove down to nab food from her hand. She recalled the way Finn's eyes used to crinkle up at the corners when he laughed.

*Is someone there?* The voice came from somewhere over Ainsley's left shoulder. She tipped her head, hearing a roaring sound in her ears. Ainsley couldn't feel her limbs in the freezing water. With her curly red hair completely immersed in the waves, Ainsley saw the upside-down image of a metal boat with a young Black woman leaning over the railing. Her mouth was moving. She seemed to be waving or gesturing. Ainsley couldn't believe another person was out here in the middle of the water. When, exactly, was she finally going to die, instead of being forced to continue on endlessly in this uncertain purgatory?

It was hard for Ainsley to decipher exactly what this woman was saying over the rush of water in her ears, but it sounded something like *are you alright, I can throw you a line, don't be scared, we'll get you warm in no time.*

# nine

## JASPER

From halfway up the mountain, Jasper saw sunlight glinting off what might be a boat on the water. He stopped to peer out, his hand shielding his eyes from the glare, but couldn't be certain there was something there. At fifty-four, Jasper's eyes weren't what they used to be, and with no access to optometrists, his sight wasn't likely to improve. Yet another element of this new existence to accept. Every single day, Iris seemed to fight against the collapse of civilization, but Min and Jasper didn't waste energy pining for what was gone. They simply got on with the business of survival.

Jasper decided to finish what he was up here to do, checking his snares and resetting them if any small animals had been caught. Then he would go down to the beach and ask Min to use her binoculars to see if that was a boat or simply more debris. In the four weeks or so they'd been living together here, a lot of useful things had washed up on shore or nearby enough to row out in Min's raft to retrieve them. One benefit of the country blowing itself up seemed to be useful elements of wreckage and garbage, finding their way out to sea. All kinds of crates, boxes, tires, glass, and packages had been washing up. Plastics, metal, clothing, even blankets had come their way like presents at Christmas. Last week, they opened a bag that contained coffee beans. Iris actually smiled at this discovery. Jasper was astonished by how the smile transformed her face. The smell of the coffee brewing over the fire made them all feel lighthearted and normal. It had been a good day, sipping morning java while chatting about nothing consequential and recalling other happy memories.

As he made his way through the undergrowth, looking for animal scat, Jasper experienced a surge of contentment that flooded him with a sense of well-being. Sure, his right leg ached, with a constellation of open cuts and muscle damage that refused to heal properly and oozed putrid green pus from time to time, but out here he felt like a truer version of himself. In his previous existence as a construction worker, husband, and father in northern Alberta, he'd tried to live like a white man, ignoring his Indigeneity to blend in better with Ginny and to get by at work. He got quite good at it. This play-acting had made him feel off-kilter, but he didn't know it until now. Out here, in the wild, with two women counting on him for sustenance and shelter, Jasper could finally breathe. In a way, it was like coming home.

His first three traps were empty, but in the fourth one he found a large rabbit. It was afraid, trembling in his large hands, so he soothed it, petting it gently before breaking its neck in one smooth motion. This would feed all three of them for dinner, making a nice change from the fish and crabs they'd been eating. He knelt down to reset the simple snare. Hunting was new for him, but he was astonished by the energy he felt after eating meat. Jasper longed to hunt for bigger game, like deer or elk, but his leg gave him a lot of trouble and he was hesitant to go higher up the mountain until it healed. He had a shotgun, but very few shells. Every day he hoped to find more weapons in the debris, or to increase their numbers with people who had scavenged more weapons than the current group possessed.

His leg burned with a hot pain as he stood up. The pinching sensation went straight up into the centre of his back, reminding him of old work injuries. He'd cut his leg to ribbons on a bunch of broken glass when trying to crawl into an abandoned tractor in a field along the BC-Alberta border. A crowd of thugs had found Jasper in a burned-out hardware store, scavenging ropes, tarps, and whatever could still be found after the armed looters had moved through, and he had to run fast to escape them. One of the nastier boys had a crowbar, but in the end, Jasper used it on the kid and then took it with him. If only he hadn't cut his leg on that glass. He worried every day now about an infection that could finish him off.

Only one trap left to check. He cradled the dead rabbit in his arms, reminding him of his girls when they were tiny. Faintly, he heard Iris's voice calling his name. It sounded sharp, like usual, but Jasper heard a panicked undertone to it. Something was wrong. He hurried out of the undergrowth and back onto the winding game trail that was the fastest way back down to the beach.

# ten

## IRIS

"Jasper! Come quick! There's a boat!" Iris felt her pulse race, staring across the inlet where a new aluminum boat with a yellow sail at the top approached the island. For weeks, Min and Jasper had been talking about the possibility of new people finding them, but Iris refused to countenance the idea. She had seen such unbelievable cruelty and death before escaping to the water. Iris preferred solitude, but finding Min had proved safe enough. Learning to co-exist with Jasper had taken a lot of getting used to for Iris, but she couldn't deny that it was useful and beneficial having him around. So far, he had behaved well enough to stay, but Iris felt in control of the situation with only the three of them on this island. She didn't think she could handle the disruption of anyone else.

The boat was even closer now. Iris turned toward the hill, where Jasper had climbed this morning to check on his traps. "Jasper, we need you!" she shouted, her throat hoarse from the effort. Min was bathing in the cove, but at the sound of Iris screaming, she came out of the waves to step into her shorts and red T-shirt, then joined Iris on the rocks. Iris reached out to hold Min's damp arm.

"Someone's coming, Min. I'm going to get my gun."

Min turned to Iris, using a calming voice that Iris herself had used many times with patients prone to panic attacks.

"Anyone who finds us now is probably safe. They will be like us, looking for land they can actually live on. They won't be interested in more violence. You don't need your gun, Iris. This is our home. A weapon sends the wrong message."

Iris's breathing was returning to normal. Holding Min's arm helped her. She needed that physical connection to another human being. "I know it's our home. We have to protect it." Even to her own ears, Iris's voice sounded pleading, which was pathetic. She remembered when she had once sounded strong and capable. Iris wondered if she would ever feel that way again.

"We will protect it," Min said.

There was no time for more, as the boat was in the cove. A Black woman stood by the railing. "Hello!" she called. "I can't believe we found you! Can I drop my anchor?"

Min looked to Iris, urging her to respond by gesturing toward the boat with her chin. She smiled, which bolstered Iris's waning confidence. Luckily, this was another woman, and not a man. With a boat almost as big as the one Iris had, although not nearly as nice. She could see fishing equipment and nets along the side of the covered cabin area. Jasper would be thrilled about the nets.

Iris took a few steps into the water. "I'm Iris, and this is Min. Welcome to our island." She forced a smile onto her face, hoping it looked as warm as Min's did.

By the time the boat was anchored, Jasper emerged from the trees to help. The young woman's name was Claudine, and she explained briefly how she had come upon Ainsley, after her helicopter fell out of the sky. Ainsley had been running a fever for the last few days, shivering and sleeping a lot under a metallic thermal blanket. Iris asked immediately if the fever could be pandemic-related, but

Claudine was insistent that she had no other symptoms and would be dead already if she had the virus. Ainsley's skin had no raised red scabs on it, which was a telltale marker of the most recent mutation, giving it the nickname the red spread.

As soon as Iris laid eyes on the tiny Irish woman, with her bruised and swollen face, she felt her heart constrict with the long-forgotten reaction of empathy, once her greatest asset as a therapist. Ainsley was like a frightened kitten, trembling and disoriented, but when she looked into Iris's eyes, something connected for Iris, the way a puzzle piece fits in only one specific spot.

Min, Iris, and Jasper all boarded Claudine's boat, but when it was time to help Ainsley off the air mattress on the floor of the dirty covered cabin, Ainsley reached for Iris. She raised a thin hand, and Iris stepped forward to support Ainsley to her feet. She was too weak to go down the back ladder into the water, so Jasper got out of the boat and then carried Ainsley like a child, with Iris walking alongside. He moved in the direction of the shelter on the beach, but Iris said, "I think my boat would be better for her while she gets her strength back."

Iris didn't miss the surprised glances exchanged by Min and Jasper. She ignored them, realizing that she didn't care what they thought. They were all trying to get through these strange days the best way they could. As Iris used to tell her clients, "We always start where we are." Claudine hung back, awed into silence by the experience of standing on land again. Iris was laser-focused on Ainsley. She was determined to get to the bottom of why she dropped out of the sky into the ocean, and nurse her back to health.

What energized Iris was having a goal again, a sense of purpose and direction. She'd been the top of her class in high school, then throughout undergrad and grad school. Iris felt comfortable being the best, anticipating bumps in the road and quickly navigating around them to get exactly what she wanted. One of the biggest losses of these last horrendous years had been the blurry aimlessness. For so long, no one could plan more than the next meal or where you might lay your head that night. Anything else was futile, which Iris found frustrating and frightening.

But now, seeing how helpless and scared Ainsley was, Iris felt once more like her old self. Capable. Not a victim, but instead a woman who had therapeutic and healing skills at her disposal, and it was time to use them again.

# eleven

## AINSLEY

Being alive, when Ainsley had anticipated her death so frequently, was exhausting. Not to mention disorienting. For a little while, when tossing and turning on Claudine's mostly deflated air mattress, Ainsley convinced herself that death was close. She could feel it, beckoning to her as it had done so often since the war on inequality began, but the fever raged and somehow didn't kill her.

When Ainsley first saw Iris, leaning over her in Claudine's boat, she felt a spark of recognition. The hunted expression in Iris's face was immediately familiar to Ainsley. It was like looking at herself. So Ainsley reached out her arm. She didn't remember much beyond that, but today, when she opened her eyes, she realized she was in a new location. Ainsley felt her body shift up and down with the current, which was normal, but this boat cabin was luxurious. She moved her head slightly, taking in the neat galley kitchen, and the carpeted stair up to what looked like a bedroom. Ainsley could hear footsteps above her, on the wood of the deck. Her head no longer throbbed. Now it felt curiously empty. At peace. She waited.

More footsteps, and then a female voice. "Hi. You're awake."

Ainsley tried to sit up, so she could turn her body to see who was speaking, but the effort of moving brought immediate agony. Muscles and joints burned, nerves screaming at her from the inside. Ainsley gasped, squeezing her eyes shut to focus on the overpowering sensations. She felt a gentle hand on her lower back and another on her shoulder. Someone was easing her into a sitting position. When the piercing aches faded enough for Ainsley's breathing to return to normal, she forced her eyes open.

Iris was there, putting pillows around Ainsley on the buttery leather couch. She moved over to the table, picking up a glass of water and a bottle of pills. Iris opened the plastic lid and shook two tablets into her hand. She held the white pills out to Ainsley. "Here's some aspirin for the pain. Claudine says you got pretty banged up in the helicopter crash."

Ainsley took the tablets, washing them down with water. Nothing seemed quite real to her. Perhaps it was the surroundings. This lavish space didn't belong here in this brutal after world. Comfort and opulence meant Thomas. It wasn't difficult to imagine him here, pouring drinks and bullshitting with his tech co-workers. If he were here, Ainsley would be dressed up to the nines, smiling by his side. Saying words she didn't believe, and playing the part of the dutiful, wealthy wife. She swallowed hard, fighting the panic rising in her chest. Ainsley's hand quivered, spilling the water onto her legs.

Iris took the glass, then sat down beside Ainsley. When she spoke, her voice was soothing, like a lullaby. "There's no need to rush. Or talk. We start where we are. No one expects anything else from you. It's okay."

Ainsley locked eyes with Iris, feeling desperate. Iris patted Ainsley's shoulder, so light it could barely be felt, but it had the effect of anchoring her here, so she didn't float away into nothing. "I know when I first came here, I used this mantra: *I am calm, I am safe, I am here. No one can hurt me.*" Iris laughed, which startled Ainsley, but she kept her attention on Iris. "Ridiculous, really, because how could I possibly be safe? Or calm? Everything was dangerous—both in Vancouver, where I lived before my house was burned to the ground, and in the middle of the fucking ocean where I could see whales and sharks, and of course no land anywhere suitable to live. But that mantra got me through, every awful day, until I made it here."

Ainsley's breath was steadier now. She leaned back, into the pillows, her eyes still holding onto Iris's. Iris added, "Saying 'It's okay' was stupid. I'm sorry about that. None of this is okay, and we have to start by acknowledging that. Everything else is madness."

Iris smiled, a sad gesture that telegraphed to Ainsley just how much anguish was inside of this beautiful, stoic-looking woman. She was still talking. And patting Ainsley's shoulder. "Claudine said your name is Ainsley, but she didn't know anything else about you. There are three of us living here. Min was first, she's from Regina, and then I came. I'm Iris, a therapist from Vancouver. And then Jasper arrived in a float plane, with no fuel, of course, so he just bobbed about on the water with the rest of us. He's a construction worker, from Fort McMurray in northern Alberta. He built us our bathroom, and the shelter, and even a small dining and cooking area." Ainsley tried and failed to make sense of these words. Iris made it sound like they had actual buildings here, but how was that possible? She decided not to think. It was pleasant to simply listen to Iris's soothing voice without having to understand what she was actually saying. "Jasper also hunts for us, which makes a change from canned food, but I have quite a bit of that still stored up and will keep you here with me in the boat until you are ready to join the others. Take the time you need. We'll do this together."

This reassurance gave Ainsley a feeling of comfort, like a roaring fire on Christmas Eve used to warm her and remind her of home. She remembered that security could be built inside of yourself. It didn't have to come from outside, where you had no control or agency. As the aspirin slowly worked to dull her physical pain, listening to Iris's stream-of-consciousness stirred a long-buried spark in Ainsley, of the bright, cheerful, funny Irish girl she used to be. Maybe, with a bit of encouragement in this strange new environment, that spark would ignite and burn once more.

# twelve

## MIN

At the first hint of light in the sky, Min got up. She had never slept well, even in the comfort of her downy queen-sized bed with Dae beside her, and out here Min missed the sleeping pills she used to take when the insomnia was at its worst. Pulling the ragged pink towel to the left, Min saw Claudine curled up on her side, knees up to her chest, sound asleep. Across the shelter, behind a flowered sheet with holes in it, Jasper snored.

Min stretched, trying not to shake the logs beneath her. She sat up, shimmying her body to the edge of the shelter to find her sandals. Min scratched at the endless insect bites along her shins. The red lumps were raised and angry looking. She attempted to give herself some relief with her fingernails without breaking the skin.

She walked across the beach to the cooking tent, grabbing the matches. Jasper always used the flint, but Min found it hurt her hands, and Claudine had brought a reasonable stash of wooden matches with her. She started the fire, using the kindling Claudine had set up last night before they went to bed, then hung a covered pot of rainwater to boil. Drinking a hot cup of water while watching the sun rise was one of Min's favourite rituals out here. She sat on the first log she had set up on her own, on day one, looking out at the explosion of purple, pink, yellow, and orange in the sky. Min raised her tin cup to her husband and her son, wherever they were. She liked to imagine them as part of the sunrise now, visiting and watching over her.

"Am I disturbing you?"

Surprised, Min turned her head to see Claudine, holding an empty enamel mug. "Not at all. I was just lost in my own thoughts and didn't hear you." Min reached for the pot of hot water, pouring some into Claudine's cup. She gestured with her head for Claudine to join her on the log.

"It's so beautiful here," said Claudine. "I can't stop staring at the trees. I thought they had all died between those blue bark bugs and the fires."

"I know. I figured I was hallucinating when I first saw the green leaves from my raft. It's a strange anomaly that somehow this particular island didn't get infected with the parasites."

"Why isn't it underwater like all the rest?" Claudine asked. "I saw the tips of land from my boat, but nothing with a beach, until I came upon you."

"I have no idea. It makes no sense at all to me. I know Jasper is itching to explore the whole place and find out what's on the other side. We don't know how big it is, or whether or not we've chosen the best place to set up camp. Those first few weeks were such a blur. I think we were all in shock and not functioning properly."

The sun was moving fast up into the sky now, warming both women. Min refilled their cups, emptying the pot. A silence fell between them, and to Min it felt comfortable. She thought about how prickly Iris was when she arrived, and how refreshing it was to sit with another woman of colour. There was so much between them that already felt understood. Eventually, even white women lost their freedoms, but women like Claudine and Min had been on the bottom of the social hierarchy for so much longer.

Claudine must have been thinking along the same lines, because she said in a low voice, "Even out here, they have the best of everything."

Min followed Claudine's gaze to Iris's boat. She thought about how cushy it had been to sleep inside of it, but she preferred the shelter. Min didn't want to owe Iris anything. Or live by her rules. She had wasted so many years tiptoeing around what women like Iris felt comfortable with. Not here. Not at the end of the world.

"Yes," Min agreed. It felt like a relief to say the words out loud. "And they don't share. It's not equal, just like before."

Claudine smiled, but Min could see the weariness underneath of it. "We'll have to fix that, won't we?"

Min thought about Jasper. He must feel outnumbered now, being the only man among four women. But Min was Korean, Claudine was Black, and Jasper was Indigenous. On this island, there were three people of colour and two white women. Numbers had to count for something. They certainly did in the before world, when the poor finally rose up against the rich, and those who had been pushed to the margins and stripped of their dignity and rights eventually said ENOUGH to the white and powerful. By then, nowhere was really safe, as the climate revolted around the same time, but there was something about Claudine that made Min come to attention.

There had to be a better way forward. Iris was not the one in charge here, even though she waved her goddamn clipboard around and was used to bossing everyone and getting exactly what she wanted. Claudine was right that Iris shouldn't have the best of everything and not have to share. Not out here. The numbers were three to two.

Min couldn't contain her smile, a grin that lit up her lined face. "Yes," she said. "Let's fix this."

# thirteen

## CLAUDINE

Claudine was on an expedition to find fresh water with Jasper. They set out together just after breakfast, which Claudine prepared and served for her, Min, and Jasper. Claudine's fishing boat had several large boxes of rolled oats in a storage cupboard, and she also had lots of canned fruit. So they dined on hot oatmeal with peach slices. It felt like being in a Michelin-starred restaurant, overlooking the water, with the sounds of the fire crackling at their feet. It was the closest to happiness Claudine had felt since her family was alive and with her.

This morning's conversation with Min had given her a jolt of optimism. It was difficult to muster up hate for Ainsley, who was sick, weak, and non-threatening at the moment, but Claudine couldn't deny that Ainsley clearly had enough money and privilege to fly in a helicopter, with hoarded fuel, while Claudine hid in a smelly fishing boat for months, trying to avoid capture as the world burned. But Iris was a different story. Locking herself in her gorgeous yacht, refusing to share what she had, and inviting another white woman to join her opulent space filled Claudine with fury.

Thousands of years of white patriarchal and capitalist power structures had eventually destroyed modern civilization, as Claudine's poli-sci professor father had long predicted would happen, but this was now a post "civilized" world. It was never fair, for Claudine and others like her, and she would die before allowing the same dangerous racist and religious ideologies to flourish here, out in the wild. There had to be a better way. She could see it in Min's eyes this morning, so Claudine took this opportunity to walk with Jasper, to get a sense of where he was at.

"How are you doing on this hike?" Jasper asked, turning from his place ahead of her on the trail. They kept a slow pace, set by Jasper and his wounded leg. "I keep moving my snares farther up the mountain, and I'm catching more rabbits and squirrels in this area, so I'm convinced there's fresh water nearby."

"I'm fine. It's so great to be walking again. I was on that boat for so long."

Jasper gave her a shy smile. For a moment, he reminded her of her dad, who always seemed bigger than everyone else to Claudine. His shadow loomed over her, giving her an example to follow. He was smart, accomplished, gentle, and kind. He did not deserve what happened to him. Not when he spoke quietly, with such gravitas and intelligence, about the warning signs that caused him to lose sleep. The Modesty laws, then the government coup, and the hate speech that was not only tolerated but actively encouraged. Her dad said the queer community and all people of colour were going to be hunted down, but Claudine kept choosing to believe this was hyperbole and paranoia. They lived in Canada, for Christ's sake—a free and diverse country. Until it wasn't.

Her dad was right, like always. And now she was the only one to survive and make it here. Claudine would not let her precious family down. She couldn't bring them back, but she could make their deaths mean something.

They kept walking. Every so often, Jasper hacked at the undergrowth with his knife, just enough to let them pass through. The ground smelled damp this deep in the forest. Claudine could do without the spiderwebs in her face, but she loved to hear the birds singing. She knew there had to be large animals nearby, but Jasper told her he had yet to be seriously threatened by anything. Right now, it seemed like a marvelous adventure to Claudine. She felt more alive than she had for ages. Her nerve endings were tingling.

Jasper stopped suddenly, throwing his right hand up to signal that Claudine should halt. They paused, hearing a snarling sound. Everything went still inside of Claudine. Jasper stomped his foot and shouted, "Hey, we're here! Outta the way now!"

Claudine laughed, joining him by clapping her hands and saying in a singsongy voice, "Don't eat us, we're just looking for water!"

Soon, the forest was quiet again. "Well done," Jasper said to Claudine. When they strolled a few more feet, a trickling sound could be heard. Claudine pulled on Jasper's arm, then pointed. He turned his head, listening intently, and Claudine took off at a run.

There, in front of her, was a small fresh water source, running down stones into a creek bed. It was an unbelievably beautiful sight. Jasper had explained that as they were in a rainforest, they could usually collect enough dew and rainwater to drink and cook, but with more people joining their settlement, they would need fresh drinkable water to keep them sustained. He knew there had to be some, where animals gathered, but he had searched for a while without finding it. The look on his face now was one of pure joy. He began to sway from side to side, his eyes closed, chin tipped toward the sky. Claudine felt moved just watching him.

After a minute or two he reached out to Claudine, and she grabbed his hands. They danced together, under the canopy of the lush verdant leaves, then they both knelt down to drink. The water tasted cool and crisp, reminding Claudine of childhood summers, when she and Patrick would stop their games to slurp from the garden hose. Jasper filled the bottles they brought with them. He splashed water over the angry red sores on his right leg, wincing a little.

"Will you be able to find this place again?" asked Claudine.

"Definitely," he said. "I've been circling it for a while, but I'm learning how to track where I am using the game trails and the traps I'm setting."

They sat by the water. Claudine pushed on the wet, springy moss near the rocks. "You seem really good at all of this survival stuff, Jasper."

"I didn't use to be. I worked outside, in construction, but I had no real connection to nature. I fished and hunted some, as a boy, but gave all that up when I got married." He paused, gazing with satisfaction over the small stream. "And now we're here, and we need to eat, so I figured it was time to become more self-sufficient."

Claudine felt comfortable with Jasper. He had an easy, undemanding energy about him. She decided to go for it, to say what she wanted to say. "Can I ask you a question? About Iris?"

He looked at Claudine, a guarded expression on his face. "What about her?"

"Does it bother you that she lives on that huge boat and doesn't share her supplies with the group? Min and I talked about it this morning. It doesn't seem fair to us."

He was still for a long moment. And quiet. Then he let out his held breath. "Yes, it bothers me. And I don't think it's fair. I've tried to understand, as Min told me that Iris was damaged and afraid when she arrived here, but weren't we all?"

"And no matter what happened to her, she still had it easier than I did. Or Min. Or you." Claudine's voice had dropped again, to that low level, out of fear that she might be overheard by the wrong person. It used to be so dangerous to say anything like this. Even to think it made her heart race while hunkered down in that boat.

Jasper met Claudine's eyes. His face was stamped with distress, and she knew in that one glance how much he had suffered. "I'm not trying to cause any trouble," Claudine continued, still in her subdued voice. "I know the three of you have been finding your way. But now there are five of us, and two of those five happen to be white women, staying away from the three of us on a tricked-out boat."

He swallowed hard. "What exactly are you saying?"

"I'm saying we need to set some ground rules. Don't you want to try to create a better situation here than the one rich white people just annihilated?"

# fourteen

---

**JASPER**

They waited a few days, until Ainsley was feeling stronger, then Claudine called a meeting after the evening meal. Min cleared away the dishes, after the fried fish, plump blackberries, and foraged mushrooms were consumed. They sat in the newly constructed dining hut, with its three walls made of skinned logs. The roof remained open, but soon Jasper hoped to cover it with evergreen boughs like the shelter, and eventually add some type of door. He had built a simple table, with five carved chairs, and the dining hut was placed to the right of the shelter. The cooking area was farther down the beach, and under tree cover. Jasper wouldn't allow any food preparation near where they slept and ate. Any smells that could draw predators needed to be a safe distance from their main camp.

Looking around the table now, he felt a surge of pride for the little home he'd created for everyone. This wasn't his family, but for now, Jasper treated each of these women as though they were his ex-wife and daughters. By feeding and sheltering them, he tried to reach out to wherever his loved ones had ended up. He steadfastly hoped they were still alive. And safe from the abuse so many women endured when law enforcement broke down.

"I think we should keep this meeting short," Iris said. "Ainsley still needs rest."

Min asked Ainsley, "How are you feeling?"

"Better, thank you." Ainsley's voice was thin, like it had been stretched. Iris had fussed over her during dinner, but Jasper had yet to talk to Ainsley at all.

Iris flipped a few pages on her clipboard and picked up her pen. "Let's get started, then. We should talk about the new water source, and make some plans for—"

She was cut off by Claudine, who leaned forward in her seat. "Excuse me, Iris. I asked for this meeting, so I would like to run it."

If looks could kill, thought Jasper. Claudine reminded him of his middle daughter, Taylor. She was around Claudine's age, mid-twenties, and always spoiling for a fight about anything she viewed as an injustice. Iris's mouth drew into a hard line. Her blue eyes narrowed. For a moment, Jasper felt afraid. He thought about Iris's gun, and how it never left her the first week he was on the island.

"We've got our own ways of doing things here. You've only just arrived, and aren't in any position to be running anything."

Claudine refused to back down. "I'm not clear on why you are the authority figure. Is it an elected position?"

Iris's face turned red. She came to her feet. "I'm not going to be disrespected by you."

Claudine stood as well, her eyes flashing.

Min reached out, placing one hand on Claudine's arm and the other on Iris. "Let's all take a deep breath. This isn't going to get us anywhere."

A brief silence fell. Jasper decided the best course of action was keeping his mouth firmly closed. Ainsley appeared to have the same strategy. She kept her eyes on the grainy sand beneath their feet.

"I think what Claudine is trying to say," continued Min,

"is that we need to have a discussion about how we make decisions going forward. There are five of us now, and what worked in the early days with Iris, Jasper, and me may not work now that we have more people. What would be fair when it comes to authority and decision-making? Any ideas?"

Her voice had a quiet command to it. Listening to Min now, Jasper could imagine her lecturing to a large auditorium of people. Iris swallowed hard, then sat back down on the edge of her chair. She looked over at Ainsley, then to Min and Jasper, but refused to make eye contact with Claudine.

Claudine eased down into her seat. They listened to the tide coming in, slapping the underside of the boats and Jasper's plane, before making a sucking noise when the current moved back out to sea.

"I didn't mean to be rude," said Claudine. "But I'm hoping we can have an honest conversation about how certain things are going to be handled going forward."

Iris spoke, her eyes on Min. The words were forced out through clenched teeth. "What 'things' are you referring to? We have a system in place and it's working just fine for everyone."

Now Min looked to Jasper. His heart started to pound in his ears. He remembered Iris's firm voice on that first day, saying with her arms crossed over her chest, "You can stay, but these are my rules for how you have to behave, or we'll ask you to leave."

"I'm not sure it's working for everyone," Min said.

Now, Jasper. This is the moment. It's time to stop being afraid of women like Iris. He drew a long, deep breath. "I agree with Min," he said.

Claudine's face lit up with a smile. She said, "No one

person should get to be in charge, without a vote. That's how everything went to shit in the before world. With only five of us, we have a chance to build something better, but not if it functions exactly like it did before."

Now Iris looked at Claudine. Her eyes were bright with anger and her voice shook. "You don't know us at all. You have no idea what I went through to get here. We're managing the best way we know how, and for you to come here and say we're doing it wrong is completely unfair."

Claudine spoke calmly, but with heat under her words. "I'm not saying you are doing it wrong, but we've all lived through hell, and white people had it better than most. But out here, that doesn't seem like a fair system." She gestured to Min and Jasper. "The three of us are living here together on this beach, sharing our limited supplies, while you and Ainsley have anything you could ever want on that yacht."

Iris jumped to her feet and helped Ainsley to stand. "We'll leave in the morning, when the sun is up." Her voice sounded brittle and rough. Ainsley seemed shocked, but Iris pulled her down the beach, in the direction of her boat.

Min hurried after them. "No one's asking you to leave. Please, Iris, let's just have a conversation. Please come back and listen to what we have to say!"

Jasper tried to follow Min, but when he stood, his injured leg gave out, causing stars across his vision in the twilight. As he felt himself falling, he thought once more of Ginny, picturing her face in his mind. She was laughing, and reaching out to him, so it must've been in the early years of their marriage, when they were both still madly in love. He held Ginny's image close, allowing it to soothe him, even as he struck his head on the edge of a chair and everything faded away into nothing.

# fifteen

## TONY

There hadn't been sirens for months now, but Tony still heard them in his mind. The way they overlapped one another, in the early days of the collapse. He could always pick out the ambulances, and Pedro would identify the police cars. Sirens upon sirens upon sirens. A symphony. Tony got so sick of them, waking him at all hours, until they disappeared, taking civilization and normality with them.

Now, he mostly heard water, destroying nearly everything in its path. He drove the old cop car that got him from Calgary to Vancouver, but he couldn't get across this bridge. Too many abandoned cars blocked his path. He could see a mountain in the distance, which was his destination to avoid the floodwaters as long as possible, but Tony knew he'd never make it there. This was the end of the road. In the early days of the pandemic, when it took more than a few hours to die, Tony used to look in the stopped cars to see if anyone needed help, but there was no point in doing that any longer. He'd seen so many corpses, covered in their red sores. All decomposing in the heat, like produce left to spoil.

He sat in Amelia's cop car, wishing he were in his ambulance. It had become too dangerous to travel with obvious medical supplies, as everyone who was still alive desperately needed them. He'd been held up at gunpoint several times for painkillers and bandages. Finally, he packed what he could in a waterproof case and left the ambulance in the road, knowing it would be ransacked and driven until the gas in the tank ran out. He set off on foot, where he found Amelia, who had been Pedro's cop partner before the Men of God seized power. She had been badly beaten, but was still conscious, her breathing ragged. Tony stayed with her until she died, lying down beside her near a dried-out ravine. He listened to her talk about the old days, when she and Pedro were new police officers in Calgary. How idealistic they were, about changing the way people thought about cops. They dreamed of a police force that was fair for everyone, not just the privileged. But it couldn't be done. The MOGs had all of Canada convinced that every last cop was corrupt and evil, standing in the way of True Canadian Values. Tony held Amelia's hand until her last wheezing breath, thinking about Pedro the whole time. When she was quiet, he took her keys and waited until he didn't see another living soul. Then he got in the car and drove west across Alberta and BC, grateful for the cans of gas Amelia had stashed in the trunk.

On the bridge in Vancouver, as the rushing water rose, Tony waited to drown. The sky was angry and grey. It poured rain, adding insult to injury. Every so often he heard thunder. His waterproof box of medical supplies sat on the front seat next to him, his name scratched into the plastic. Tony hoped that someone else would find it, floating in the wreckage. He left the windows of the car open for this purpose. His corpse would remain in the car, but the bandages, salves, sutures, and pharmaceuticals would drift away, to seek out any humans who had been lucky enough to make it.

The water came even higher, breaking glass and causing the bridge below him to groan in complaint. The noise was loud, but Tony preferred to tune back into the sirens in his memory. He thought again about his ambulance, and the calls he used to make in his job as a paramedic. No, it was much more than a job. It was a calling. The same way his husband, Pedro, had felt called to serve as a cop. They understood each other very well. The deep need to give to those who were afraid and in pain. Even when it cost an equal amount of suffering to those doing the giving.

In his last moments, Tony could feel Pedro here. His big laugh. Those bear hugs. The way he would wipe tears from Tony's face after a particularly grueling call. Whenever there were dead infants or children, Tony wept. Their bodies had seemed so small and vulnerable. His shoulders would shake with the sorrow he could no longer contain inside of himself, and Pedro would hold him close, telling Tony it would be different one day when they had kids. He missed that soothing presence more than anything. After all Tony had seen and experienced since Pedro was murdered, he longed most for his arms around him.

There was water in the car. This wouldn't take long. He tried to stay focused on Pedro. The life they had built together in their sixth-floor condo in the southwest corner of Calgary. Before it was flattened by the tornado. No, don't think about the wreckage. The screaming. The limbs torn off. The bloodied bodies in the rubble. Tony couldn't imagine anything worse than the tornado, and then the hailstorms that pounded the prairie crops, but these storm cycles turned out to be only the beginning. After that, there was nowhere to go in Canada where you could be gay and not be branded a criminal. He helped as many sick and injured people as he could, but Tony and Pedro had to separate for their own safety. Saying goodbye was like cutting off his own oxygen. They should've stayed together, because once the MOGs were in control of the government, Pedro was killed anyway. Tony bitterly regretted not remaining with Pedro. At least they could've died together.

He closed his eyes. The water coming into the car was cold and refreshing. Pedro, he thought, Pedro. I love you. I always loved you, and I will see you soon.

# sixteen

## DIAMOND

Diamond was rowing when they came upon the car on the bridge. They noticed the old faded RCMP logo and the red and blue lights on the roof. It was late afternoon. The sky was black and stormy, the wind pushing the boat along in the churning water. Rain splashed against Diamond's neon green jacket. Diamond had found this wide wooden rowboat a few weeks ago, and it was the only reason they didn't drown like most other people in Vancouver when the tsunami hit. If you turned back, for someone you loved, or worse, to get something from your house or car, you drowned. Diamond had a backpack of supplies, covered with a protective plastic sheet. It was always on their body. Once they got the boat, Diamond added anything else they could find: a few blankets, jugs of water, canned food, buckets, utensils, and bars of soap. It wasn't much, but enough to survive for a few months if Diamond were careful. They were only seventeen, but had been fighting publicly for nonbinary and queer rights since their eleventh birthday, when Diamond told their parents they didn't want to identify as female. Diamond knew how to fight, and ride the wave of fear when threatened with death if you didn't shut your fucking mouth. They weren't ready to die quite yet.

Diamond rowed closer to the car. Water was rising, up to

the door handles, but Diamond could see a person sitting inside. Probably just another corpse, but some instinct urged Diamond to check. When the rowboat was close enough to the bridge to bump the metal of the cop car, Diamond shouted over the rush of the water. "Hey! Are you alive? Do you need help?"

The person in the car turned his head, giving Diamond a scare. Was it safe to rescue a cop? Diamond wondered. They hadn't seen a cop in so long. How the hell had this guy made it this far, in that car? Cops were public enemy number one for the last year or so, when they tried to stop the MOGs from storming the capital buildings and were vilified online and through their bullshit puppet media mouthpieces. Diamond criticized the police plenty when they did nothing to stop the Father First and Modesty Act garbage, and they did a whole video series a couple years back about white supremacy in law enforcement and the justice system, but at the end it seemed the cops were trying to stop the Men of God. Maybe for that reason Diamond was curious about this guy. They'd like to get a few questions answered about what really went down. Not that Diamond's video subscribers would be able to hear the story, but maybe one day the internet would be resurrected.

The guy in the car gestured with his hand for Diamond to keep moving. He didn't appear to be white, which was a relief. Maybe Latino? In this dim light it was hard to tell.

In less than an hour he would drown if Diamond left him. It felt strange, even now, when death had been an everyday occurrence for years, simply to row away and leave him here. Ever since Diamond's mom died, doubled over in agony from stomach cramps and dehydration after drinking contaminated water on their journey together to the coast, death felt much more personal. Now Diamond understood why their mom felt so gutted by Dad's death. He didn't support Diamond's gender identity changes, so his death meant something different to Diamond than their mom. But losing a person you counted on to be there for you, that was something Diamond could only grasp now that they were entirely alone in the world.

"Are you sure?" Diamond called. "Why don't you swim out the window? This boat won't be great in the middle of the ocean, but it's definitely better than a cop car."

The guy shook his dark head, hair hanging in his eyes. His face was so sad. Diamond felt their throat constrict while looking at him. Then he reached into the seat of his car and handed Diamond a big plastic white case with the remnants of a red cross scratched off the side. Medical supplies. They reached over, trying to balance one hand on the oar while the water bashed around the sides of the boat. Diamond grabbed the case, setting it carefully on the bottom of the rowboat.

"I have some food and water. There's probably nowhere to go, but I'm alone. And scared. I'm only seventeen." Diamond paused, seeing the effect their words were having on the older guy. He appeared to be listening, so they kept talking. "I could really use some company."

The man clamped a hand over his mouth. He brought his other hand up, pressing his fingers to his thumb, then raising his fingers up and down in a flapping gesture. He performed this pantomime of speech up by his face, then clamped that hand over his mouth as well.

Understanding dawned for Diamond. "You don't talk?"

The man nodded. He shrugged, a gentle expression on his face. Damn, Diamond thought. I guess I won't be getting that info about the RCMP after all.

Diamond leaned forward, offering him their hand. "I

don't mind," Diamond said. "I'm nonbinary, which is illegal now as you know, so I'm hoping you don't want to arrest me. I came all the way here from Saskatoon before my mom died, and I have nowhere to go, but you can come with me if you don't mind my company. Or you can stay here. It's your choice. But if you want to die, give me time to row away so I don't have to watch."

He looked through the car window at Diamond's face. The rain battered the car. He passed a small wet leather satchel out the window to them, then he crawled out and into the rowboat.

# seventeen

## AINSLEY

Ainsley sat in the shelter next to Jasper, changing out the cold cloth on his forehead. She gazed to her right at the bathing cove, as it was Ainsley's favourite spot out here. Above the cove was an area they used as a lookout, with a sloping hill and grassy outcrop. Ainsley dubbed this Cat Point, for the shrub on the plateau was shaped like a cat head with cute pointy ears. Claudine provided some bandages from the first aid kit in her fishing boat, so the new open cut on Jasper's forehead was covered in gauze, but he burned with fever, delirious and weak. His right leg oozed from the cuts that hadn't healed. The pus was yellowy-green and smelled foul.

Ainsley talked a lot to Jasper, to keep them both occupied. She prattled on about Galway; her childhood orange cat, Mr. Muggins; endless visits to the principal's office for the mischief Ainsley and her four siblings would get up to; the first fumbling kisses she had with Finn behind the church, his lips warm and soft; midnight Mass on Christmas Eve, the trees at the front of the nave lit with brightly coloured bulbs and decorated with paper snowflakes. Jasper may not have paid any attention, but Ainsley needed to hear every word, so she could remember who she had once been.

She tried to do what she could around camp to help, but Ainsley was still sore from the helicopter crash. She moved slowly and got winded easily. Claudine and Min had really stepped up since Jasper became ill. They checked his traps, spent hours fishing, and maintained Jasper's measures for keeping dangerous animals away from the beach. The business of day-to-day survival was grueling and time-consuming. When Ainsley stopped to think about how simple her life was before the collapse, she wanted to weep. Those with money didn't have to do anything for themselves. Thomas and Ainsley paid people to make their complicated lives run in an effortless manner. Out here, the rules had changed.

Jasper made a moaning sound. Ainsley said, "There, there. Just rest now," in a soothing tone. She pretended that Jasper was her three-year-old son. He was prone to ear infections as an infant, which grew into bad colds when he was a preschooler. His lungs must have been weakened already, leading to so many breathing complications when the volcanic ash settled over Seattle. Thomas always said their son would outgrow his health issues. He was wrong about this, like so many things, but Ainsley kept quiet and didn't argue. He was the tech magnate, so she figured he had to know more than she did. But their son never saw his fourth birthday. And a year later, Ainsley still couldn't bring herself to repeat her children's names. She felt shame when she thought of both of them: hot, violent anguish, like the lava that poured from the Yellowstone volcano, at how badly she'd failed as a mother and a wife.

The altercation between Claudine and Iris a few days ago, just before Jasper fell and hit his head, brought that shame back to the surface for Ainsley. She experienced the same guilt by association that had plagued her for the twelve years she'd been with Thomas. A sort of imposter syndrome. Ainsley had propped Thomas up, boosting his ego, working out for hours to look the part of a rich wife so she wouldn't embarrass him. She felt like a Barbie doll, sculpted out of plastic, standing on marble floors in designer dresses and heels, to be admired by drunk men who believed they were captains of industry. Ainsley was extraneous. Window dressing, at best. She willingly laid down her own abilities to bolster her husband's, and now, on an island in the middle of the ocean, Ainsley had accidentally aligned herself with another woman who fancied herself in charge.

Her face burned with heat. She applied more aloe from a plant she found in the woods to Jasper's leg wounds, wishing she had access to Iris's stash of painkillers to offer him more relief. The night Claudine and Iris had argued, Ainsley asked if she could stay in the shelter. Iris only shrugged at this request, so Ainsley moved out of her boat that night and now slept near Jasper. She felt useless to do the hard work around camp that Jasper, Min, and Claudine were doing, but Ainsley thought she could take responsibility for his care. She used to be a mother, after all, even if her son and daughter had died under her direct supervision. When they had no more nannies and tutors working for them, and Ainsley was the one in charge, it all went to shit. But some of that was the chaos of the civil war in America, and not her fault. Or so she told herself when the despair rose up in her throat.

Here, though, Ainsley was determined to keep Jasper alive. They needed him. He had built this sleeping shelter, mess hall, cooking hut, and their privy. He kept them fed. Since he'd gone down with his infected leg, tossing and turning with a high fever and chills, the mood in the settlement had changed. Become more urgent, somehow, as the women realized just how precarious their situation was without Jasper. No one seemed to want to admit that they needed one another. It was too fresh, too vulnerable, to allow yourself to rely on someone. But now, he was seriously ill, and the fear that had been stuffed down and locked away was fighting its way back to the surface.

"Water." Jasper's voice was strained, but he offered a small smile to Ainsley. She reached down for the mug that came from his plane. It was black, with a photo of a sprawled-out striped tabby cat that looked like Mr. Muggins, and the words *I hate Mondays.* Jasper had told Min that his ex-wife had given it to him years ago. Ainsley poured boiled water into the mug, and supported Jasper's head as he took a slow drink. He leaned his head back on the pillow and gazed at her with bright eyes.

"Are you cold?" Ainsley asked. "I can get you another blanket."

He shook his head.

"Do you want anything to eat? Maybe soup? We have a little dried fish from this morning."

Jasper didn't bother responding. He simply looked at her. Ainsley set his mug down by her feet. She held his warm hand. They sat in silence together, the minutes ticking on with no sense of urgency.

She was determined to keep him alive.

# eighteen

## CLAUDINE

Claudine climbed the back ladder of Iris's boat. When she got to the top, she knocked on the shiny wood railing. Min had told her not to set foot on the deck unless she was invited. Iris had a handgun and boxes of bullets. She took her safety seriously, and might fire first and ask questions later.

Claudine did not want to make this visit, but a few days had passed since Iris threatened to take Ainsley and leave, and Iris remained holed up on her boat. Ainsley had joined Min, Jasper, and Claudine on the beach, which probably pissed Iris off, but Claudine figured she had to at least make an effort at peace with Iris. She could've pulled her anchor at any time and sailed away, but she was still here. Claudine hoped that meant she was worried about Jasper, but she had no way to know unless she asked.

Iris opened the door to her cabin and poked her head out. It was early afternoon, and bloody hot. The sun was relentless, with not a single cloud in the summer sky. Min had created a calendar near the dining area, using charcoal scratched onto a skinned log. They all figured it was early August, but they were only guessing. Time had taken on a strange elastic quality. Claudine could hardly believe she used to fixate on the clock in the upper right-hand side of her computer, tracking each second that went by as she coded or taught students or schemed with hackers about infiltrating MOGs corrupt government systems. How far away that seemed now. How meaningless, to be so consumed with the passing of time.

"What do you want?" Iris's voice was sharp.

The metal of the ladder was hot under Claudine's hands, so she dropped them to her side and attempted to balance on the rung using only her feet. "I wanted to apologize for our argument." The word *apologize* stuck in Claudine's throat, but she forced herself to continue. "I simply wanted to start a dialogue, but now Jasper is sick, and we need all of us to pull together and get him through this."

Iris leaned against the doorframe. Her arms crossed over her body. "How is he doing?" she asked.

Bingo, Claudine thought. There was a human being in there after all. "He's got a high fever. Those cuts in his leg seem to be infected." Claudine wiped sweat away from her forehead. "Any chance I could come inside? It's really hot here on the ladder."

Iris seemed to consider it, which was surprising, but then she shook her head. "I'm hot too. Let's have a swim, and we can talk about it."

"Sounds good. I'll meet you in the cove."

Claudine climbed back down the ladder, immersing her body in the salt water. There was no point in stripping off her shorts and tank top. They would dry soon enough in the heat, and they reeked of dried sweat, so could use a rinse. She swam around the boats, Min's raft, and Jasper's plane, to the shallow cove to the right of their sleeping area. A few trees provided dappled shade here, making it a pleasant spot to bathe.

Soon Iris appeared, in a red polka-dot one-piece bathing suit. Fucking hell. Did she think this was a tropical photo shoot? Claudine owned four changes of clothes. Ainsley had the outfit she wore when the helicopter went down, and absolutely nothing else. Claudine's warm feelings toward Iris disappeared. She forced herself to breathe deeply and remain calm. Min had been coaching her these last few days.

Iris dunked her blonde head underwater and came up to the surface with a sigh. "That feels so good."

A silence fell between them, other than small splashing sounds as they treaded water. "Ainsley has been taking good care of Jasper," said Claudine. "She's still bruised up, but she's refused to leave his side. Min and I have been trying to handle the fishing and the hunting."

She waited, hoping for some kind of a response from Iris. After a while, Iris said, "Okay."

Claudine's anger flared, like a match bursting into flame. She stood on the rocky sand, wading toward Iris. "Look, there are five of us here, and only three of us are doing any work to keep us going. We don't want to lose Jasper. Right before he fell, cracking his head on the log chair, you stormed off the beach with Ainsley, saying you were leaving. But you are still here." Claudine knew her voice was getting louder. It felt good not to hold back, to stop tiptoeing around, to actually say what she wanted to say without moderating it so carefully. "Ainsley says you used to be a therapist. Can't we at least talk honestly about Jasper? We need you to help us, Iris. Can't we try to be a team in order to keep all of us alive out here?"

The last few words came out in a gulp as Claudine's throat closed up. Tears pooled in her eyes. Goddammit. Stop pleading. Never show them the depth of your feelings. She wanted to hit Iris, so she turned her body away, lowering her clenched fists under the water.

Iris fixed her eyes somewhere behind Claudine, who looked toward the beach. The leaves and boughs threaded together over tarps above the shelter fluttered in the afternoon breeze.

Iris did not speak for a long time, but when she did, her voice was tight and lifeless. Almost robotic. "I know I have to do better. I get so afraid I can hardly breathe. I don't want to care about any of you. It hurts way too much. But something about Ainsley really got to me. Helping her was helping me. But then that night you started to shout at me, and I was right back in the before world, with my house set on fire and a knife at my throat and the men, one after another on top of me, tearing at me and screaming…" Her voice was frantic now, rising and falling in strange places, but she didn't even sound human. She wouldn't make eye contact with Claudine, who wanted to respond but didn't have any idea what to say. Iris's eyes were dry, unlike Claudine's.

"I couldn't leave, not with Jasper like that. I was so afraid of him when he first got here. I wanted to kill him, for what those men had done to me, but he never once hurt me." She paused once again, cupping water in one hand and splashing it up onto her neck. The gesture seemed to bring Iris back to herself. Her face softened, and her voice became normal again. "Where can I go, anyway? There's nowhere to go. We're all trapped here whether we like it or not."

Now Iris glanced at Claudine. The only thing Claudine could see on her face was sorrow, etched into every pore. "I am sorry," Claudine said. "For all of it. For all of us, and what we've each endured. But please, Iris, come and talk to Min and Ainsley. And me. Let's get through this awful shit together. Talking about it has to be better than not talking about it. Right?"

Iris bit her top lip. She sank down into the water. Claudine waited.

When she popped back up to the surface, she wiped at her eyes. Then slowly, languidly, Iris swam toward the beach.

# nineteen

## MIN

Claudine had worked some kind of wonder with Iris. Min hadn't talked to Claudine about it yet, but Iris was there, on the beach, asking how she could help Ainsley with Jasper.

Min was cleaning fish in the cooking area. It was not a job she enjoyed, but it reminded her of her college days as a pre-med student, before she switched over to climate science. As she filleted the glistening pink meat, Min smiled at the pleasant sound of Ainsley and Iris chatting. They were working together to get Jasper in a sitting position for a sponge bath. He was almost unresponsive now, which worried Min tremendously, but it was enjoyable to see Iris engaged in his care. She'd even brought out a number of first aid supplies from her boat, like antiseptic cream years past its expiry date. They were all just hoping for a miracle at this point.

If Dae were here, he'd have some ideas about the wounds on Jasper's right leg. They'd been there ever since Min met him, and she knew they caused Jasper trouble by watching him grimace and shift his weight off that leg, but now Min feared a sepsis infection. In the civilized world, that could be treated with antibiotics, but out here in the wild, it seemed like a death sentence.

Jasper had really come alive these past few weeks. Despite

his sore leg, he seemed refreshed and inspired by his newfound existence as a hunter and gatherer. Min shook her head as she laid the salmon in the cast iron frying pan. She thought she had abandoned all hope that life would be fair, but of the five of them, it was astonishing that Jasper was now in the most danger. Min wouldn't have predicted that, but then again, forecasting anything in this unstable after world reality was a foolish endeavour. Min thought she would grow old with Daeshim, in their split-level in Regina. She expected Chul to settle down and give her grandkids one day. All those dreams, gone up in smoke.

Min put the pan of fish aside, then scooped up any guts she missed to add to the bait bucket.

Walking down to the edge of the water to wash her hands, Min glanced at the wood pile by the fire. She sighed. It was low, which meant either she or Claudine would need to restock. God, she missed Jasper. Min tried not to panic, thinking about how they would manage if he died. How long could any of them really expect to live out here, with no support system or safety net of any kind? Just five people against the elements. And this was the heat of summer. When the rainy season began, there would be a whole other set of challenges that Min felt unprepared for. It was daunting. And exhausting.

She rinsed her hands and the water felt so good that she walked in and began swimming. Her neck felt grimy, so she scrubbed it with a bit of sand. Before she knew it, Min had floated quite far out. The beach looked small from this view. She remembered the sharks she'd glimpsed during those long weeks on the raft. At first, she'd felt afraid, then she gave in to the inevitable. Starvation or sharks. She couldn't decide which was worse. But then she came upon the island.

Floating on her back, Min heard a rhythmic sound. It reminded her of the slicing echo her one oar made in the water while on the raft. She closed her eyes, enjoying the hot sun on her face, listening. After a few minutes, she pushed her body into an upright position in the water. Min looked out to the horizon. Something was there, moving up and down on the waves.

Her heart started to pound. Was this good or bad? She thought about Claudine and Ainsley's arrival, and how the ripple effect had sent tremors of change through the settlement. When Min couldn't sleep, and she got up and walked around on the beach in the dark, she dreamed of a huge ocean liner coming by to rescue them. To bring the news that civilization was re-forming somewhere. Surely it was just a matter of time until Vancouver dried out from the tsunami and survivors began to rebuild. They would come to their senses, recognizing what the violence and bloodshed had cost, draft new laws to stop the awful Men of God, protect the environment, share the remaining resources, and learn to live peacefully with one another. That was the only course of action that made any sense to Min. But of course, kindness and reason had failed to prevail before.

Someone was definitely coming. Not in an ocean liner, but rather a small rowboat of some kind. Min swam closer, then waved her arms and shouted, "Hello! We're here, on this island!" just in case the person needed shelter or could tell them what might be happening in the world now.

# twenty

## DIAMOND

Diamond felt a physical shock when they heard a voice shouting. Tony had been drifting in and out of sleep, his head against a blanket on the side of the boat, but he sat up with a start at the voice. He and Diamond looked at each other, then in the direction of the sound. What they saw when they turned was impossible to comprehend. Close up, a pair of human arms waving in the air. And then, beyond that, like a painting from a museum, a real-life glimpse of trees, on land, swaying in the summer breeze.

Rowing harder, Diamond came up alongside the woman in the water. She was middle-aged, and Asian, with a welcoming grin on her face. Diamond had so many questions: Why in the hell are you swimming out here alone? Is that an actual island or a mirage? Looking at Tony, it was obvious that he had many of the same thoughts.

The woman was talking while treading water beside the rowboat. Diamond and Tony leaned down to hear her. "I bet you were surprised to see me waving! I heard you rowing and came closer to investigate. We're desperate for any news, and you must really want some land. Follow me, let's get your boat tied up, and you can meet the rest of us!"

She began to swim toward the beach, not waiting for an answer. Stunned, Diamond shrugged at Tony, who shrugged back. Diamond rowed hard, following the woman to shore.

When the boat was tied up, alongside four other watercrafts, Diamond came unsteadily to their feet, stepping out into the shallow water. They marvelled at the sensation of standing upright, of being out of the boat, of looking at another person who didn't appear openly hostile. The woman came close, offering a hand, but Diamond turned back to assist Tony. He came slowly out of the boat, seeming to savour the experience like Diamond was. They walked together, out of the water and onto the sand.

"Welcome," the woman said with a broad smile. "I'm Min. I was the first one here, but soon after some more people joined me. There are five of us." She gestured to Tony and Diamond. "I guess there are seven of us now, if you should choose to stay."

"I'm Diamond, and this is—"

Min said, "Wait, let me get everyone else before you tell us who you are." She took a few steps away from the water and toward a large shelter at the start of the trees, cupping her hands to her mouth. "Ainsley, Claudine, Iris—please come here for a moment."

Diamond and Tony waited. There was so much to see here. Sand, leaves, rocks, little log buildings with thatched roofs and doors in a row near the treeline, a fire crackling on the beach, a water jug, wooden crates holding dishes, pots, utensils. It was a feast for the senses. Diamond loved the smell of smoke. The safe kind, from bonfires instead of forest fires. It had been so long since they'd smelled it.

Three women walked toward them. Two were white and one was Black. Diamond worried immediately about the white ones. A lot of Diamond's first videos were about the role white women played in allowing the collapse to happen. Diamond fidgeted under their gaze, adjusting their T-shirt and torn khaki pants. They put a hand to their short black hair. Diamond was half Iranian, but most people assumed they were white.

The young Black woman grinned. "Oh my God, are you Diamond?" she asked.

Shocked, Diamond said, "Yes, I am."

"I used to adore your videos! You were so fierce and strong. You inspired me and my friends so much in college. I told everyone to watch your stuff."

"Thanks," Diamond said, flattered by the compliments. "Not that they really changed anything."

"Courage always changes things." She stepped forward and extended her hand. Diamond shook it. "I'm Claudine, and this is Ainsley and Iris. We all use she/her pronouns."

Diamond experienced a rush of relief, like water flowing through their veins. They had tried so hard to communicate how important pronouns were to those who had spent lifetimes being misgendered. To have the government of your country say pronouns "didn't exist" felt to Diamond and others that as people, they didn't exist either. But here, at the very edge of civilization itself, Diamond felt as though Claudine could really see them. "Thank you for telling me," Diamond said. "I love that. I'm nonbinary, and I use they/them pronouns."

Each of the white women stepped forward to shake Diamond's hand. It was obvious they had never heard of Diamond, but that was to be expected with anyone older than about twenty-five. Ainsley was tiny and seemed friendly. Iris looked elegant and intimidating. Plus, she appeared to have a very large stick up her ass.

Diamond smiled at Claudine, hoping to telegraph their gratitude, then gestured to Tony. "This is Tony," Diamond said. "I found him in a cop car on a bridge in Vancouver.

I don't think he's a cop, but he hasn't said a word since I met him."

The women nodded at Tony, except for Iris, who narrowed her eyes. "Why doesn't he talk?" Iris asked.

"I don't know," Diamond said. "He showed me his name on the outside of his kit, but I can tell you he's gentle and kind."

Iris didn't look convinced.

"There's no problem with Tony," Diamond reiterated in a firm voice.

"Welcome, Tony," said Ainsley.

Tony hung back, behind Diamond.

Min asked, "Vancouver's still completely flooded, then?"

Diamond nodded. "Yeah. It's fucked. We've just been floating around for ages, going nowhere, until we heard you calling to us in the water, and saw the island behind you."

"We keep waiting for it to dry out," Claudine said, her voice tinged with sadness. "And for all the assholes to die off so we can go back and start to rebuild without all the angry religious bullshit."

Diamond laughed, then asked, "Is this all of you?"

"There's just one more," Min said. "His name's Jasper, but he's not well at the moment. We're very worried about him."

Diamond and Tony exchanged glances. "Not well?" asked Diamond. "Is it the red spread?"

"No, not that," Min answered. "When Jasper came, he had an injured leg. Cut on some glass. It hasn't healed correctly and now I think he has an infection. I took a couple years of pre-med, and my husband was a doctor, so I've tried to do what I can, but he seems to be getting worse."

Claudine said, "He built everything here. And he hunts

and fishes for us…"

As she was speaking, Tony turned and walked quickly down the beach to the boat. Everyone seemed puzzled, but after rooting around in the rowboat, Tony returned with his waterproof white medical case, holding it up in front of him like a shield.

"He's this way," Ainsley said, leading Tony toward the shelter.

# twenty-one

## TONY

As Tony hurried behind the short red-haired woman, he experienced a surge of well-being. Finally, something familiar. A feeling of being needed, not hunted down. In his heart, Tony wanted to give and to help. There were just so few safe outlets for that since civilization imploded. He tried, in the early days, but people got violent so fast when it all spiralled out of control. But hearing that this guy had a cut leg and an infection? Tony had a chance to fix this, and that jolt of hope brought his long-buried feelings right up to the surface.

At the log shelter, Ainsley moved to the side so Tony could see a big man curled up in the fetal position on the wood. Tony opened his plastic case, rooting quickly through bandages, pill bottles, ointments, and suture kits to find the antibiotics. When he found the broad-spectrum tablets, he pulled them out and handed them to Ainsley. He felt Jasper's forehead, not surprised to feel the heat pulsing from his skin. Then he examined his right leg, which was a mess. It was too late to sew up these cuts, but he could drain the pus and bandage the leg. He could treat this sick man. Hopefully, with a little luck, his life could be saved.

Ainsley didn't seem to mind that Tony didn't talk. She was an effective nurse: getting water, urging Jasper to take the pill Tony placed in Ainsley's hand, sterilizing the knife blade, and holding Jasper still as he cut into the worst of the infection to drain the poison from the skin. She even found a stick for Jasper to bite down on while Tony treated him, dabbing the cuts with alcohol, but the patient was drifting in and out of consciousness and didn't seem to be in unbearable pain.

Tony was vaguely aware of other people standing back on the beach behind him, probably watching him work, but he was dialled in and focused on his patient. Just like it used to be. Pedro always said that Tony had healing hands. Cleaning Jasper's leg, Tony felt like he was caring for someone he loved, which made no sense, as this was a stranger. But nothing had made sense for a long time. Except this. Caring for the body, which was caring for the person's soul at the same time.

Ainsley helped Tony loosely bandage up the leg when the draining was complete. It would look jagged when it healed, but these wounds needed air and time. Now they had to wait, to see if the expired antibiotics would be strong enough to fight the sepsis. These primitive conditions didn't help, but at least Jasper was up off the ground in this impressive, covered shelter. That had to count for something.

When he put his supplies away, snapping his kit closed, Ainsley drew close. She placed her hand on Tony's upper arm.

"Thank you," she said. He could hear some kind of lilting accent under her words that made the sentence sound musical. It was pleasant to listen to. He loved the feeling of her hand on his arm. For just this moment, Tony didn't feel so alone.

Diamond hadn't made physical contact with him. It could be the no-talking thing, that made Diamond wonder

just how damaged Tony was. He wasn't quite sure himself.
Tony used to talk a lot. He was the extrovert while Pedro,
the macho cop, was the introvert. But all the death and
violence had shut Tony's systems down. He'd open his
mouth, and nothing would come out. His words had gone
underground, steeping in sorrow in his bones and tissue.
For many months now, Tony thought he'd never speak
again. But he also hadn't considered another person finding
him, offering a lift in their boat, and then encountering
a small community of people surviving on an island that
was actually livable instead of destroyed or drowned. He
thought he'd given up all his hope, but hope was pushing
up now from the centre of his being, like a stubborn plant
in early spring.

"Is there anything I can do for you?" asked Ainsley.
"Anything you need?"

Tony looked at her kind, freckled face. She rubbed his
bicep, running her fingers lightly up and down his grungy
skin. Then he couldn't see her, at least not clearly, because
out of nowhere he was crying. Tony sank to his knees in
the sand, weeping out the grief that had been lodged inside
of him. His shoulders shook and his lungs heaved. He
heard animal noises, then realized they were coming from
his own mouth. Ainsley was beside him, holding him close,
and Tony clung to her like he had once held onto Pedro.

# twenty-two

## JASPER

When Jasper opened his eyes, he knew something was different. His head wasn't pounding like before. He'd been floating, in and out of awareness, for a long time. Vaguely aware of others, talking to him or around him, and touching him, but none of it felt quite real. Jasper's leg had stopped hurting, or he stopped noticing that it hurt, but now he felt a steady throbbing sensation.

He raised his head, peering down the length of his body. There were new white bandages wrapped around his thigh and calf. Jasper pulled himself up to a sitting position, then shifted his flowered sheet curtain to the side.

By the light, he guessed it was mid-morning. And hot. The salty seawater smell was pungent. He saw a new rowboat tied up. Iris and Ainsley were by the fire. A man Jasper had never seen before was chopping wood with Jasper's axe. He was compact and muscular, with long, dark hair. Jasper hoped someone would come tell him what was going on.

"Ainsley!" he tried to call, but his voice came out in a croak. He knocked a few times on the wood of the shelter, which caused Iris to look over.

"He's awake!" Iris said, her voice drifting over to Jasper. He watched both women stand and hurry over to him. Ainsley gestured to the man, who walked over from the other side of the beach.

Ainsley was the first to reach Jasper. She smiled, and it lit up her whole face. "Hi," she said. "Welcome back."

Iris added, "You had us worried."

"What happened?" To his ears, Jasper's voice sounded strange. Far away, and so hoarse.

"It was your leg," Ainsley explained. "You fell, more than a week ago now, hitting your head on one of the chairs. Iris brought some creams from her first aid kit, and we used bandages that Claudine had in her boat, but you ran a high fever and seemed to get worse. Until Tony came."

Both women stepped aside to reveal this mysterious Tony. He looked to be around Jasper's age, somewhere north of fifty.

Ainsley patted Tony on the shoulder, then proceeded to introduce him. "He doesn't speak, so we don't know much about him, but he came a few days ago with Diamond. That's the new rowboat. Diamond is young, almost eighteen, and they found Tony in a cop car and rescued him. He has medical supplies, and he cut into your sores and drained the pus from your leg."

Jasper was only half listening to this stream of information. His head felt curiously empty.

Tony leaned forward to feel Jasper's forehead. He nodded, like he was pleased. Then he peeled back some of the bandages and inspected Jasper's leg.

Iris handed Jasper a glass of water, which he drank in one long gulp. She took the glass, squeezing his hand.

"Do you need the chamber pot?" asked Ainsley. "Or some food?"

Jasper shook his head. He swallowed hard, looking at their pleased expressions. When he was in and out of consciousness, he had thought of Ginny and his girls. He remembered when they were a family, before everything broke apart and was destroyed. Jasper longed for them. To be close to them. Needed. Loved. It had felt possible, somehow, with his fever raging. But now, his ex-wife and his daughters were disappearing. He was here, on this island, and he would probably never see his family members again.

Jasper said, "Thank you, Tony. And Ainsley. And Iris."

They sat down beside him in the shelter. He had more questions, but his energy was fading fast. For now, this was enough. To still be alive. To imagine he might recover, and make some kind of life work here in this place, and with these people.

Jasper realized, looking out at the water, that the face he really wanted to see was Min's.

# twenty-three

## IRIS

Seeing Jasper come back to life was a miracle. Iris realized that all four of them had been holding their breath while he'd been ill, stuck in a strange holding pattern. They got on with the business of day-to-day survival, which was arduous and grueling, but without acknowledging it, each of them had been waiting to see if he would live or die.

Iris had become convinced he was going to die, after all those days with no improvement, until Tony came onto the beach with his medical kit. He moved to Jasper with such a sense of purpose, going to work on his leg and producing antibiotics like the world hadn't actually cratered in on itself. It was inspiring to witness. Watching him work, Iris felt a small stirring of hope for their future. Tony didn't seem like a doctor, but he must be, as he was so capable and sure of himself. None of them were certain, because he refused to write anything down or speak. He was a mystery, but it seemed as though Tony had saved Jasper's life, which was worth celebrating.

She was sitting at the dining table in her boat, reading through her clipboard notes. Checking on her supply lists was Iris's favourite calming activity. Claudine had called another meeting, by the fire this evening, and Iris was trying to decide how to proceed. When Jasper was so sick, and Claudine had swum with Iris, she found herself opening up to the younger woman. A tenuous truce had been reached between them, but Iris could feel the shift away from that peace now that Jasper was regaining his strength. Some new decisions would have to be made.

Iris breathed slowly. In for five, hold for two, out for seven. All hope is not lost, she told herself. *I am safe, and no one can hurt me.* But the familiar mantra failed to work its magic. Iris knew shifts in energy. She felt them coming, like changes in the wind or the undertone to the colour of the sky, and she managed by controlling whatever she could control. But with the arrival of Claudine, and now Diamond, who were already thick as thieves, Iris could feel her early alliance with Min breaking up and moving away from her grasp.

Pushing the yellow curtain aside, she saw the group of six forming by the fire. She would have to go and join them, whether she wanted to or not. Iris stood, holding her clipboard tight in her sweaty hands. With a loud sigh, she dropped it back onto the table. The sight of the clipboard irritated people. Iris would try her best to make do without it.

She took the back ladder down into the water, then made her way slowly to the fire pit. Jasper patted the empty space next to him on Min's log. Iris sat down.

"You look better," she said.

"I feel better."

Ainsley smiled at Iris and Jasper from her seat across from them. "He's promised that he won't do too much too fast, but it's obvious he really wants to hike up the hill to check on his traps."

"And use my fishing nets and equipment," added Claudine in a teasing tone.

Jasper said, "What I really want is Diamond and Tony's rowboat. That's the ideal vehicle for small excursions around the island. I want to see what's on the other side."

"When that leg's all the way healed, and Tony gives you the nod, we'll go together to see what's out there." Diamond grinned at Jasper. She was a gorgeous girl, thought Iris, with her sparkling hazel eyes and short black hair. Oh shit, she wasn't a girl. Diamond was nonbinary. Iris had to keep reminding herself to use they/them pronouns when referring to Diamond, or Claudine would get prickly and mad.

Min handed around a soggy box of cookies, something that had washed up to shore earlier that day in a beat-up envelope lined with thick bubble wrap. They were stale and broken into ragged chunks, oatmeal with chocolate chips, but the sugar tasted delightful on Iris's tongue. She wanted to ask what they were meeting about. Iris longed to run the discussion, but it felt so pleasant to sit here as a group, eating cookies and chatting about nothing too contentious.

She decided she could wait. There was no reason to rush. No clients were waiting for their session. Iris's life had been ruled by fifty-minute blocks for her entire adult life. Having so much empty space with no way to measure it should've been welcome, but it continued to frighten her. Structure was so much safer and more predictable than no structure.

Claudine cleared her throat and stood up from her log stool. Here we go, thought Iris, her pulse fluttering in her throat. Let's get this over with.

# twenty-four

## CLAUDINE

Claudine looked at the six faces sitting around the fire. To her, they were beautiful in this early evening summer light. In all that time Claudine hid in the fishing boat, expecting to be discovered and killed, she never imagined she would sit peacefully with a group of people on land again. Laughing. Eating crumbly old cookies. Feeling a little bit like a normal twenty-four-year-old Info Tech teacher again. If only her mom, dad, and Patrick were here with her. It made no sense that they were the ones to die instead of her, but Claudine was doing her best to learn to live with the unfairness of everything that had happened. Asking why was not a helpful exercise. Now Claudine was determined to move forward.

"Thanks, everyone, for coming. While Jasper was sick, we put some of these discussions on hold, because he was the priority. But now, thanks to Tony, his leg is healing, and the infection appears to be clearing up."

This prompted a spontaneous scattering of applause around the group. Tony turned his face to the side, tucking his chin down like a duck hiding in its feathers.

"There are seven of us now. And more could come at any time. Before Jasper fell, we had a discussion about some systems we could implement here so that things feel fair. What destroyed the old world cannot be allowed to wreck this new group. We have to do better, so I was hoping we could brainstorm a few ideas together."

Claudine smiled, trying to take the sting out of her words. She waited, certain Iris would be the first to speak.

"What is it about our group here that doesn't feel fair to you?" Iris's voice was calm, but deliberately so. The muscles around her mouth looked like they were drawn tight.

Stay calm, Claudine reminded herself. Nothing about this was going to work if Iris stormed out again. "Part of what doesn't feel fair involves resources and how we share them. In the world we all escaped from, the rich hoarded what they had, refusing to share. As the government got more unstable, and the climate crisis got worse, those of us who were marginalized and broke lost our jobs and our homes and we didn't have enough to eat, so we tried to fight back." These were simply the facts, but Iris seemed like she might argue with this statement, so Claudine decided to swiftly change gears. She remembered the pain on Iris's face when she talked about the men with the knife to her throat, and her house in flames. Claudine wanted to talk about the horrors of the fucking white supremacists, and the significant part they had played in the destruction of the before world, but she worried that Iris would take that personally as well.

Claudine sighed, then put her hands out in front of her, with her palms out. "What I'm saying is that we need all of us in order to make it out here. We have a real chance to create a new settlement here, something that works for everyone, not just a privileged few."

Min jumped in with, "Maybe we should start by forming some committees for the work that has to be done. Hunting, fishing, cooking, cleaning, bathrooms, building, exploring, and so on."

This got a few nods around the group. Iris was staring into the fire. Claudine decided to capitalize on any form of agreement. "Min is right," she said. "We should all say what we'd prefer to do, so we can spread the workload around fairly, and that should make our day-to-day lives easier. Let's take this one step at a time, building something we can all be proud of. Something better than what we just escaped from."

What Claudine itched to say was this: We can never really trust each other while Iris sleeps alone in her boat with a loaded gun, hoarding her food and supplies while the rest of us try to make a new life here together on this beach. She has to start sharing with us, and sleeping in the shelter with us, or she should leave so we can get on with this important work. But Claudine knew it was too early to speak this kind of blunt truth. She would have to learn to compromise. Min was exceptionally good at compromise, so Claudine would try to learn from her.

Iris was still staring into the crackling fire, apparently deep in thought. Claudine tried to summon her father's quiet yet authoritative professor voice. She could imagine him saying, "Easy, chicken. Rome wasn't built in a day. We only go as fast as our most hesitant team member." Thinking about Dad made Claudine softer and gentler. Less furious.

Claudine moved closer to Iris. She crouched down, so she was eye level with her. This would be painful, as Claudine hated the sight and the sound of the item she was about to request. To her, it represented control and hierarchy and fear. But Claudine thought it might also extend an olive branch of sorts to the most fearful member of this settlement.

Waiting until she knew the whole group was watching and listening, Claudine asked, "Iris, would you be willing to get your clipboard and write down the decisions the group makes so we have a record?"

# twenty-five

## AINSLEY

Ainsley felt conflicted looking across the fire at Iris, who had perked up since fetching her beloved clipboard. She couldn't help remembering how generous Iris had been during Ainsley's first days here, banged up and exhausted from the chopper crash. Iris had shared aspirin with Ainsley, allowed her to sleep on the sofa of her luxury boat, and made food for her. She could feel Iris's kindness bleeding through her hard exterior.

But that was then. Now, with the group of seven around this bonfire in the dusky evening light, Iris seemed like an obstacle blocking where everyone else wanted to go. And that made Ainsley sad. It was difficult to see what privilege looked like in yourself, but in Iris, Ainsley could see her own societal status reflected back to her, like staring into a cracked, distorted mirror.

Ainsley tried to listen as Iris created lists of who would serve on which committee, but Claudine's speech about the rich hoarding what they had as the climate crisis wiped out the poor rang in her mind. It was true. She and Thomas had done exactly that, hiring more guards to patrol their estate, and hiding out with their children when the fighting outside their locked gates escalated. They had hoped it wouldn't reach them, but of course it did. The mob was only after Thomas at first, allowing Ainsley to get away with a nanny and the two kids, but then the Yellowstone eruption happened, and she had to get her sick son away from the blanket of falling ash. He couldn't breathe, and Ainsley's friend Janna knew someone who still had access to their helicopter, and she thought safety might still exist outside the borders of the United States.

There were so many things Ainsley should've done better. Thomas was born and bred as an elite, but at Ainsley's core she was not. She had allowed herself to be lost. Unconcerned with the plight of others. Corrupted by her own insulated status as a wealthy white woman. When her housekeeper asked for money and forged papers to travel out of the country at the beginning of the civil war, Ainsley begged Thomas to help. He refused, saying it was better not to get involved in matters that didn't concern them. Ainsley remembered washing her face at her marble sink, looking in the mirror at Thomas's reflection as he sat shirtless in their king-sized bed, scrolling through his phone. He had no interest in the details about Luiza and her family. He didn't care, and Ainsley didn't want to upset him. So she did nothing. One day, when the laws about illegal citizens got stricter, Luiza didn't come to work. Ainsley thought about her almost every day, wondering what happened to her and her family, and if Ainsley's assistance would've made a difference.

Something about Claudine's impassioned words tugged at a loose thread of Ainsley's conscience. She would not stay quiet, like she had done since she married her husband. He was gone. Luiza was gone. The entire old world was gone. This was Ainsley's moment to practice courage, to remember the person she used to be.

She stood, clearing her throat politely, like it was a school PTA meeting. "Excuse me," Ainsley said.

The voices died out. Even the noise of Iris's ballpoint pen scratching across her paper ceased, creating a strange vacuum of sound. The tide was coming in. The fire crackled and spat. A lone bird sang, somewhere unseen in the trees. Everyone waited, looking at Ainsley.

Now, Ainsley told herself. Speak. Summon that red-haired Irish lass with the tiny frame but the huge, echoing belly laugh. She's not gone. She's here, inside of you. She is you.

"I'd like to tell you something." Her voice was thin, but holding its own. Ainsley made herself look at each person as she spoke. "My husband, Thomas, was CEO of a tech company in Seattle. When the mob came, they beat him to death with his golf clubs in our living room in front of me and our two kids. We ran after that, across the abandoned border. But I can see now how I was part of the problem. Responsible, even. Rich and spoiled. Intentionally turning my back on what was really happening in the world. I could ignore it, because I felt protected in the old world, right up to the end. But here, tonight, listening to Claudine talk about fairness and not allowing what destroyed civilization to inevitably cock up what we've got here, I get it. And I'm devastated by my part in it."

Ainsley felt Min's warm hand slip into her palm. Min squeezed, letting Ainsley know she was being heard. She didn't know she was crying until she felt the tears on her stained and torn sky-blue sleeveless blouse, the only shirt she owned. Ainsley felt as though something patched up inside of her was coming loose.

"My kids were only five and two. Just babies. And I couldn't keep them alive. I haven't said their names out loud, or even in my mind, because I'm overwhelmed by shame. I stayed with Thomas for them, trying my best to keep them safe, and it all failed. I failed. But I've also hurt you—Claudine, Diamond, and sweet Min—because I didn't care what might be happening to you." She paused, looking around the faces in the firelight. Her voice rose and fell as she forced out her confession. "And Jasper, you too. Probably you, Tony, as well. I don't know your story, because you don't talk, but we had loads of money, Thomas and me, and we didn't share it with anyone. We tried to keep it, to protect ourselves, so maybe I deserve what I got. It's my penance, for being a selfish and horrible cunt. I'm sorry I couldn't see it. I didn't know. And I don't think I deserve a place here, with all of you, who welcomed me and cared for me, even though you didn't know how very rich and cruel I was."

The tears were coming faster now, cutting off Ainsley's ability to speak. She doubled over, at the waist, wailing the way she heard Tony cry his first day on the beach.

Ainsley felt Min draw close, then more arms, hands, and heads came near, in a wider circle. She heard words being said in low tones, but couldn't make sense of them. Ainsley wept until her insides were swept clean, then in the centre of her empty being she imagined the two names she had locked away for safekeeping, written large on the blank wall of her soul: Ava and William.

# twenty-six

## MIN

M in had no idea Ainsley was a mother. She had thought about Chul, nearly every minute of every day, so knowing Ainsley for weeks and only now finding out they were both mothers was a shock to her system. Of course, people handled grief in their own private ways, and judging those with different coping systems was a waste of precious time and energy. But your children? To Min, that felt like it was on another scale or level.

Still, she was the first to slip her hand into Ainsley's and then wrap her arms around Ainsley's diminutive body. Pain was pain, and Ainsley's was visible for all of them to see. Min also felt relieved, in a way that was challenging to pinpoint, by her acknowledgement that the wealth Ainsley enjoyed had indirectly wounded most of the survivors sitting here around this fire. Ainsley's privilege had made the world less safe for the people of colour who lived here now. And Diamond, who was nonbinary. Ainsley came here in a private helicopter, for Christ's sake, while Min floated for weeks under the punishing sun on a rickety homemade raft.

Now that Ainsley's storm of grief had passed, everyone was refueling with cookies and cool water, collected earlier from the stream, stored in the large insulated drinking jug Diamond had brought with them in the rowboat. Tony had built a box for the red water container, and they had fastened the top of the jug to the wood and tied the contraption to Iris's boat, so the water stayed cool in the ocean. It sure beat the tepid rainwater they used to collect. Drinking cool water helped bring the body temperature down.

When Min settled back into her seat, a plastic mug of water in her hand, she noticed Jasper's eyes on her. Min offered him a small smile. This had been happening more and more since he had recovered from his infected leg. Jasper would offer to help Min when she was engaged in a particular task, like cleaning fish or scrubbing out the frying pan. Earlier this week, when she couldn't sleep in the predawn hours and was walking along the shore, Jasper came to join her. They didn't talk, but she found his presence comforting and welcome, which unsettled her.

No one seemed to know quite what to say after Ainsley's vulnerability had been put on full display. Min noticed that Iris seemed even more tense. It looked like Claudine might be gearing up to take over, and Min worried she would push too hard in this sensitive space. She could hear Dae's voice in her ear, saying with a laugh, "Go ahead then, mother. Make everyone feel comfortable. It's your specialty." Min smiled to herself, glad she could still summon his presence when she needed her husband most. She could only make things right for other people in her previous life because Daeshim was there to make things right for her.

Min decided to stay in her seat, but she spoke with a firm tone. "Thank you, Ainsley, for sharing so much of yourself with us. That had to be painful. Being brave always is."

Others nodded around the fire. The light was slowly seeping out of the sky, the sun inching closer to the water. "We've made a good start here," she continued. "With committees sketched out for the basic things we need to survive. Claudine has also brought up the important issue of fairness, and what that fairness should look like in our little settlement. I think we should keep talking about this, but let's not rush anyone." Min said this for Iris's benefit, who glanced up and met Min's eye with a grateful expression on her face.

"It will be dark soon," said Min, "and we all need to get some rest, but the one word I keep thinking of is 'safety.' What would make each of us feel safe here? Should we think about that overnight and revisit the subject tomorrow? Iris can bring her clipboard out, and throughout the day she can write down everyone's responses. Then we can go from there. Would that work, do you think?"

More nodding. Min felt warmed inside, the way she felt after a particularly hard-hitting climate lecture when she sensed some of the audience's resistance melting. A decade ago, Min loved nothing more than to hear people fired up after one of her talks, plotting and planning what they could do to be involved to mitigate the disaster already unfolding.

"Could I say one thing?" Iris asked.

No, Iris, please don't blow this now, Min thought. We've come so far. Don't make it hostile. Please.

Min attempted to send this message to Iris by furrowing her brow a bit, with no idea if she'd succeeded or failed. She forced a smile onto her face. "Sure," said Min.

Looking directly at Min, Iris said, "One thing that would make me feel safe is separate sleeping quarters for men and for women on the beach. I would like to feel more a part of things with everyone, but sleeping where men are nearby is…" her voice faltered, then came back in a whisper, "… difficult for me."

Min turned her body slightly toward Jasper. "Would this be possible, Jasper? A separate shelter being built?"

His answer was gentle. "Sure. I could build that."

Iris looked over at Jasper. Her eyes were dry, but wide. She nodded once, to acknowledge his reply, and then a silence fell over the group.

# twenty-seven

## JASPER

After Iris's question about the separate shelters, the meeting seemed to wind down. Tony agreed to do the nightly animal perimeter watch, checking to be sure all food waste was properly disposed of, and nothing seemed to be prowling in the forest behind the shelter. The wolves were sporadically howling, as usually happened when darkness fell, but they were farther up the mountain and couldn't be seen. Both Iris and Ainsley hurried away, and Diamond and Claudine drifted together in the direction of the bathroom. That left Jasper alone with Min.

He felt unexpectedly nervous, wiping his sweaty palms on his ragged black shorts. Something about Min reminded Jasper of his youth. Her kindness, and razor-sharp intelligence, stirred up sensations that he hadn't experienced since he was a teenager. Since landing on this island, Jasper had observed himself from a distance. There were a lot of things he saw that he didn't like. His desperation to fit in, to pretend to be white by his proximity to Ginny, to deny his Indigenous heritage because it seemed like it might be a hassle for others. Long after his divorce, Jasper was still defining his identity by Ginny's standards, instead of his own.

In those first weeks here, when he felt lost and ashamed of how hard he'd worked to hide himself away, Min was a type of balm for Jasper's soul. Just being near her calmed him, made him feel both strong and capable. They worked well together. He knew Min's husband and teenaged son had died, and Jasper had been careful never to pry into these personal areas. But lately, since he'd come back from his long fever and infection, Jasper couldn't ignore that he felt like a lovesick puppy around Min.

"Should I put the fire out?"

Swimming in his own thoughts, Jasper came back to reality with a jolt. Min was standing near him, with drink glasses in her hands. The fire was burning down to its embers.

"No, it will be out soon enough. I might sit here for a little longer. You're welcome to join me if you'd like." He held his breath, waiting for her to reply. She seemed to be thinking it over.

"Okay." Min held up the cups. "Let me go drop these in the kitchen area and I'll be back."

She walked away down the beach. Jasper let out his breath. He limped over to the wood pile and added two logs to the dying fire, then he sat down on the first log that Min had used when she was alone on the island, before Iris and Jasper came. Even though he'd built and designed other chairs out of logs, he preferred this seat. He knew Min did as well.

He watched her walk back to the fire. Jasper recognized that this was not an appropriate time to develop feelings for someone. Min was fragile, like everyone here, and Jasper would likely be dead now if Tony hadn't come along when he did with a bottle of antibiotics in his medical kit. He wondered if this new attraction was because of his near-death experience. None of them knew how much time they had left in this strange life they were living. The precarious nature of this experience made every moment feel more urgent and valuable to Jasper.

Min came and sat down beside Jasper on the log. He felt his throat go dry, so he swallowed hard. His heartbeat sounded loud in his ears.

"So tell me, Jasper, did I make things better tonight, or worse?"

"Better. Definitely. I think you make everything better." Oh shit, why had he said that? Jasper could feel his cheeks burn in the gathering darkness.

Min turned her head. "That's kind of you to say." She reached out with her hand to pat his, which was resting between them on the log. Without thinking about it, he turned his palm upwards and closed it around hers. Jasper's heart was galloping now. Min squeezed once, then pulled her hand away and placed it on her lap.

Jasper said, "I don't know why I did that. I'm sorry." He looked away from her, at the last stirring oranges and yellows of the sunset.

"Don't be sorry. I'm just afraid of more complications right now. I think we should focus on the challenges ahead before we get into anything else."

"Sure." Jasper's voice sounded strange, like someone was stepping on his vocal cords.

"We were all so worried about you when you were sick, Jasper. You've done so much for all of us, and you mean so much to us."

All of us, Jasper thought. Not Min personally. But what did he really expect? He was the one who nearly died, not her. Iris wanted a separate shelter for the women so she could feel safe. Maybe Min wanted that, too, but just hadn't asked. Don't be a jerk, Jasper told himself.

He turned his face back to Min. She looked sad in the

waning firelight. Jasper gave Min a smile. "All of you have come to mean so much to me as well. I'm glad I've been given a bit more time. We still have a lot of work to do here."

"Yes, we do." They sat together in silence, both lost in their thoughts, before Min added, "And I think you make everything better, too."

# twenty-eight

## TONY

Tony had been working with Jasper for a few weeks on construction projects. Diamond and Claudine helped out, and so did Min and Ainsley when they weren't busy with the cooking and cleaning tasks. Everything was running more smoothly since that first fraught evening meeting, where Ainsley broke down in tears. Committees had been formed, each with a team leader, and it seemed like people were gentler with one another and more conciliatory with decision-making now.

When Iris had come around with her clipboard to ask about safety, Tony took the pen she offered and placed it against the paper. Random thoughts and images went through his mind, mostly of Pedro and their chocolate Lab, Maxwell, in happier days. Watching TV or reading, while petting Max's silky head. Choosing a mellow bottle of red and opening it with a spirit of celebration, even if it were just a Tuesday evening and they both happened to be off work at the same time. Sunday mornings in bed, Pedro's stubble dark on his chin. All of it meant safety to Tony. Yet none of it would translate here.

He had shaken his head, unable to write a single word. Iris took the pen from his hand, saying, "It's okay, Tony, really. Don't worry about it." Her voice was tinged with compassion. It was the first time Tony could glimpse the therapist she used to be.

Jasper and Tony worked well together as a building crew. Jasper still tired easily, and Tony felt protective of Jasper as his patient, so Tony shooed him away from the heavy lifting. Jasper designed the buildings, explaining carefully how to saw the logs and shape them so they fit together at the ends. Claudine and Diamond had enormous energy, because they were young and fit, so Tony left some of the most arduous building work to them. He enjoyed the sensation of being exhausted at the end of the day. It was refreshing to be so tired that he could sleep without dreaming.

The town was coming along well. Jasper and Min had been calling it a settlement, but that seemed too formal to the younger people. Once, Ainsley said it reminded her of sleepaway camp at home in Ireland, so she suggested that for a name. Claudine and Diamond bristled at the thought of including the word 'camp,' so Iris said, "It's our town, isn't it?" and that was the name that stuck.

Now they had a women's sleeping shelter, with a roof made of interlocking logs, covered by a tarp from Iris's boat. Laid over the tarp were sets of overlapping evergreen boughs, which helped to deaden the sound of rain. Next to that was the original shelter, for Jasper and Tony, with similar improvements made to their roof. Down the beach a short distance was a covered dining area, with a long table and eight chairs, where they ate most mornings and evenings together. Closer to the water was a cooking hut, with a covered trough built to store water brought down from the freshwater stream in buckets and old scoured jerry cans. The next construction project was a medical building, where Iris had generously offered a few locking cabinets from her boat to store Tony's precious supplies.

When the medical centre was finished, Iris requested a

covered space the group could use for meetings and games. Diamond was in charge of entertainment, as they used to produce a lot of videos before the internet went down, and Diamond was tremendously excited by what they referred to as "the rec room." Tony had no idea what this would look like, or why it seemed so important to people, but he was willing to build it if it kept the peace around town.

Tony was in charge of the medical decisions. He recognized that his inability to speak was a liability for leadership, but up to now he'd managed to communicate without words. Ainsley was the best at understanding him. Somehow, the two of them seemed to be able to reach each other. Tony had no clue why this was the case, but he was grateful for Ainsley. She had become his voice out here, looking after him in a way that profoundly moved Tony.

He looked around now, from his space on the warm sand where he was threading together large fronds with chunks of moss to create insulation for his medical clinic, and marveled at how their town hummed with vitality. Iris worked with her clipboard in the dining area. Ainsley banked up the drinking water station with rocks. Claudine and Diamond were up the mountain, pulling in small game from Jasper's snares. Min washed dishes near the cooking hut. Jasper measured along the sand for the new rec centre, stepping back every so often to think and imagine what should go where.

Tony hadn't known any of these people a month ago, when he sat in Amelia's police car, waiting to drown. He wanted to see Pedro again, more than anything else. But then Diamond came by, finding him like a needle in a haystack, and he swam out and into their rowboat.

He still felt shellshocked, like his true essence was buried away and no one had the key to unlock it. But he could also imagine one day opening his mouth and words tumbling out of him again. With these six people, he'd found a new home. There was so much he didn't know about what had happened to all of them, but with each passing day, it mattered less and less. They needed each other. Plain and simple. The rest was extraneous.

Finished with her decorative water work, Ainsley sauntered up the beach to Tony. "Need a hand?" she asked with a bright smile, her curly red hair bright in the sunshine.

Tony nodded. Ainsley sat beside him, and he handed her a stack of fresh green moss.

# twenty-nine

## DIAMOND

Diamond was hunting with Claudine. It was Diamond's favourite thing to do. So primal, snapping little forest creatures' necks. Jasper had taught them both how to skin the animals and joint them. And now Ainsley was taking the pelts and repurposing them into clothing, so nothing the island gave up was being wasted. They knew there might be deer, and were actively searching for them, but so far, no joy.

Being alone with Claudine felt exciting to Diamond. Claudine knew who Diamond was, from their videos, and that continued to thrill Diamond after a few weeks of living here. After hiding out, and grieving their mom's sudden death, being recognized by Claudine was like belonging somewhere again. Stepping back into the spotlight. Not being strange or freakish, but inspiring instead. Claudine's respect made Diamond feel invincible. And attractive, for the first time in a long time.

"Do you want to take a break? Have some water and hang out before we bring these to the hut?" Claudine turned to Diamond, holding the dead squirrels, rabbits, and birds up high. She was backlit by the sun, under a canopy of leafy trees, and Diamond was flooded by a wave of desire.

"Good idea," Diamond said. They both settled in, leaning against two trees. Diamond found a stick and scraped their teeth with it.

"Do you think Tony's ever going to talk again?" This was a favourite question of Claudine's. She found his silence endlessly fascinating.

Diamond shrugged by way of answering, then added, "And no, I don't know why he doesn't speak. He didn't exactly tell me while we were together in the boat. But I do get the feeling something awful happened, and he hasn't been able to come to terms with it."

Claudine rolled her eyes. "Oh, did something awful happen? Like the fucking world ending? Poor baby. Good thing nothing bad happened to either of us." She laughed—a harsh, biting sound.

"There's different levels of awful."

Claudine stopped laughing. "I do know that, but comparing doesn't really help anyone. We've all been through hell, okay? I outlived my parents and my brother, lying on the floor of a smelly fishing boat under a mouldy tarp to avoid mobs who wanted to kill me. All because my skin isn't white, and the religious nuts that took over the government made that a crime. And you were speaking out against the politicians who outlawed gay rights long before that, so you were targeted and threatened because you refused to back down. You kept on making videos. And I kept watching them, and started helping people fight back by stealing identities and bank accounts online. We got dealt shitty hands, but neither of us went silent. We're still fighting. We're still here."

Diamond said, "Tony's still here, too. He didn't need to say anything to bring Jasper back to life, or to help build the town we've got. I think you should go easy on him."

Claudine smiled. "Okay, I'll be nicer to your boyfriend if it means that much to you."

"He's not my boyfriend. But you should be nice to him anyway."

"Fine. Just don't ask me to be nice to Iris."

Leaning over the dead game, covering the distance between them, Claudine rested her palms in the dirt and stared Diamond square in the face. Diamond felt their heart start pounding. "What about you?" Claudine asked. "Should I be nice to you?"

Diamond didn't trust their voice to work. They dropped the stick, then nodded. Claudine scooched her body closer, running her fingers down the side of Diamond's face. Everything seemed to slow down, like video running at half speed. At seventeen, Diamond had never been kissed, but they'd imagined it many, many times. With boys. Or girls. Or other nonbinary people. Diamond didn't care. They just wanted to feel alive, and attractive, and wanted by someone.

Claudine's mouth brushed against Diamond's. It felt warm. Wet. Sensual. They kissed back, exploring with their tongue, feeling all there was to feel. Diamond's hands ran down Claudine's shoulders and touched her breasts. The sound of their panting was loud, overwhelming the subtle noises of the forest.

Moving the dead animals aside, Claudine laid Diamond down, sitting astride them.

"Should I stop?" she asked, ready to tear off her tank top.

"Fuck, no," Diamond answered, pulling Claudine down onto them.

# thirty

## CLAUDINE

Claudine had never been with a woman before. She'd only ever had sex with men, white men to be more precise, but something about Diamond reminded Claudine of the internet, which stirred a powerful yearning deep in her being. And Diamond was famous in the before world, so Claudine felt like she already knew them. Having Diamond here added glamour to this whole adventure. And they didn't identify as a woman, Claudine reminded herself.

They skinned the game together in the cooking hut. Diamond had blood and entrails all over their hands and arms. The first time Claudine did this job with Jasper, the ripping sound of flesh separating from fur made her sick. She ran to the toilets and vomited. It reminded her of the bloodshed Claudine and Patrick had to escape, by hiding out in their cousin's boat. But now, Claudine had come to enjoy this ritual. It was raw and animal in and of itself. Real, instead of virtual. Butchering animals to feed the group awakened a primal instinct in Claudine. The whole process made her feel powerful.

Claudine skinned the pelts with the old rusty knife, preparing them for Ainsley to repurpose into clothing. Apparently, Ainsley had studied fashion design in university, but dropped out when she met her billionaire tech husband. She lost everything in the helicopter crash, so her committee position was clothing and comfort items. Over dinner the other night she mentioned making new pillows using feathers and hides. Claudine loved seeing people coming into their own unique identities here on this island. It brought hope right back up to the surface when she worried it had been lost forever.

As she skinned a rabbit pelt, the knife scraping quietly against the hide, Claudine watched Diamond work. They looked sexy, like a contestant on a survival show. Diamond had been mildly embarrassed by their breast binder, but Claudine kissed the dirty fabric wrap around their chest and said it was fine. Claudine asked if it hurt, and Diamond only shrugged.

Now, Claudine sighed, wondering if she'd taken advantage of Diamond, who was not quite eighteen. She could tell Diamond was a little infatuated with her, and had been since they arrived, but Claudine was tired of being careful. Things were finally starting to improve with their town, now that Iris had stepped aside and stopped fighting Claudine every step of the way. Diamond was an important ally to have, against Iris, and now Claudine suspected Diamond would be even more loyal after their romp in the woods.

She didn't mean to be so mercenary, even in her own thoughts. Claudine enjoyed the release as much as she imagined Diamond did, but she would have to be careful. Looking after another person's feelings was not something Claudine was prepared to do. It was enough to manage her own, and try to keep this fragile town on the path to fairness and equality. Diamond was young, and impressionable, but Claudine was young as well. Only twenty-four. She had big plans to rebuild the internet, and re-imagine what society could've been if it hadn't imploded. Diamond was a fun distraction, but Claudine would have to be sure they didn't expect more than she could give.

Claudine set the rabbit and squirrel furs aside. She still had to pluck the feathers from the birds they'd caught. She came up behind Diamond, who was attempting to clean up the wooden counter.

"So that was fun," Claudine murmured into Diamond's ear. "But I think we should keep this a secret for now. You know, not put too much pressure on ourselves."

She felt Diamond stiffen up. Oh God, thought Claudine, they're disappointed. She held her breath, hoping this situation wouldn't spin out of control.

Diamond didn't move. Under their breath, Claudine heard them say, "If that's what you want."

Claudine pushed her body between Diamond and the cooking hut table. Diamond's eyes were on their bloody hands. "Hey," Claudine said. "Talk to me."

Without making eye contact, Diamond murmured, "I've never even kissed someone before. This was all new for me. And I loved it, but now you wish nothing had happened between us."

Claudine shook her head, stepping back a bit in case anyone could see them through the window. "I didn't say that I wish nothing happened. I just don't know how other people will feel about this. I'm older, and I don't want you to think I'm taking advantage of you. I think you're gorgeous, and sexy, and I have a great time with you. But out here, it's day-to-day, just to survive. I'm not sure there's any point in planning for more."

Diamond still looked crushed. They wiped at their eyes with their elbow, as there was so much blood on their hands. Claudine could see their vulnerability clearly on display, but couldn't take responsibility for it. She simply didn't have space for it.

Claudine tried again, in a softer tone. "What I'm trying to say is that I want to keep our friendship as our first priority. We can have a little fun whenever we can find time on our own, but let's not complicate matters by making anything obvious in front of other people. That way we won't have to answer any questions or put up with a bunch of knowing looks whenever we spend time together."

This seemed to help to calm Diamond down, so Claudine waited, and then said in a slightly firmer tone, "Okay? Does that make sense?"

Diamond nodded, swallowing hard and clearing their throat a few times. Claudine rewarded them with a bright smile. She leaned down and lifted the full bucket of blood and innards.

"I'll go bury this while you clean up and then we'll go for a swim." Diamond nodded.

Claudine turned and went out of the hut. She would have to be careful here or this situation would get away from her.

# thirty-one

## AINSLEY

Min and Ainsley worked together at the dining table. Ainsley called this their sewing circle. They had feathers in a large, covered bowl, animal hides, grass, moss, leaves, shells, and some bark, along with raggedy items of clothing other group members had donated or had washed up to shore. Jasper had carved needles from animal bone, and they used fishing line as thread. Ainsley wanted to see what she could create for them to wear when the weather got colder or when their own meagre supplies of clothing and blankets wore out. She was determined to make her three years of fashion design mean something out here so she could contribute to the growing town.

"I've never sewn a single thing in my whole life," Min confessed, threading shells on a string of copper wire. "I was a very bad mom that way. I was too busy in the lab or writing research papers to do much of anything too domestic with Chul."

Ainsley laughed. "I had a whole staff of people to be domestic, so I never sewed after college either. I didn't have to." What a waste, she thought, but did not say.

Min said, "I didn't cook much either, but we've all had to learn how to do that here."

"Whether we want to or not." Ainsley laid out the tanned pelts they had collected so far, trying to imagine the most useful garment or quilt she could make with these. It was boiling hot right now, and so difficult to imagine that one day they might be freezing, but Ainsley was trying to plan ahead for the upcoming fall and winter.

In her mind, she could imagine herself wearing a fabulous dried grass skirt with a crop top made from animal hide with shells as tassels. Ainsley's current clothes could probably stand up on their own, in spite of repeated washings with a pinch of the laundry powder Iris had finally shared with the group, and she was sick of the sight and the feel of them. They reminded Ainsley of being rich, something she was trying hard to get away from. This was a whole new world. She wanted to dress for it.

Ainsley picked up scissors and started to trim one of the squirrel pelts. She held it up to her chest, trying to imagine how it could work as part of a top.

In a quiet voice, Min said, "I was really surprised to hear you say you had children."

Ainsley's hands stilled on the fur. She looked up and into Min's kind face.

"It's just that we're the only two mothers out here. Before that night, I thought I was the only one. It's a specific type of anguish, losing your child."

"Yes," Ainsley replied. A hush fell between them, making this dining space feel like church to Ainsley, the one she remembered from her childhood in Ireland.

"I lost my husband Daeshim at the beginning, in one of the earliest pandemic waves. Before we knew how bad it would all get, with the fevers and the red sores and the lungs filling with fluid and drowning you a day after infection. He was an ER doctor, so on the front lines. Chul was only fourteen then, but he took care of me when Dae died. He got me out of Regina, and found us a family to travel with. But Alberta was so cold in the winter, and there was no power, and one morning I couldn't get him to wake up." Min's eyes were dark with pain. "Fifteen, and frozen to death. Why him and not me? I stopped eating and drinking on that goddamn raft, and I still couldn't seem to die."

Ainsley nodded. "We've all wondered why we should survive when those we love didn't." She paused, amending her words. "Those we were responsible for." Ainsley could see them then, her little girl and boy, standing side by side with their reddish-blonde hair and blue eyes, looking at her. They had needed her, and she had failed them. Ainsley's heart constricted, the walls of her soul flooding with agony like water over a barricade.

Min got up and came closer. She touched Ainsley on the arm. "I suppose we look after each other now, and hope that's enough to reach them. It's all we can do. Try to stay alive, whether we want to or not. For each other."

Ainsley heard her but couldn't think of anything to say in response. She looked down at Min's hand, but she couldn't feel it on her skin. It was like she was already dead.

# thirty-two

## MIN

Min was in the bathroom in the middle of the night, trying not to cry out with each stomach cramp that doubled her over in pain. She'd had violent diarrhea on and off for the last few days. Min put it down to the new mushrooms and berries the cooking committee had been adding to their meals. Jasper suggested they take all new foods slowly and carefully, with a single person testing each one first before serving it to everyone, but Min's digestive system was not pleased with something she'd been consuming.

Tony had been keeping a close eye on Min, noticing that something wasn't quite right. He'd offered her some antacids from his medical supplies, but she declined. What Min longed for was an ice-cold can of Sprite, her favourite cure for any stomach upset. When Chul was a pre-teen, he often complained of a flu bug, just so he could get a few cans of Sprite. The thought made Min smile, even while she was angrily shitting herself in a log outhouse, the smell vicious and nauseating. It felt so good to think of Chul and not be in pain for once.

She used a lot of the moss to clean herself up, almost emptying the container Jasper had built to store it. First thing in the morning she would have to get more. Ainsley had asked if the moss could somehow be shaped into a toilet roll, which made everyone laugh. Any excuse to feel normal was welcome here, but Min was so accustomed to the moss now that it was hard to even remember the convenience and comfort of toilet paper.

Min picked up Iris's little battery-operated lamp and stepped out of the women's bathroom. The outline of a person standing near the men's facilities surprised Min. She let out a sharp gasp.

"I came to be sure you were okay. Sorry to startle you." Jasper, come to check on her.

Min lifted her lantern so she could see Jasper's face. He smiled. She felt her heart skip a beat, then waited for the inevitable prickling of guilt to follow. But this time, in the pitch dark, she didn't feel bad. Jasper was a good man. Dae had been dead for over two years. Not one of the seven survivors here on this island knew if they had a single day to live or another ten thousand. All of a sudden, Min couldn't see what she'd been so worried about.

"I should go wash my hands," she said.

"I'll come with you, unless you'd rather be alone."

"I don't need to be alone."

They walked together, to the bathing cove, where Min leaned down to wash her hands in the salt water. She splashed some on her warm face. When she stood up, she saw stars in the outline of her vision. She wavered on her feet, then felt Jasper reach out to support her with his hands on her thin upper arms.

The next thing Min knew, she was weightless. It took her a moment to recognize that Jasper was carrying her in his arms.

"No, your leg," she whispered.

He said, "I'm fine. It's you I'm worried about now." He walked a few uneven steps, toward the shelter.

"Jasper. I want to talk to you."

In the moonlight, his face so near to hers, Min felt overcome by a foreign sensation of gratitude. She needed this man. Here, in this after world, Jasper made sense to her. Min would have to let both Dae and Chul go. They were already gone, into some other realm where she could no longer reach them, but Jasper was right here in front of her. She wrapped her arms around his neck and squeezed, for all she was worth, holding onto him like he meant survival itself. Jasper answered by tightening his grip on her, burrowing his face next to Min's.

It started to rain, the sky spitting fat drops that splashed onto their skin. Min looked up, laughing at the sensation of being carried, in the middle of the night, on an island in the middle of the Pacific Ocean. It was ridiculous. And wonderful, in its own strange way.

Without saying a word, Jasper moved with Min in his arms toward Tony's medical centre. They had built two rudimentary beds, creating mattresses out of dried grass sewn into a pair of Iris's sheets, and Jasper settled Min onto one of these with the care of a nurse handling a newborn. Min relished the love she could feel in his touch. It was simple and pure, a thing of beauty.

He moved to sit across from her on the other bed, the rain gently battering the thatched roof, but Min grabbed his arm and pulled him back to her. He lay down beside her. Min reached for his hand, holding it between both of hers. Jasper turned his face to look at her in the low light of Iris's lamp. His eyes were so kind.

"Min."

"Jasper," she answered back. "I've been afraid. To care too much. To need you. Because of Dae and Chul."

"I know. It's okay."

"No. It's not okay." Her voice became cloudy, choked off by tears that threatened to fall. "I already need you, and have for some time. I'll never stop being afraid, and I loved my husband, I really did, but he's gone. And you're here. I don't think there's any point in waiting around."

With his free hand, Jasper wiped the tears from Min's eyes. He stroked her black hair. When he spoke, his voice also sounded strained. "I loved Ginny, too, but that was over years ago. I wasn't a good husband to her, and I let my girls down when they were younger and needed me. It's the biggest regret of my life. But they are all gone—Ginny and Dae and our children. Maybe now, after we've lost everything, we can start over. Or at least try."

Min's stomach cramped again. She brought her legs up, breathing through it. Jasper seemed to know what was happening, as he shifted his body to the side to give her more space. He put his arms around her. It felt so good to be held.

She moved her face closer to Jasper's and kissed him. Just once, lightly, to practice. He responded with warmth, but allowed it to die out quickly. Min laid her head on his shoulder. She knew if she needed the bathroom again, urgently, Jasper would help her get there. He'd make sure she had what she needed. The thought brought a feeling of joy to her weary body.

Min felt Jasper reach across her to extinguish the light, and then they slept.

# thirty-three

## IRIS

" **I** know lots of people who went to therapy, but Thomas always said it was for weak people without enough common sense to solve their own problems." Ainsley made a face, then followed this up with, "I'm sorry. I don't mean to be offensive."

Iris laughed. "Believe me, I've heard it all. 'Therapists are quacks, it's a total waste of time, touchy-feely nonsense, witch doctors.' I'm not offended. I'm glad you asked me for a session."

They were sitting in the newly constructed rec room, leaning against pillows Ainsley had sewn, sipping mugs of tea. It was almost normal. Cozy. Safe, even.

Iris had already explained to Ainsley that this couldn't possibly be therapy under the old world's terms, because they were friends who saw each other outside of the treatment space. Normally, boundaries were a critical piece of the therapist/client relationship, but here that type of separation simply wasn't practical. To which Ainsley shrugged and said, "We'll just have to make new rules, then."

So that's what they did. Iris got out her clipboard and wrote out potential treatment options, feeling her competence slowly return, like she was turning up a dial. What was therapy, after all, but helping other people while trying to protect yourself from becoming too embroiled in the other person's pain and problems? Maybe there was a way for Iris to try to heal herself while healing others. She figured it couldn't hurt, and it would give some shape to her otherwise far-too-open days.

Ainsley was a terrific first client in this new setting. She had never been to therapy before, so had no preconceived notions. Both women agreed to simply share honestly with one another, or as close to honesty as they could manage in any given day, and only in this space. Iris hoped this would provide the sense of boundaries, knowing that certain types of vulnerable sharing only happened here, and not in the shelter or around the dining table or a bonfire on the beach. Iris hadn't wanted to bring therapy into her boat, as that encroached on her personal space in a way she couldn't countenance, but this recreation room was different. She could set rules and keep them in here.

Iris finished her mint tea (she only had a handful of tea bags left, but Claudine kept experimenting with herbs from the forest to make a similar flavour) and set her cup down on the wooden table in front of her. "Is there anything in particular you wanted to talk about today?"

"Besides the scandal of Jasper and Min in the medical centre, you mean?" Ainsley grinned, showing her dimples.

Iris smiled, but it was her professional version. The one that said, I'm willing to engage with you in whatever way you need, but the clock is ticking.

Ainsley looked out the window, an open space cut into the logs. They could hear the tide coming in, crashing up against the beach. She was quiet for a long time, then she said, "I guess I wanted to tell someone what I've been thinking these last few weeks. And you seemed like the best fit."

Tipping her head to one side, Iris waited until Ainsley turned her head back to face her. "Why's that?" she asked.

"Because you're trained to listen. And to care. You're the closest thing we have to a priest out here, Iris."

"I can't absolve you of any sins. I'm not licensed for that."

Ainsley smiled. "I know that. I'm not looking for forgiveness. Just someone I can tell my feelings to. These last few weeks, building this town with everyone, I've realized how fucking unhappy I was before, in my marriage and my rich, stupid life. I was invisible, a shell of who I used to be. Nothing at all, really. It makes me wonder if my kids could even see me properly. I mean, I know they loved me, and I loved them, but I was there for Thomas, to be whatever he wanted me to be. And I despise that now. I wish, so badly, that I could go back and tell him to fuck off. That I could be the girl I used to be, instead of the pretend woman I became."

She paused here, and Iris recognized the moment to intervene with her therapeutic wisdom. But she chose not to speak. Iris waited, recognizing that Ainsley was getting to a discovery all on her own. Perhaps everyone here simply needed a chance to talk without being interrupted. To unburden themselves with no other expectations.

"I was filled with shame, for so long, but now it seems to be changing into something else. I couldn't say my own children's names to myself, or even remember their faces, at first. But the night I lost it around the fire with everyone, when Claudine was talking about privilege and fairness, I could see their names, in my mind. And later, their faces." Her voice, with its pretty Irish lilt, got softer now. Iris had to lean forward to hear her.

"I'm not sure what any of this means, except that it's better that they aren't lost to my memory. They are no more, my darling Ava and William, but I did my best to save them. I would've died in a heartbeat so that they could live, but some things are out of our control. I was their mother, and I tried to keep them with me, but I couldn't do it. And now I have to let that go."

She wept. Quietly this time, and controlled. Iris stood and came over, sitting beside Ainsley on the bench, hoping her presence would provide some comfort. What would it be like to be a mother as society crumbled around you? Iris was relieved to never have to find this out. She had been viciously attacked by a group of men, but at least she did not get pregnant. Shuddering, Iris forced herself to focus on Ainsley. Stay here, stay present, be there for your client. This was Therapy 101.

Iris said, "That sounds like a healthy response to unbearable pain. You did your very best to save them, but as you said, some things are out of our control."

Nodding, Ainsley wiped at her tear-stained face. Iris reached for her box of tissues, passing them to her client. She could've been in her minimalist office right now, with those calming white walls. Some things transcended tragedy, and this normalcy of therapist and client felt like one of them. It was holy ground, what the two of them were doing here. A chance to close up a gaping wound. To make sense of the unimaginable, through words and the compassion and time of another person.

"And as for Thomas," continued Iris, "you can tell him to fuck off any time you want to. Even if he's dead."

"I can?" Ainsley asked, amazed.

"Sure. We can do it together, if you like."

"Yes, please." Ainsley grinned, her face lit up. She looked like an entirely different person to Iris.

"Okay, on the count of three. One, two, three!"

Both women screamed, "Fuck off, Thomas!"

They laughed, imagining the rest of the group stopping their chores outside to listen, then Ainsley and Iris repeated the directive to poor dead Thomas, again and again, their voices mingling together and being carried out the open window by the coastal breeze.

# thirty-four

## AINSLEY

Ainsley pulled a few of her new clothes behind her, bundled in a blanket, around the curve of the bathing cove. She stood waist-deep in the water, the morning sun in her eyes as she gazed out over the ocean. She couldn't help thinking about the helicopter crash, which seemed like a long time ago now. Ainsley felt like a different woman. She had been reborn out here.

"Bye, Ainsley!" Claudine shouted from the boat, her hands forming a trumpet around her mouth.

She turned to see Jasper, Claudine, and Diamond, rowing away from Ainsley and the shore, heading east. For weeks, Jasper had been longing to get out in the rowboat to see what was on the other side of the island, but he hadn't been able to go with his leg and then with Min being sick. But at long last, the three of them were going on a day trip.

Ainsley called, "See you soon, intrepid adventurers! Find us some treasure!"

Diamond waved, an exaggerated gesture, and Ainsley watched them get smaller and smaller against the horizon. She sent up a prayer for them to return safely.

She pulled out the clothes she had sewn, experimenting with skinned tree bark Jasper had peeled for her, tightly woven grasses and leaves, and bits of fabric other townspeople were willing to donate to the cause. Ainsley wasn't likely to win any fashion awards for her work, but it felt so damn satisfying to make something with her own two hands. To rely on her wits and her ingenuity. There was no one to ask for permission out here. No powerful husband to consider, or to defend her fashion ideas to. Just Ainsley. And the pure freedom of not needing to appear a certain way any longer. She could be herself again, wearing a haphazard collection of feathers and leaves, and there was no one to impress.

She wanted to see how these new clothes held up in water. Ainsley pulled one garment out, and then the next, running them through the salt water and laying the clothes next to her body. The whole process felt sensual. One of Ainsley's favourite elements of this new life was no mirrors anywhere. She loved not looking at herself, worrying about how her hair was styled, obsessing over the size of her hips after a few stolen bites of pasta. What a stupid waste of time that narrow existence was. Ordering designer dresses online to wear once to a party she didn't even want to attend. Counting every calorie in her green salad to feel thin next to the other wives and girlfriends. Playing a game with ever-changing rules that Ainsley felt she could never win.

But now, she was truly free from all of it. Ainsley gathered her new clothes in her arms and lay on her back, floating in the waves. The sky was clear, impossibly bright and blue. She thought about Jasper and Min. They made sense together. Both so practical and smart, but also sweet, kind, and generous. It made Ainsley smile to think of them around the fire the other night, holding hands like a pair of teenagers.

Ainsley was swimming in her lacy matching lilac underwear and bra. She'd have to figure out how to make herself new ones, something that didn't make her think of her old life. Ainsley was done with that now. With one hand holding her clothes, the other one slid down the length of her body and into her panties. Ainsley moved her fingers, lazily, without haste, enjoying the sensation of the water and the sun on her nearly naked skin. She came suddenly, gasping alone in the water, laughing at the sheer animal pleasure of what she'd impulsively done.

The clothes seemed to be holding together, even when soaked through. Ainsley thought about helping Iris, Min, and Tony with meal preparations, since almost half the town was away for the day and wouldn't be completing their usual workload. She should go in, even though this aimlessness was pleasant and relaxing. Simply being alone out here felt like luxury.

When Ainsley tried to stand up in the water, she realized she had floated quite far from the cove. The rocky outcropping of the Cat Point cliff was behind her, and she would need to swim back. She heard a loud sound, in the distance, something she couldn't quite place. Oddly, the water below her felt like it was sucking her down. She had to fight to stay on the surface. Kicking, struggling, Ainsley saw some of her newly designed clothes stretch away from her. She tried to cry out, but suddenly she was underwater, and didn't know why.

When she popped back up, swallowing huge lungfuls of air, Ainsley saw a wall of water coming toward her. It made no logical sense. The sound was loud, reminding her of the fancy water feature at Thomas's favourite French bistro in downtown Seattle. She looked away from the enormous wave, just for a second, in order to turn her head back to the beach.

Everything slowed. She saw people, her people, gathering

on the sand by the shelter. Tony was far away, but it seemed like he might be running in her direction.

After that, Ainsley was underwater. She was hit, like a punch, by a force much stronger than she was. Her feet were above her head. Her lungs screamed. Her head pounded, but there, close enough to touch, were her two babies. They waited for her, Ava and William, the way she had been waiting so long for them.

# thirty-five

## JASPER

Jasper rowed, in a steady rhythm, listening but not really paying attention to the chatter between Diamond and Claudine. Every so often one of them laughed, the sound like a punctuation mark. They never seemed to run out of things to say to each other. Most of it was nonsensical to Jasper—assignment operators and loops and unique visitors and SEO.

He preferred to stay in his own thoughts, but Jasper couldn't ignore the sense of foreboding he felt. At first, he thought it was due to Min's digestive troubles, but those seemed to be over now. She was regaining her strength and vitality. To Jasper, Min was beautiful. He simply couldn't believe it when she told him she needed him. It was almost too good to be true, but he knew Min didn't say things she didn't mean. When she looked at him, that night he waited for her outside of the bathrooms, he could tell that something had changed between them. To kiss her was like coming home on a frigid, snowy night, and lighting a fire to slowly warm up.

Maybe that's where the worry stemmed from. The feeling that the other shoe could drop, that experiencing fleeting joy out here was tempting fate in some sinister fashion. Jasper had wanted to get to the other side of the island for a long time, but his bum leg had stopped him from doing a trek over the mountain on foot. He'd been taking small hour-long trips in different directions from the fresh water source, keeping an eye out for wild animals while taking comfort from the rifle slung around his neck. Diamond had brought it with them, but they only had one box of shells. Jasper guarded it fiercely. He'd been trying to get a rifle or a shotgun when he raided the burnt-out husk of a hardware store in order to stock his float plane, but then he'd been chased out. Ripped his leg open on the goddamn broken tractor window where he hid. But now he finally had what he wanted in his possession. Jasper had the rifle with him today. He wasn't about to take any chances.

"Should we check out that little beach?" Claudine pointed to the right, at a small patch of rocky sand breaking up the treeline.

"It doesn't look like much," Diamond said.

"Let's go a little bit farther." Jasper's arms were getting tired, but he didn't think they were all the way around the other side of the island yet.

He wanted to be sure they had picked the right location for their town. They had two separate sleeping shelters now, male and female bathrooms (so Iris would use them), a dining hall, a rec room, Tony's medical centre (which Jasper would always have a tender spot in his heart for), a cooking hut, and their bonfire area with logs and chairs. Plus, the bathing cove was a favourite hangout spot for everyone, underneath Cat Point, and the copse of trees on the opposite side of the beach from the bathing area was ideal for tying up the boats and his plane. It was hard to imagine anything more suitable, but curiosity had been eating at him for weeks now. Min, Iris, Ainsley, and Tony seemed content not to explore further, but Claudine and Diamond were eager to see what else they could find, on this miracle piece of land that somehow wasn't underwater or destroyed by the forest fires and blue bugs that had been eating the trees and causing the drought and destruction in other places.

Diamond shouted, "There! Look! It's a boat!"

From his position at the back of the rowboat, Jasper peered around Claudine and Diamond, who sat at the front, to see what the fuss was about. His eyes were definitely not what they used to be, but he could make out the shape of a multi-storied yacht not far from the shoreline. For a second, Jasper's stomach dropped, like he was on a roller coaster. Someone else was here, sharing their island space without any of them being aware. If this person were wealthy, Jasper had no idea what that could mean for their tiny town.

The anxiety he'd been fighting off returned with a bang, making his skin crawl, and suddenly he wished they'd listened to Min and hadn't made this voyage.

# thirty-six

## CLAUDINE

The sight of the enormous sleek ship surprised Claudine. She knew it was theoretically possible to find other people living here, as the seven of them had been doing, but to see proof with her own eyes was different, somehow. It was unexpectedly sinister.

"What's with all the black marks?" asked Diamond in a low voice.

Claudine said, "Looks like spray paint to me. Graffiti." On one side, just above the water line, big block letters read FUCK THE RICH. KILL THEM ALL.

Jasper had yet to say a word. At the front of the rowboat, Claudine turned. His face was ashen. He'd stopped rowing, and they bobbed in the water, staring at the yacht.

"Are you okay, Jasper?" Claudine leaned back to pat him on the knee.

His voice was quiet. "I think we should go. Head home."

Diamond spun around to look at him. "What? No way. Can you imagine what might be in that thing? Food, blankets, clothes, maybe even weapons or more shells to hunt with. We came to see what's here. We can't leave without seeing what we can take with us."

Jasper said, "It's too dangerous. We have no idea who might be living here."

Diamond turned to Claudine. "But you want to rebuild

the internet! Who knows what kind of radio equipment might be in this yacht. And there might not be any people at all. They could be long gone. Dead."

At the mention of the internet, Claudine could feel any resistance crumbling. Diamond was right. This could be a gold mine for them.

Diamond said, "Let's vote. I say we pull the boat up to the narrow little shore, take the gun with us and do a little exploring. Claudine, what do you say?"

Claudine knew that Jasper thought this might be unsafe, but it felt cowardly to row away, like a dog tucking its tail. This was their home now. They had a rifle for protection, and there were three of them. She really wanted to know what was inside that fancy boat.

"I agree with Diamond. We should see what's here. But we'll stick together, Jasper. It will be fine."

He shook his head. "I think we should leave it alone. This could be trouble."

Diamond said, "The vote is two to one. Let's row in."

Claudine reached for the rifle, laying it across her lap. She nodded to Jasper, hoping to reassure him.

After a long pause, Jasper started rowing toward the rocky shore.

Claudine couldn't wait to see what she could use in that yacht to try to contact the rest of the surviving population. Deep in her soul, she believed there were still people out there, like the ones who were here. Those who had survived hell would want what Claudine wanted—a fairer society, one that didn't hoard money or persecute others for their skin or beliefs or gender. Obviously, the old systems had failed, catastrophically, so anyone who made it through would be able to see the value in starting fresh. Like the seven of them were doing here. It had to be possible to recreate what they built in their town again, on a bigger scale, with more supplies and resources available.

Claudine dreamed of having electricity again, and luxuries like laundry facilities, cinemas, restaurants, soft mattresses, and much better leaders. Ones like Claudine herself, who had a clear vision of what it would take to create a government that made a safe space for all of its citizens. Later, when some form of civilization was rebuilt, Claudine would get the internet functioning, with safeguards against the cyberattacks and political coups and identity thieves. She could see it all in her mind, playing out like a video, so close Claudine could almost taste it.

# thirty-seven

## DIAMOND

Diamond was suspicious of the rich and powerful, just like most everyone else, but they weren't in the habit of running from a challenge. Jasper was far too conservative, in Diamond's opinion, but part of that might be how sick he had been, and now his fresh romance with Min. The seven of them had all found a way to get along and live with one another, so why should this be any different? Sure, the yacht was intimidating, with its size and the angry spray-painted graffiti, but Diamond figured the boat was as likely to be empty as it was to be occupied, and that was worth a risk or two.

Once the vote was cast and the decision made, Diamond felt stirrings of excitement. They reached over to Claudine, squeezing her hand. This was their moment, together, and in spite of Jasper's fears, the three of them were going to see what was here for the taking. Anything that made their town better was worth the danger. Diamond had missed this feeling, the one where you balanced on a knife's edge, knowing that death was possible, if not probable. Going forward to face it made Diamond feel invincible. It had worked before, in the other world, and so there was no reason why it wouldn't work here.

A strange sound came from behind them, like a firework going off. The three of them looked at each other, immediately alarmed. The water got choppy below them, as if they were in a storm, but the sun was shining, and the wind felt normal. Jasper rowed faster, trying to get them to shore, when they were drenched by a giant wave they hadn't seen coming. And then another one.

"Hang on!" Claudine shouted.

Diamond hit their head on something, losing a sense of where they were, and then they were underwater. Fighting to the surface, Diamond grabbed a big breath, rubbing at their eyes. The rowboat was overturned. Diamond couldn't see Jasper or Claudine anywhere. The yacht was just ahead, not far away, so Diamond grabbed hold of the rope at the front of their boat.

"Jasper!" Diamond called. "Claudine! Where are you?"

They ducked down, under the surface, trying to see under the boat. Claudine was there, breathing in the open space below the upside-down seats, attempting to hold the rifle up so it wouldn't be drenched. Diamond popped up beside Claudine.

"I can't find Jasper. Swim out with me." Claudine nodded, terror in her eyes. Diamond took a lungful of air, grabbing Claudine's hand and yanking her away from the overturned boat and back above the water line.

Diamond shoved the rope into Claudine's hand. "Here. Hold this and don't let go. Hang onto the front of the boat."

Swimming, Diamond went around the boat to find Jasper, clinging to one of the oars, still attached in its metal ring. Flooded by relief, Diamond said, "Jasper, follow me. Claudine's at the front. Let's pull the rope and get to shore."

It was hard to be heard, over the sound of the pounding waves. Diamond felt battered by the water, but somehow the three of them managed to swim, pulling hard on the rope, until rocks could be felt under Diamond's feet.

Breathing hard, together they pulled the boat up onto the sand, then flipped it over. The yacht nearby was swaying in the violent waves. On the tiny strip of beach, a much smaller area than the seven of them had on the other side of the island, a firepit had been swamped by the wave that overturned their boat, so ashy logs floated near Claudine, Jasper, and Diamond.

"What the fuck just happened?" Claudine asked, but before anyone could answer, a loud male voice boomed from the direction of the water.

"Hey! Who the hell are you and why are you trespassing on my beach?"

# thirty-eight

## RON

Ron stood on the lower deck of the yacht. He was shirtless, wearing only a pair of slouchy grey boxer briefs. His bare feet roasted on the hot deck.

He'd heard a strange noise outside and came to investigate. He was sitting alone in the huge living room when the boat began rocking suddenly from side to side. Ron was drinking his homemade sour mash concoction, smoking a cigar, and brooding about his former life. He could waste hours obsessing over two of his three children. He and Cindy had worked so hard to raise them right, taking them to church every week and expecting them to make intelligent choices. But Paul and Patsy got mixed up with the wrong crowd as teenagers, bringing shame to Ron. He strongly supported the new government, proud to finally have Ron's value system leading the country as the Men of God. But when the rioting got worse, and Ron couldn't keep all the beggars and thieves off his property, he told Cindy to pack for the three of them, and they flew out of Winnipeg in his crop-dusting plane. Ron had no idea what happened to Patsy and Paul, but they had made their bed and would have to lie in it. As an evangelical Christian father, Ron prided himself on upholding high moral standards. Those who didn't obey him, even his own children, found themselves cast out. This was how Ron showed his love.

What he had heard was a strange popping sound, and then the boat shook. The others were making themselves scarce, as usual, so it was left to Ron to investigate.

He stood by the railing and saw an overturned wooden boat, in the water, with three heads swimming toward him. Ron stared, wondering if he were imagining this. Where had they come from? Ron had assumed everyone else was long dead, but he thought that when his plane went down, as well, and yet Spence had come along and rescued him.

Now these unknown people were on the beach, gasping and lying around. Ron could see that the Black girl held a rifle.

"Hey!" he shouted. "Who the hell are you and why are you trespassing on my beach?"

All three scrambled to their feet, looking up at Ron on the deck above them where the boat was anchored. The man was tall, and nearly as old as Ron, with dark hair and skin. Could be Indian or maybe Mexican, Ron thought. He watched the guy draw close to the two young women, pulling them to his side in a protective gesture.

"We got washed out by that strange wave," the man called. "We've been living on the other side of the island, but wanted to see if anything was over here."

"Is that right." Ron gestured widely at the beach and then at himself. "As you can see, I'm here. What are you planning to do with that gun?"

The Black girl slung it over her shoulder. "Hopefully nothing," she said. "But you never know when you might need it."

Ron bristled at her overly familiar tone. It was young people like this that had destroyed the world, with all their rage at the rich and the stable. When Godly men like Ron were respected, and in charge of things, there was a certain order to society. People knew their place in it, which made things function smoothly. Predictably. But then the weird young kids and the fragile snowflakes rose up, causing chaos and unleashing hell, and everything went to shit.

"There's no need for any violence," Ron snapped down at her. "Your lot already did enough of that over the last few years."

The other girl stepped forward, toward Ron. She had short dark hair and looked pissed off. "No, it's actually your lot who did all this."

Ron laughed. What a joke.

The man said, "We'll be on our way, then." He walked to their little wooden rowboat.

"Are you alone here?" This was the Black one again, tipping her head up to look at Ron by the railing of the boat.

"No. There are a few of us."

"Where do you live?" she asked.

"Why do you care? What's it to you?" Information was power out here, in this new world, and Ron wasn't stupid enough to give away anything for free.

"Come on," the dark-skinned guy said on the beach, gesturing to the girls. "I think we should go."

The three of them huddled together, talking quietly among themselves. Other than the rifle, they didn't seem like they had anything worth stealing, but that rowboat might be a nice thing to get around in. Ron considered his options, hoping Spence stayed away until they were gone.

But then, sure enough, there was a rustling sound in the trees, and out came Spence onto the beach, a deer carcass hanging from his bare black shoulders.

# thirty-nine

## SPENCE

Spence almost fell over when he saw three strangers on the beach. How long had it been since he'd seen someone besides Ron and Kanda? Weeks, certainly. Possibly even months. Some days, it felt like years that he'd been living this half-life here. He felt checked out of reality, floating through time like a ghost, as though none of this was actually happening. Without Yvonne, everything seemed false and improbable.

He staggered under the weight of the dead animal. Spence tilted to the side, trying and failing to draw a proper breath, in the grip of a full-blown panic attack. He was vaguely aware of people around him, removing the deer, helping him sit down, saying reassuring phrases.

When he came back to the present moment, Spence was looking into the face of a Black woman. She was about a decade younger than he was, but she reminded him so much of Yvonne that he began to weep. Sobs racked his brawny frame, causing him to feel like he was being sliced open from the inside. The pain was hot, piercing him through. This woman had her arms around him. He breathed into her neck, imagining that Yvonne could still be alive. And close. Carrying Spence's child, along with every one of the dreams they once held for their future together.

"Pull yourself together, for God's sake." Spence could hear Ron's acidic voice, floating somewhere above him, destroying the comfort of this woman's embrace. He pulled back, suddenly acutely aware of the blood from the deer on his skin, trying to make sense of three new people standing on their beach.

Spence wiped at his eyes with the back of his dirty hands. "Sorry about that," he apologized.

The young woman smiled. "Nothing to be sorry about. We're the ones crashing into your space." She extended her right hand to shake his. "I'm Claudine." With her head, she gestured behind her. "This is Jasper. And Diamond."

He squeezed her palm, trying not to think about how she'd just been rocking him like a child in her arms. "Spence."

"Do you catch a lot of deer?" Jasper asked. "Or any other big game?"

"Some. Ron made a bow and arrow and we've brought down some wolves. Not much to eat, but good fur pelts. He really wants a bear."

Jasper said, "On the other side of the island, we trap rabbits and squirrels, plus do a lot of fishing, but I haven't gone after anything bigger yet. I don't want to disrupt the ecosystem too much, and so far, we've managed to avoid predators on our beach."

Still peering down from the lower deck railing, Ron called out, "I hate to interrupt the circle jerk, but we've got to get that deer ready. I thought you said the three of you were on your way back to wherever you came from?"

Spence flinched at his voice. He turned his back to Ron, in his flimsy, disgusting boxer briefs, and spoke in a low voice. "Listen, Ron's a pain in the ass. There are three of us: me, him, and a young woman named Kanda. When my prick of a boss got the virus, he gave me this boat and I sailed here, wherever 'here' is, from Portland. I found Ron in the middle of the ocean and should've left him there. Kanda was on a homemade raft, and she came on board too. You said you're from the other side of the island? How many of you are living there?"

Claudine said, "Right now, there are seven of us. Jasper is amazing with construction, and he's built us a little town."

"Do you stay on your boat?" asked Diamond.

Spence nodded. "It's huge, so we each have a bedroom, but Ron's fucking trashed the place. It's been complicated." He sighed, glancing over his shoulder, to see Ron frowning down at them. "I'd love to ditch him."

Jasper said, "We do everything by committee vote. It's important not to destroy what we've worked so hard to build."

He seemed to be saying this directly to Diamond and Claudine. Spence felt his stomach clench, like he was going to be sick. "Please don't just leave us here," he begged. "It's been especially rough on Kanda. She's only nineteen. I do my best to get food to her and help her out, but she mostly hides in her room with the door locked, to avoid Ron. He's a racist, and a fucking MOG supporter. He's said despicable things to both of us, but Kanda seems to have taken it to heart. I think she's given up. We can leave Ron the boat. I don't need it. Please take us with you."

When he looked down, Spence saw he was gripping Claudine and Diamond's arms, trying to hold them here, with him. He saw a look pass between Claudine, Diamond, and Jasper.

"Where is Kanda now?" asked Diamond. "I'd like to meet her."

# forty

## KANDA

Kanda lay on her bed, curled on her side in the fetal position. She ran her hand lightly over the mattress cover, simply to have something to watch. In her mind, she was back in her first-year philosophy classroom at the University of Alberta in Edmonton, typing furiously into her laptop, ideas sparking so fast she could barely capture them in words. Back then, when Kanda dreamed about running for prime minister to rid Canada of the Conservative men who ran the country backwards, right into the Dark Ages, she brimmed with hope. And vision.

When class was over, she'd cross the campus to meet her girlfriend, Celeste, at the pub. They'd have a few beers, sitting so close together that all other thoughts would fly out of Kanda's head. All she'd be left with was pure sensation: the anticipation of later, in bed, when she could touch and kiss every inch of Celeste's incredible body, lost in her smell and taste. Saving the fucked-up world could wait when Celeste was around.

Kanda only had four-and-a-half months with her. The happiest time of Kanda's life. But when she went to register for her next semester, she found an angry red bar across the screen, shouting in all caps: "INELIGIBLE DUE TO SEVERAL SECTION BREACHES." Kanda was both lesbian and Thai, and with the MOGs taking the government over by force right after Kanda's eighteenth birthday, she could no longer live on campus or attend classes. The best period of her life was abruptly over. Celeste was allowed to continue, in her bio-chem program, where her dream was to be the scientist to develop the right vaccine that would finally end the mutating pandemic that tore so violently throughout North America and then later the rest of the world. But Celeste was white, and had access to privileges that Kanda could only dream about.

Now, she tried to force her thoughts away from Celeste, so she wouldn't have to imagine her twisted and bloodied corpse on the pavement. And all that came afterward, with Kanda so blinded by rage that she slaughtered as many men as she could, one after the next, to punish them for what they did to Celeste. No, stop thinking about it. Kanda's breath became hollow, until she was lightheaded. Her cabin spun around her. She waited to pass out.

Ron's voice was shouting something or other outside, but she tried to ignore him. Ron brought it all back for Kanda: the white-hot fury, her grief over Celeste, the price women and people of colour had to pay to suffer at the hands of ignorant fools like Ron who held all the power. Kanda heard footsteps, then a light knock. She was so close to losing consciousness, her favourite state to be in, so she ignored it. The door handle jiggled, then something snapped the flimsy lock, and Kanda opened her eyes to see Spence, cloudy in her vision, standing in the doorway.

"Kanda," he said, "I'm sorry to barge in, but we have three visitors, from the other side of the island, and they wanted to meet you."

She turned her head, making a scratchy noise on the mattress cover, and tried to focus. Someone came close, crouching down just by Kanda's face. She looked familiar, somehow, but that made no sense at all.

"I'm Diamond," the person said. "Are you okay? Can you sit up?"

Diamond. Surely not the same person who used to make videos about queer and nonbinary rights when all that Father First and Modesty shit started? Celeste had introduced Kanda to Diamond's channel, and they both fell a little in love with their anger and passion. Kanda hadn't been drinking or eating much lately, trying to finally fade away into nothingness, so she must be hallucinating. She tried to sit up, but the effort required was too great, and she fell back down.

Kanda whispered, "Diamond," like the word was the answer to a complex thought problem.

Diamond stroked Kanda's cheek, with kindness and care in their touch. "Yes, it's me." They laughed, and Kanda thought it sounded like music. "We're building something cool, right here on the other side of this island, and if you want to leave this boat, you can come be a part of it."

It was challenging to understand what they were saying. Building what? How could Kanda leave? She could barely stand.

There was a sound, of someone drawing close, and Diamond disappeared from Kanda's sight. She closed her eyes, concentrating on breathing in and out, only hearing snippets of conversation. Something about talking to the others. Being careful here. Not making any promises. Then Kanda thought she heard Spence, saying, "Please, we'll do anything you ask." Talk of a rowboat, and others expecting them back soon.

Kanda felt her shoulder being shaken. She forced her eyes open. Diamond was there again, smiling. God, they were beautiful, with those hazel eyes and cute pixie hair. Kanda loved the sensation of looking at this stunning creature. They felt like possibility, and hope. The way Celeste had seemed so long ago.

"Listen, Kanda, we're leaving now, but we'll come back for you. Let Spence take care of you. He says you haven't been eating or drinking. We're building something I think you'll want to be a part of. It's not like this, here with Ron. It's better. Fairer. We've got big plans for the future. You can leave here and come to us. Just get better, okay? And we'll come back for you."

Diamond squeezed Kanda's hand, then lightly kissed her cheek. Whoever was in her cabin shuffled out, Spence closing the door behind him. More voices in the hallway, likely Ron spouting some bullshit or other.

Kanda placed her hand on her cheek where Diamond's lips had been. *We're building something. Better. Fairer.* The words rattled around Kanda's mind. She had no idea what they meant, but they seemed worth holding onto.

# forty-one

## TONY

When Tony first noticed the rogue wave approaching, as big as a building and terrifying to see from the beach, he ran to the shoreline, waving his arms above his head and hoping that Ainsley would see him. She was far from the bathing cove, floating on the surface. The water sounded louder than usual, reminding Tony of a freight train. He felt a strange shaking sensation under his feet, bringing him right back to sitting in that police car on the bridge as the ocean rose higher and closer. A tremor went through his body, weakening his legs and making it a struggle to stand.

"Ainsley!" Tony tried to scream her name. In his mind, the sound was vivid. Piercing. But he had no way to know if his voice was audible to anyone else. Or if he could even be heard over the rush of the waves. Tony's heart raced. He could see she was in immediate danger. Kicking off his shoes, Tony ran. He was going to save her.

At the water's edge, Tony felt himself get yanked backwards. He fought against whoever was holding him, trying to gesture toward Ainsley. He was a strong swimmer. He could reach her in time.

"Tony, she's too far out. Come on, hurry, we need to get to the trees." He turned to see Iris, pulling his arm, dragging him away. She grabbed Tony's sneakers from the sand, then they both ran toward the shelters, where Min was waiting for them. There was no time to think.

The wall of water struck their side of the beach with a force that was difficult to comprehend. Tony felt frozen in place. He found it challenging to breathe. In his mind, he was transported back to the day the tornado ripped through Calgary, flattening buildings like they were toys. He recalled the deafening whine of the wind, followed by the screaming that haunted him every time he closed his eyes. Now, he heard the medical centre break apart, along with the dining area and the cooking hut. Tony and Jasper had interlocked each log with great care, never imagining that the tsunami wasn't quite finished with its rampant, careless destruction.

Min, Iris, and Tony clung to one another, standing in the men's shelter. The water came up to where they were, splashing over their feet, and then quickly receded, taking so many of their supplies with it. Without a word, the three of them ran onto the wet sand, grabbing what they could and hauling it back up to the treeline. Tony went for his locked cabinet of medical supplies, Min headed for the cooking area, and Iris grabbed what she could from the damaged dining area.

Tony tried to see Ainsley, but couldn't. In between waves, they continued their supply rescue mission, running back to the shelter when more water pummeled the beach, but Tony noticed both Min and Iris also peering out to sea. The worry between them was palpable. It was impossible not to think about the rest of the group, out in the rowboat circling the island. Had this sudden flooding affected them as well? Were they alive? Or injured and in need of help?

When the water started to calm down, Tony pointed to the area beyond the bathing cove.

Quickly, Min said, "I'm sure she's on the other side of the cliff, where we can't see her, just waiting to be able to get back to safety. Ainsley's a good swimmer, Tony. She's going to be fine."

Tony glanced at Iris, waiting for her to say something similar, but her face was pinched and pale, the way she used to look when he first arrived here. She didn't say anything, simply shook her head.

He took off toward the cove at a run. Min called after him, "Be careful, Tony—don't go too far!" In the water, he started to swim, as fast as he could, thinking with each breath please, please, please. As a mantra, it kept him focused. He thought about how in sync he and Ainsley had become. She seemed to know what he was thinking, and what he needed, even when he wasn't sure himself. Ainsley would smile at him, when he least expected it, and it made him feel warm. She would bring him his cup of tea in the morning, a weird concoction of grasses and leaves that she steeped in boiling water. Her blue eyes were as sad as Tony's brown ones, and in them he thought that he could see Pedro, their dog Max, and the two young children that Ainsley had lost.

He was around the side of the cliff now, the area you couldn't see from the beach. Min was so confident that Ainsley would be here, treading water and waiting for the tsunami to die down so she could come to shore. Tony had begun to believe it himself. But there was no sign of her anywhere. That red curly hair, so distinctive in the sun. There was nothing. No sense that she had just been floating here, with the new clothes she had sewn and was so proud of.

He dove down, the salt stinging his eyes, peering in the murky gloom of the water for his friend. Coming back to the surface, he looked in every direction. The sea was still churning, angry over something Tony couldn't visualize, and Ainsley was gone. Like Pedro, and Max, and Amelia, who gave him the keys to her cop car so he could get to the coast. Like everyone in the before world, no matter how hard Tony had tried to save them, one by one. He had snatched Jasper back from the jaws of death, so Tony had begun to believe that hope was a worthwhile venture. But not now. Not here, where you had thirty seconds of warning before nature destroyed everything you had built, and battered those you loved simply for swimming in its waters.

Hope was as dangerous as this place. Kicking his legs to stay afloat, then falling below the surface when the current got stronger, Tony screamed with all of his might underwater, where the others couldn't hear him.

# forty-two

## MIN

When Tony came in from the water, he looked haggard. Much older somehow. He walked with his shoulders hunched over. Seeing Tony like that frightened Min. It made her growing fear for Jasper slide up another notch. Why did they have to go to the other side of the island at all? And why today, when a goddamn wave the size of a skyscraper had to come out of nowhere to wash them out?

She settled Tony in a chair, one of the few that hadn't broken into pieces, and grabbed a blanket from the women's shelter to put around his shoulders. He was soaked through and shivering like a kitten. A fire may have helped, but their fucking fire pit had been built too far down on the beach and it was washed away. All of the chopped wood was soaked. Everything would have to be carefully rebuilt, and planned with more foresight in case this happened again.

Min missed her fancy lab equipment. Her computer models, that predicted the upcoming disasters and laid out emergency plans with step-by-step instructions. Even the weather app on her phone would've been helpful today, to know that tsunami waves were expected. Out here, with no technology of any sort, Min felt hamstrung as a scientist. Useless. Jasper could build, Ainsley could sew, Iris could offer therapy, Tony was some kind of medical professional, Claudine a teacher, Diamond an influencer. Some more practical vocations than others for the end of the world, but without her lab and her research team, Min's skills amounted to nothing. This surprise flood should be her area of expertise, but there was nothing she could do to anticipate or prevent it.

Iris was knee-deep in the water, trying to spot and grab any missing materials from their buildings on the beach. Min went to join her. She was especially upset over the loss of her special log, as she had pulled it from the forest on her first day here and set up the campfire next to it. It was where Jasper first hinted at his feelings for her. It was Min's security blanket on this island, and now it was God knows where.

In the light of what happened to Ainsley, a hunk of wood was nothing. Min knew this, but she couldn't focus on Ainsley now. Not when Jasper and the others were still not home. Min had to keep busy, or she would fall to the ground in a weeping fit that she might not recover from. She had to believe that Ainsley was okay. She must have seen the wave, and swum to safety on the other side of the cliff, then made it to higher terrain. Ainsley would appear soon, along with Jasper, Diamond, and Claudine. They simply had to. Min couldn't countenance any other option.

Iris waded over to a shiny metal serving spoon, lifting it out of the water and cradling it to her body. Min wanted to talk, to ask for reassurance about Jasper and Ainsley, but Iris's face had that old familiar stony expression on it. Min got the message and held her words in. They both turned to look at Tony, still quaking in a log chair. The blanket had slid down to the wet sand, and he didn't seem to notice.

Walking farther out, Min peered around the cove, hoping

desperately to see the rowboat coming their way. But there was nothing. Only more endless choppy ocean waves. The late afternoon clouds were darkening, threatening rain. Min heard a new scraping sound, turning her head in the other direction, toward the drenched but still standing boats. She blinked in the sunshine, unable to believe what she saw. It was her log, bumping against one of the floats on Jasper's plane. Min brought her fist to her mouth, stifling a smile. This had to be a sign. Jasper was okay, and coming back to her. The log wasn't washed out to sea. Tonight, Min could sit on it, with Jasper's comforting form beside her. This thought helped Min's rising panic recede enough for her to breathe a little deeper.

"Iris," she called, pointing to the log. "Can you help me bring that in?"

# forty-three

## IRIS

After Iris helped Min drag her stupid heavy log out of the water and back onto the beach, the two of them collected as much wood as possible from the forest so they could get a new fire going. They built it between the rec centre and the men's shelter, as it was the driest spot they had that wasn't in the trees.

Iris hated building fires, which Min seemed to know instinctively, so Iris helped collect the wood and then left Min to actually start the thing. The flames were still too close, too personal and frightening. Once the fire was lit, Iris was okay, telling herself it was contained and small, like a fun campfire from her youth. Not out of control, burning her precious possessions to the ground and causing her lungs to scorch with inhaled smoke while the men held her captive inside—laughing, taunting, grabbing at her with their disgusting hands.

Tony sat by the fire, his clothes finally dry, but Iris could feel his grief seeping through the humid air and into her body. He and Ainsley had grown quite close. Min chirping on about how Ainsley was fine, and would appear at any moment, grated on Iris's frayed nerves. Iris could recognize this as a coping mechanism, in a clinical sense, but that awful wave had the power to rip their log structures apart in an instant. What chance did a tiny Irish woman have against that?

It was now early evening. They should be preparing dinner, but the cooking hut was gone. None of them seemed able to voice their fears about Ainsley being dead, and certainly Min was worrying herself into a state over Jasper not being back yet. No one was hungry, so Iris didn't think eating was a priority. She stood near the fire, keeping an eye on Tony, but also looking longingly to her boat. It got banged around in the storm, taking on some water and striking Claudine's fishing vessel, but thankfully, made it through intact. Iris wanted to be alone, to process her thoughts and to cry over Ainsley. They'd been allies, in a way, and her loss felt so pointless and futile. It brought Iris's fear right back to the surface, in an unpleasant rush, and Iris felt both angry and miserable at the same time.

Min was bustling around, laying the mattresses from the smashed medical centre out to dry near the shelters. She'd already stacked the wood they'd recovered from the buildings for Jasper to look at, to see what might still be salvageable when they rebuilt. But he wasn't even here. All three of them—Jasper, Claudine, and Diamond—could've been swamped by that wall of water just like Ainsley was.

Iris tried to resist the lure of her boat. Suddenly, she felt naked and exposed, like her carefully constructed defenses might be crumbling. She'd been sleeping in the women's shelter for weeks now, helping out around town more, and meeting one-on-one with Ainsley for therapy sessions. Oh God, thinking about Ainsley made Iris's throat feel like someone was squeezing it. The blood drained from her head; there wasn't enough air for her to breathe. Panicked, she ran—faster than she had since the world had collapsed around her and she had fled in her asshole client's boat—into the refuge of the rec centre. Iris fell onto one of the log benches, burying her face in a pillow Ainsley had sewn with such care. She wept, hard and furious, her body convulsing beyond her control.

When the storm of grief was over, Iris opened her eyes, blinking in the gloom of the building she'd requested for the purpose of therapy and relaxation. Tony and Min were both there, standing nearby but not touching her. Iris sat up. She knew her hair and face were a mess but for once she didn't give a shit. Ainsley was dead, the others were missing, their little town mangled. At any moment, the rest of them could get sick or injured or die by an animal attack or an earthquake or an even bigger tsunami wave. What were they even doing here, pretending to be a normal little civilization, talking about issues of fairness and safety? What would make Iris feel safe no longer existed. Not here, not anywhere.

As the therapist, Iris should ask Tony how he was doing. She should gently confront Min's blind denial, suggesting with kindness that Ainsley had died earlier today, her body washed out to sea. They would never see her again, and they should mourn together, as a group. But Iris worried that her centre would not hold if she said these things to Tony and Min. She hadn't cried a single tear since she had been violently raped at knifepoint by a group of foul men in her own home, forced to watch as it burned around her. Like Tony's words, Iris's tears had gone underground, locked up where she couldn't reach them. She was numb instead. That's how she was able to get through each day. Without that armour, she didn't know how she would survive.

Her breath came in little hiccupping rasps. "Can we sit down beside you?" Min asked.

Iris wanted to say *no, please leave, I came in here to be alone and to fall apart completely*, but instead she found herself nodding.

Tony sat on her right, and Min on her left. They were close enough to reach out and touch her, but they did not. Iris was aware of the cloud of Min's fear and Tony's sorrow. It swirled around the room, and she breathed it in, where it comingled with her anguish. And her rage against those men who had treated her so callously, a plaything for their power-hungry lust. They had taken so much from her, the confidence and competence that made up her identity. She found the presence of Tony and Min comforting, like a child in the presence of a parent, tasked to care for her. Iris wondered if this was how her clients felt in a session with her. The rain started, fat drops pinging on the thin yellow tarp covered with evergreen boughs above their heads.

She lost track of time, but after a long while, through the open door and window, the three of them heard a voice call, "Hello? Anyone there?"

It was Jasper. Min jumped to her feet, racing out of the rec centre faster than Iris or Tony.

# forty-four

## JASPER

Having rowed the boat for hours in the punishing sun, Jasper's arms were shaky and sore. Their water bottles had been lost when the boat was overturned, so no one spoke unless absolutely necessary due to their aching throats. Claudine took the next shift, and now Diamond was rowing them home in the rain. Jasper couldn't wait to arrive. He worried about the beach (he knew the fire and the cooking hut were down too close to the shore), and Min was in every one of his thoughts. What he wouldn't give for a phone so he could text and ask if she were all right. He knew she would be panicking over him as well. Not being able to communicate unless you were in the exact same physical space could be a real pain in the ass sometimes.

When they were in sight of the beach, he felt his heart lift with joy. The feeling turned to dismay quickly, when Jasper saw the wreckage of the buildings, but everything up by the treeline seemed to have fared well. But no one was there. His heart moved up his chest into his throat. He turned back to look at Claudine and Diamond, who were exchanging concerned glances with one another.

His voice cracked as he cried out, "Hello? Anyone there?"

Min flew out of the rec centre like she was being pursued. Jasper couldn't stop the grin from spreading across his face.

He didn't even attempt to conceal it. She ran, right into the surf, pulling Jasper toward her when she was waist-deep in the water. He felt her cling to him, Min's heart pounding against his own. The rowboat tipped back and forth, but Jasper cupped his hands around her hair and pulled her in for a deep kiss. Diamond and Claudine whooped and cheered behind them, but Jasper didn't stop. He kissed his beloved until he ran out of air.

"Jesus, get a room already," said Claudine.

"Can I ask you to move aside for a moment so I can get this boat into shore?" Diamond asked, laughing.

When Jasper pulled back, he saw that Min's eyes were shining with tears. Still holding onto her, he tried to get out of the front of the boat, not an easy endeavour with his bum leg.

Claudine steadied the shaking rowboat. "Woah, you're going to flip us again! Can't you wait two minutes and get out on the beach?"

Jasper sat back down. Min held his hand, walking beside them to shore. She helped him out, where they embraced again, and Iris and Tony gave Claudine and Diamond a hand as they disembarked.

Min whispered to Jasper, "I thought you were never coming back. That wave…"

"I know," he whispered back. "It capsized us, but we were okay. I was worried about you, too."

"Do we ever have a lot to tell you," said Claudine.

At the same time, Diamond asked, "Where's Ainsley?"

Jasper saw Iris's face fall. Min shook her head, fighting back more tears. Tony sank to his knees on the sand, his head hanging low.

It seemed like the world went still. No birds were singing. The wind died down, the rain turned silent. Jasper thought about the look on Ainsley's face when she remembered her kids, refusing to say their names out loud. Ainsley had such a bold and bright laugh. No one who heard it failed to have their spirit lifted by it.

Jasper sat down by Tony, putting an arm around his shoulders to draw him close. Min crouched on Tony's other side, then Iris, Diamond, and Claudine pushed in. They stayed in a circle, with no one speaking, but no one moving away.

When Jasper looked up, he saw that Iris was crying, and this surprised him even more than everything else that had happened that day.

# forty-five

## DIAMOND

Diamond was eating the last of their fried halibut. Tony had gone out beyond the bathing cove, where they had some of Claudine's fishing nets set up, and found three fish for a late dinner. Min had fried it in the cast iron pan over the campfire, in a new location near the men's sleeping shelter. It tasted so good, fried with a little salt and pepper from Iris's boat, spitting in its own grease. Rain was still lightly falling while Tony gutted and cleaned the fish, so Diamond had suggested eating in the rec centre since so much of the beach had been damaged by the tsunami. But Jasper was adamant that no food should be in their sleeping or living areas. He was paranoid about predators, Jasper was, even though they hadn't seen any wild animals in their town. So they ate by the fire, in the on and off rain, as new construction would begin tomorrow to rebuild what was lost.

There was a strange mood among the group. Diamond hadn't been particularly attached to Ainsley, so her death didn't rock them like it upset the others. At first, Diamond struggled to figure out Ainsley's mysterious bond with Tony. Diamond was the one who rescued him, for shit's sake, and yet once they got to the island, he seemed to prefer Ainsley's company over anyone else's, which made no sense to Diamond. And for some unknown reason,

Iris was a mess over it all. Diamond felt like everyone was behaving in a strange way, which was inconvenient as they had so much to discuss from their trip.

Claudine was across from Diamond. Her face looked gorgeous in the firelight. The tide was coming in behind her and it was what they used to call "golden hour" when Diamond was shooting their videos. Diamond tried to make eye contact with Claudine, but she seemed lost in her thoughts along with everyone else. Feeling jealous was a stupid exercise. Diamond did understand this on an intellectual level, but they couldn't deny that Spence's reaction to Claudine was upsetting. He seemed to fawn all over when he saw her, grabbing her and sobbing like a baby. Diamond wasn't interested in sharing Claudine. They'd been fucking for more than a month now, and Diamond had learned so much about their own body. And Claudine's. Touching her, deep in the woods, making her moan and squirm with pleasure, gave Diamond a feeling of power and purpose. It made them feel special, to be desired by someone bold and strong like Claudine. Everything was more bearable here in this strange after world place because Diamond had someone to get close to.

Spence better not get in the way of that. He was Black, which seemed to bond the two of them instantly, and Diamond couldn't compete with that. But Kanda was a fascinating and unexpected development. She was sick, and weak right now, but definitely young and attractive. Diamond couldn't stop thinking about how Kanda might fit in over here. With Claudine, Kanda, and Diamond, there would be three young people to help balance out the more conservative olds who tended to run the place. Diamond hated being told what to do by the old. That's how the other world got blown up. It was someone else's turn to lead, and with Kanda on board there would be three young visionaries to shake things up and really get some progress happening. Min, Jasper, Tony, and Iris were all relatively decent, as people go, but Diamond felt impatient for their time as the leaders to be over.

The key to getting Claudine on side was that fucking yacht of Spence's. Diamond had asked if the group could see the radio, and they saw Claudine's eyes light up at the tech possibilities. Claudine believed that she was the one to eventually rebuild the internet, so she could communicate with others and find out how the climate recovery efforts were proceeding in other places. Getting the internet up and running somehow would be great, or even just reaching a live, breathing human on the other end of a radio signal, but it wasn't Diamond's key focus. They were dialled in on what was happening here, at least before the destruction today, where the town was making real progress with committees and honest conversations about privilege and equality. Diamond knew there had to be a better way to live than what had passed for fairness in the old world. Even as a kid, when everything was relatively stable, Diamond could see that the functioning political structures were seriously messed up. Trying to achieve gender equality and evolve out of racism and xenophobia seemed impossible with a patriarchal hierarchy baked into the whole society. It was never going to work.

But now, out here, it might actually be possible. Diamond missed their mom, and some of the friends they'd made through the anti-MOG and pro-queer marches and video shoots, but most of their teenage years had been wasted fighting for the simple right to exist. At the cusp of turning eighteen, Diamond was exhausted, and angry, and determined to unearth a better way of life out of the ruins that had inevitably been created by the religious and greedy white men who caused so much pain to so many people.

Now, they really wanted to talk about Ron, Spence, Kanda, and that enormous boat over on the other side of the island, but it didn't seem like the right time with Ainsley gone. Soon, Diamond would get Claudine alone, and they would make a plan together, then convince everyone else to let Kanda come over here. She was being mistreated by that fuckwit Ron, who represented everything wrong with the before world, and Diamond was determined to rescue her and form a solid youth coalition in this town.

# forty-six

## CLAUDINE

Claudine brought her blue speckled enamel camping mug to her lips, savouring the slow burn of the amber whiskey as it slid down her throat. She thought of Iris's dead client, who was generously, posthumously, unknowingly donating this tribute to Ainsley around the campfire. The sun was just starting to set as the rain stopped, and the six of them were raising a glass to their dead friend (that might be a strong word for Claudine to use when describing Ainsley, but when she remembered pulling her freezing, trembling body out of the ocean, Claudine certainly felt something in the neighbourhood of sorrow).

Over the fish dinner, no one had spoken. It was eerily silent, contrasting sharply with the usual dinner chatter. It had felt wrong, somehow, knowing Ainsley had just been swept out to sea and drowned, to start talking about their visit to the other side of the island. Decisions were going to have to be made, and soon. But Claudine was trying to slow down, instead of rushing in and accusing others of racism or elitism or sexism or any of the other isms that she often saw and experienced with people, as that hadn't gone so well for Claudine at first. Min was good at picking the right, most sensitive time to speak about potentially prickly topics, so Claudine waited for her or Jasper to start talking, but it didn't happen that way. It was Iris.

When they finished eating, Iris spoke to the group in a subdued voice. She stared at no one in particular, but at some unknown spot above everyone's heads. "Today has been a very hard day for all of us. Ainsley went for a swim in the bathing cove, because she wanted to test her new clothes in the water, to see how they would hold up. When the first enormous wave came, Tony ran down to the shoreline, waving his arms to warn Ainsley. I could see he was going to rush in to swim out to her, and I was afraid for his safety. I grabbed his arm, telling him to come back onto the beach, that it was too dangerous."

Her voice wobbled, and she paused, sniffing a few times to try to regain her sense of control. Claudine looked over at Tony. His head hung low, dark hair obscuring his rugged face.

Iris continued, "I'm sorry, Tony. I was just reacting, purely on instinct. I knew we had to get to higher ground, and by then Ainsley had floated so far away from the cove. She was quite far out to sea."

Min, sitting next to Tony, reached out and patted his shoulder. He put his head in his hands.

"The three of us waited it out in the men's shelter, running out between waves to grab our pots and cooking stuff and some of the chairs that had been broken, dragging it all to the trees. When the water got calmer, Tony swam out, around the cove, searching for Ainsley. We couldn't see her anywhere. Min hoped she got to higher ground and would come back to us, but as the afternoon wore on, it didn't seem likely."

Claudine felt a sudden lump in her throat. How much of this was due to Ainsley, she wasn't sure, but hearing Iris talk like a caring person, instead of a raging bitch, was unexpectedly heartwarming. It was a relief to know she was in fact a human being, who felt things like the rest of them. The whole group was spellbound, listening to her.

"I know we all had different interactions with Ainsley, and we will all remember different things about her. But it's important that we grieve as a group. Together. She was the first person to ask me for some therapeutic sessions out here. We didn't meet one-on-one for long, but I know I'll never forget the work she did in our little rec centre. She dug deep, to understand who she was before, with her husband and her kids, and who she was now. I saw her change, over the last little while, and she really inspired me with her courage and transparency."

Claudine noticed that both Min and Jasper had tears in their eyes. Tony still hadn't looked up. Claudine could feel Diamond's eyes on her, but she decided not to make eye contact. Lately, Diamond wanted so much of Claudine. What was fun at first was now stifling. The sex was a good distraction from the monotony of life without an internet, but Diamond was six years younger than Claudine. She remembered how emotionally needy and clingy some of her high school info tech students had been, before Claudine was fired for her skin colour under the True Canadian Values bullshit. Diamond reminded Claudine of a few of her most insecure students. She would have to find a way to get out of this emotional entanglement, but it wasn't going to be easy.

Something about Spence had moved Claudine. He was so raw, when he saw her, falling apart so spectacularly in front of people he'd never met. And he was hot, as well, with that dead deer dripping blood down his bare shoulders. Seeing another Black person made Claudine feel hopeful. Less alone, and more connected somehow to herself. While Claudine held him as he wept, she felt a stirring in her body that she'd never experienced messing around by the little mountain stream with Diamond. This felt different. More primal and urgent. Almost spiritual, in a way she couldn't even articulate to herself. Claudine couldn't wait to finish with this Ainsley memorial and move on to discussing Spence and that incredible yacht with all of its possibilities for her communication plans.

By the end of the meal, Iris stood up, talking about her dead client's bar in her boat and how she'd like to get some Irish whiskey so they could all toast to Ainsley and tell a few stories about her. This was good, Claudine thought, as it meant they could put a pin in this grieving and get on with the next order of business tomorrow morning. Rebuilding the beach, and getting Spence and Kanda over here, along with his impressive boat.

That asswipe Ron could fend for himself, or die, for all Claudine cared, but the invitation to their town would certainly not include him.

# forty-seven

## TONY

All six of them had been up at dawn, to start the hard work of rebuilding what had been destroyed. Jasper was thrilled to find a crate from a hardware store, containing nails, hinges, hammers, screws, and other assorted useful elements, washed up in the bathing cove. He said it was perfect timing, proving that their needs were being looked after. Every time something floated their way, it was like Christmas morning for the town. Sometimes it was disappointing—fresh fruit or frozen goods that had spoiled long ago, but often they found something useable or distracting. The day they got a bunch of Lego sets was especially satisfying. The group laughed a lot that day, trying to build spaceships and dinosaurs and even a small TV set with instruction booklets that were nearly unreadable from so much time in the water. It reminded Tony of teambuilding exercises through the ambulance service, back when he was young and in training.

They worked all day, with Jasper fully in charge of the operation. He decided where the new cooking hut should go (farther back, under the tree cover, straight up from where the boats were tied on the opposite end of the bathing cove), and he gave all the orders. Jasper said the cooking hut was first, then a more permanent fire pit. After that they would rebuild the mess hall and the medical centre, in a treed area behind the washrooms, farther from the beach in case of future flooding.

It was bloody exhausting. Tony's muscles ached. He had little cuts on his hands and arms from hauling wood and sharp leaves. His head pounded from not drinking enough water in the heat. But he preferred to stay busy. It kept his thoughts at bay. He didn't feel guilty about not saving Ainsley's life if he worked until he was ready to drop.

There was a weird vibe going on with Claudine and Diamond. Tony wasn't sure exactly what was happening between them, but they always volunteered to go together up the mountain to the stream to fill up the water bottles, buckets, and jerry cans. They would be gone for a long time. Tony saw the way Diamond looked at Claudine around the fire in the evenings, with a naked sort of longing in their eyes. He worried something had gone wrong between them when they went to the other side of the island. Tony knew he couldn't get involved in everything, but Diamond had saved his life, and he couldn't help feeling protective toward them. So young, and so vulnerable. So sure they were the one to provide solutions for the problems. Was it better, Tony wondered, to know only chaos and turbulence in the world, like Diamond did at seventeen, or to have forty-plus years of modern civilization to look back on before it was obliterated, like Tony and some of the others did? He thought about this question a lot, but had no real answer.

Dinner was finished, the last of the dishes washed and put away, and now the town was meeting in the rec room. Claudine asked for a discussion about what they found on the other side of the island. Tony had a sick feeling in his stomach about it, like he used to have when he went out on particularly distressing calls. The suicides, the domestic violence incidents, the car crashes where you pulled bodies out by individual parts. At least he'd had Pedro to go home to. Max would lay his silky head on Tony's knee, and Pedro would rub his neck and shoulders, saying, "I love you," every so often to anchor Tony there, and distract him from the horrors he had seen. Tony would do something similar for Pedro after a hard day at work, touching him to bring him away from the pain and back to Tony. They knew how to get back to each other. Something about Ainsley, an indefinable quality of compassion and sensitivity, helped Tony feel more grounded here. Less alone. But now that comfort was gone, like Pedro and Max were gone, and Tony felt unmoored.

Claudine cleared her throat, then began speaking to the group. "I know we're all wiped out, with Jasper as our relentless taskmaster, but we have a situation from the other side of the island that we need to talk about." Jasper covered his face with his hands, peering through his fingers for comic effect. Everyone chuckled.

"We didn't want to talk about this yesterday, as everything with Ainsley was so fresh and upsetting, but we don't want to leave this too long." Claudine paused, looking around. "We found three people living over there, in a huge and fancy yacht."

This news caused a stir. Min appeared less shocked than the others, which didn't surprise Tony. Jasper must've talked privately to her about this already.

"Who are they? What are they like?" Iris asked with fear in her voice.

Claudine answered, "There are two men and a young woman. I think two of the three of them would be solid additions to our little town, and Diamond agrees with me."

"Jasper said the older man was abhorrent," Min said.

"That's the word he used."

Tony's sick feeling returned with a vengeance. He watched Jasper's face. He was upset.

Claudine nodded. "Agreed. He's nasty, old, and white—a definite MOG supporter. He'd be nothing but trouble. Inviting him here would be a terrible idea."

"Splitting them up is also a dangerous plan. None of us want Ron as an enemy." Jasper's voice sounded louder than usual in this confined space.

"Who owns the yacht?" asked Iris. Trust Iris to be concerned with an impressive boat, thought Tony.

Diamond said, "Spence does. He's in his thirties, I think, and Black. He said he picked Ron up in the water when Ron's crop-duster plane crashed, and he wishes every single day that he'd left him there."

Claudine came to her feet. She spoke with passion, her arms crossed against her chest. "Spence begged us to bring him and Kanda with us. They're desperate to get away from Ron. It doesn't seem like the right thing to do, to just abandon them over there. And Spence can hunt. He shot a deer. He's strong and kind and could be a big help to us over here with the rebuilding and the food committee."

Tony glanced at Diamond as Claudine was praising Spence. Their face clouded over, and Tony knew he had solved the mystery of what went wrong between them.

# forty-eight

## JASPER

Jasper did his best to listen to the conversation in the rec centre, but his thoughts were scattered all over the place. He felt a knife edge of fear that made his blood run cold. Iris was peppering Claudine and Diamond with questions, and her rigid body language showed that she was as afraid as Jasper about what these three new people might mean for their town. Once again, Jasper wished with all his heart that he had listened to Min and stayed here. No exploration was worth risking upsetting what they'd been trying to do as a group.

As usual, Tony said nothing, but he looked *green around the gills*, as Jasper's mother used to say when he was a boy, hoping to get out of going to school by mustering up a stomach bug. Iris would fight just for the sake of fighting, everyone knew that by now, and Min would be measured, careful, and reasonable, as she always was. These were just a few of the many qualities he both admired and loved about her. As a climate scientist, Min understood better than all of them how precarious their situation here was. She told him last night that the tsunami waves were likely caused by an earthquake on the ocean floor. It could happen again and again, and with no warning. Those ocean tsunamis had already wiped out the big coastal cities. What chance did the six of them have out here, in this tiny place, marooned and cut off from any other living souls or civilization of any kind?

But there weren't six of them any longer. There were now nine, with Ron, Spence, and Kanda on the other side. Should've been ten, if Ainsley hadn't chosen that godforsaken moment to test out her new clothes in the water. Jasper could feel his breathing becoming ragged. His whole body was tense, like a power current ran through it.

Min grabbed Jasper's hand, holding his sizeable paw in between her thin palms. She squeezed, and he turned his head to meet her eyes. She breathed deeply. He watched her, his body matching her breathing rhythm, until he calmed down. Jasper felt overcome with gratitude for this woman, who knew what kind of help he needed even before he did. He tried to imagine his ex-wife, Ginny, doing anything as practical as breathing with him, and failed to summon any memory other than her telling him to stop kissing his white bosses' asses and stand up for himself in order to earn more money.

There were a lot of voices talking at the same time in the rec centre. Suddenly, Jasper was angry. He said, "What is it you want?" in a tone that caused the other chatter to quickly die down.

"Who are you asking?" Claudine wondered.

"You," Jasper answered. "And Diamond. When we got to the other side, and saw that yacht, I said I had a bad feeling and we should leave. Both of you hoped no one was there, that the ship was abandoned, and so I was outvoted. Then we had the wave, and we capsized, and swam over to the beach, and Ron came out to shout at us. It was two to one then, and I get the sense the vote between us stays the same now. But I'm asking what it is that you actually want. All three of them over here, or just Spence and Kanda?"

Jasper could feel every eye shift from him over to Claudine and Diamond. The quiet in the room was unsettling. He realized that a lot was riding on this answer, for all of them.

Diamond said, "I want to invite Kanda. She's weak and demoralized, tormented by that MOG bastard Ron, and she belongs over here with us."

"No Ron? Or Spence?" asked Jasper.

Diamond shrugged. "Definitely not Ron. I'm undecided about Spence. Kanda's the one who needs our help."

Claudine narrowed her eyes slightly. "Jasper is right about Ron. He's disgusting and will not fit in over here. But Spence is different. We can use him here, and he'll understand the rules and boundaries we've established to make things run smoothly."

Diamond rolled their eyes. "You only want him because he freaked out for some reason when he saw you, bawling and holding onto you like a scared kid. He's unstable. I say we send a group over there to bring Kanda back here."

"You sound like you're picking teams in gym class," Iris said. "I don't think either of you realize how disruptive these three people could be for us. It sounds to me like you would be inviting a whole lot of trouble, which doesn't seem worth it."

Jasper said, "Well said, Iris. I agree. I vote no on all three of them. It's too risky, to invite one or two and leave one person behind, alone on their beach. They have no infrastructure like we've tried to build. They just have that huge, swanky boat, which they've treated like a frat house anyway. We can't afford to make enemies out here."

"We need to hear from everyone," Claudine said, with an edge to her voice. "Min, what do you think? I'm hoping you can be reasonable about this."

# forty-nine

## MIN

Min was feeling conflicted after everything she'd heard. She knew Jasper would be crushed if she didn't side with him, but Min had never been one to back down from a challenging situation and she wasn't about to start now. It was obvious that Jasper and Iris were dead set against inviting these newcomers in. Diamond and Claudine both wanted them. Tony would vote, with his hand raised when the time came, but he had been profoundly shaken by Ainsley's death, and Min thought he was likely to side with Iris and Jasper. That made Min an important vote. It was easier with seven people, as they never had a tie, but the group had already decided that a tie meant waiting on whatever action was being proposed. They agreed not to move forward with an important motion unless there was a clear consensus.

Now, Min sighed. She took a moment, looking around the room at these faces that had come to mean so much to her. Min imagined Ainsley in her usual seat, offering up an encouraging smile. When Claudine had rescued Ainsley after her helicopter crash, Ainsley had been so bruised and battered, but when she recovered, she became a valued member of the town. Ainsley had refused to leave Jasper's side when he was so ill, in those frightening days before Tony arrived with his medical kit of antibiotics and supplies. Would he still be alive today, sitting beside Min and directing them all on how to rebuild their structures, if Ainsley hadn't been there to take charge of Jasper's care? The clear fact was, they needed each other to be able to survive in these primitive conditions.

She cleared her throat, intentionally waiting just a little longer before speaking. Min used to love this tactic as a conference speaker at emergency climate summits. Knowing you had the audience in the palm of your hand, and could command the attention of an auditorium full of people, even if in the end no one did anything to stop the climate catastrophe that was clearly on its way.

"I appreciate hearing the different points of view on this matter. It's good that we can all share so openly with each other, even when we don't agree. We've built something much more respectful and democratic than the type of top-down decision-making we had in the before world. Jasper and Iris are right not to want to risk this, with the addition of new people, as it took us awhile to get our committees and conversations to this healthy place."

Min paused, noticing the tension on Jasper's face ease with her words, although he wasn't going to like what she had to say next. "On the other hand," continued Min, "Claudine and Diamond have expressed valid concerns about this young woman who seems trapped over there, and the man who can hunt, as they are both asking to get away from the older white man."

Her voice dropped, into a quieter, more thoughtful tone. "We all need each other out here. We were all broken, in one way or another, when we arrived. And we are still hurting. The kind of pain we endured will take a long time to heal, plus we've just been handed another blow with Ainsley's death. We've learned to lean on each other for comfort and for our survival. I'm wondering if these three people, on the other side of the island, deserve that same chance."

Iris said, "But this man Ron sounds far too dangerous. He won't be likely to listen to a group of women and people of colour. I don't think it would be safe to have him here."

"Okay," Min said, "that makes sense. But I think Jasper makes a solid point, about not making an enemy of this man. Inviting two out of three people here sounds cruel and discriminatory to me. Isn't that what we've been trying to avoid when we've had these careful discussions about fairness and equality?"

Diamond's eyes flashed. "You didn't meet Ron, Min. We did. And after less than an hour we couldn't wait to get away from him. Trust us on this."

Min noticed that Jasper was chewing on the inside of his cheek. He did that when he was angry, and trying not to show it. She moved closer to him on the bench, hoping her physical presence would help to ease the blow of her words. "I think we have to clarify what our expectations would be, for all three of them, if an invitation is extended for them to come live in our town. We might need to brush up on our ideas about justice, and what we'll do if our behavioural guidelines are breached. We'll have to revisit the earlier discussions about weapons, and how they are stored, and who is allowed to sleep where, and outline for them how we make decisions and run our day-to-day lives. Then I suggest we offer all three of them the choice to join us or not, provided they can agree to what we are asking from them."

Everyone seemed to be thinking over this proposal. Min let a short silence fall, but decided to finish her thought before anyone else jumped in. "I was the first one here. I had no idea if I'd ever see another living person when

I found this place. But then, one night, there was Iris. And shortly after that, Jasper in his float plane. And then Claudine, who brought Ainsley, and finally Diamond and Tony, who saved my Jasper's life when his leg got infected." Min wiped at her eyes, sniffing a few times. Jasper placed his hand on her knee. "At no point did we consider turning any of you away, because we knew from experience how arduous and harrowing our escapes and ocean voyages had been. We accepted you, one by one, experiencing some tension and arguing from time to time, but eventually relying on each other. Then learning to care for one another, and even some of us falling in love." Min smiled at Jasper. "I think we can't call ourselves a better society than the one we came from unless we keep open minds about every new traveller. We should hold firm boundaries, for sure, but refusing anyone a safe harbour here, like the one we were offered, feels cruel to me."

Min's throat was dry, so she reached forward for her pink water bottle and took a long drink. The antagonistic mood in the rec centre seemed to have softened somewhat.

Claudine said, "As usual, Min is the best spoken of us all. Well said. I don't mean to rush this, but I'm thinking we should take a vote and see where we're at."

"What specifically would we be voting on?" Jasper asked.

"How about this?" said Claudine. "We firm up our town rules, using Iris's fabulous clipboard to write everything down and make sure it's clear. I don't think Spence and Kanda will have an issue with our committees and voting systems, but Ron certainly might. We tell them what we would expect, then invite them to come live here if they can agree to slot in and help, without causing any problems to our way of life."

"So the vote is for inviting all three of them to live here?"

Iris clarified. "With the understanding that any number of them could choose to stay over there or come over here?"

Claudine nodded, then she asked, "Does that sound right to everyone?"

More nods, all around.

"Any other questions?" Claudine waited, and no one spoke. "Okay, all in favour of what's been proposed: the tighter rules that Min talked about, then inviting all three of the new people, Kanda, Spence, and Ron, into our town?"

Claudine raised her hand. So did Diamond. And Min.

Jasper, Iris, and Tony did not move.

Interesting, thought Min.

Frustrated, Claudine lowered her hand. "With six of us, we're at a deadlock. Before we abandon this discussion for a later time, does anyone voting 'no' want to change their mind? I'd like to remind you all that Spence has a massive yacht, with all kinds of useable furniture, blankets, cookware, and supplies, to say nothing of a fancy-ass satellite radio system that could actually help us communicate with the outside world, if the world still exists anywhere else, that is."

Diamond added, "And a young nineteen-year-old woman who is scared out of her mind, alone with two men, and could really use the comfort and support we could all give to her."

Claudine's hand went up again into the air. "Anyone? Tony? Jasper? Iris?"

Each one of them shook their head.

"Thanks, everyone," Min said. "Let's table this vote for now. We can all spend some time thinking about this, then we'll discuss it again."

# fifty

## CLAUDINE

A full week had gone by, with the six of them working themselves to the bone every day to rebuild their damaged structures, then meeting around the fire or in the rec centre at night for more discussions, but they were still at a stalemate when it came to inviting the others. Iris had made page after page of notes on her beloved clipboard. Sheets of pros and cons—endless brainstorming on a justice committee with discipline tactics in case people (which Claudine and everyone else knew really meant Ron) broke the rules, how to handle differing ideas about religion, which had been so catastrophically mishandled in the before world, and about a million other things that Claudine couldn't give two shits about. What she wanted was the satellite communication system in that yacht, to get going on her plan to rebuild some version of the internet. And Claudine also wanted to feel what she had felt when Spence grabbed onto her. She longed for that excitement again.

Claudine and Diamond were losing patience with everyone. This was taking too fucking long, and Kanda might be hanging on by a thread. So the two of them hatched a plan. They would go themselves, as emissaries from the town, to talk to Spence and Kanda. Claudine thought Jasper and the other oldies were being too fussy about making an enemy out of Ron. Screw him and his delicate feelings. If he wanted to be part of their town, he could stop being such a loathsome prick, and then he would be invited. Claudine couldn't waste any more precious time thinking about him. It was time for action.

That afternoon, Claudine and Diamond went with Jasper to the freshwater stream to fill up their containers. He had the best sense of direction, so Diamond attempted to casually ask him where he thought the best path might be to get to where the others were, just in case the decision was made to invite them over. Claudine froze up, knowing it was a clumsy effort to get information, and Jasper held to his line that it was too risky to go through the mountain. Too many wild animals, undergrowth, and other invisible dangers. Diamond shot back that the rowboat wasn't so safe last time either, but Claudine met their eyes behind Jasper's head and slashed her hand across her throat, to get Diamond to shut up.

Now, late at night after the others had put out the fire and gone to the shelters to sleep, Diamond and Claudine snuck out to the dining area, newly placed in the trees behind the bathrooms. Claudine brought her large flashlight, which still had batteries thanks to a small store of them in her fishing boat, and they went over the plans. They were calling it Operation Kanda, even though Claudine had every intention of bringing Spence back as well. They would leave at dawn, doing their best to find their way through the underbrush of the forested hills, to hike over to the other side of the island. They had a machete, water, some smoked fish, blackberries, a bag of long-expired potato chips Diamond had been saving, a crude hand-drawn map, and Claudine was bringing the rifle. Better to err on the side of safety.

Claudine wanted to prepare Diamond for the fact that things might change between them, depending on how everything went tomorrow. She planned to say that no labels should be put on their relationship, and suggest that they hold loosely to the concept of commitment. But after the travel arrangements had been made, both of them were hyped up and excited over the upcoming mission, and before Claudine knew it, their clothes were off, and they were fucking on the table where everyone ate their meals. This might make the inevitable conversation more challenging, when it finally happened, but who knew if they would even be able to find the other three on foot, or if they would agree to come back with Diamond and Claudine? There were too many unknown factors, so Claudine figured she'd wait on making any changes.

After, they lay together on the table, Diamond's head on Claudine's chest. "How many health code violations do you think we just committed?" they asked.

Claudine laughed. "Hang on, I'll ask Iris to get her clipboard and she can write us up." Diamond's left hand was tracing lazy circles on Claudine's side. It tickled, but also felt comforting. The two of them used to sleep on opposite sides of the women's sleeping shelter, but one night, Claudine woke up to find Diamond snuggled in beside her. She worried that this made their sexual relationship blatantly obvious to everyone else, but Claudine had to admit this was probably true regardless of the sleeping arrangements. There wasn't much room to hide out here, living together on a beach with threadbare sheets and towels hanging up to separate the bedrooms. Claudine didn't want anyone thinking that she was serious with Diamond. Jasper and Min were an exclusive thing, and Claudine doubted they were even screwing, as Jasper was still sleeping in the men's shelter with Tony, to make Iris more comfortable. What Claudine had with Diamond was much more open-ended and flexible. But she wasn't at all sure that Diamond saw it the same way.

Claudine shifted her body under Diamond and moved to sit up, reaching for her clothes.

Diamond stretched, like a cat. "Let's stay a bit longer. It's so peaceful to be alone with you."

"We better get some sleep. We've got a big day tomorrow."

Diamond leaned over to brush their mouth against Claudine's. Between kisses, Diamond said, "Operation Kanda is a go. I can't think of anyone I'd rather go on a secret mission with."

# fifty-one

## DIAMOND

It felt like Diamond and Claudine had been walking forever. They took turns with the machete, cutting down anything that impeded their path. Claudine held the compass from her fishing boat, stopping every so often to compare it to the map they'd composed together over the last few days. It got dark the farther they went in the forest, the thick leaves blocking out the sun. Diamond shivered now, enjoying the rare feeling of being cold. There was a musty smell here, like clothing that had remained damp for days. Still they walked, hoping they were making progress toward their goal.

A few times, they heard a distant crunching sound that had to be animals. Once they heard panting, a little too close for comfort. They stopped, waiting for whatever it was to appear, but thankfully, so far, they hadn't really been afraid. Claudine had the rifle slung over her shoulder, and she wouldn't hesitate to use it if something pounced. The exhaustion was starting to set in, but suddenly Claudine paused, raising her hand to indicate that Diamond should catch up to her.

"Listen to that," Claudine whispered.

Diamond concentrated. Waves. Like the ones on their beach, lapping up to shore. Grinning, Diamond hugged Claudine. "We did it," they said. "We found them."

Claudine smiled back. "Let's stay in the trees, like we talked about. Scope out the yacht from the forest and see who's around."

They crept forward, until they could see the small beach. The yacht swayed gently in the current. A fire was burning on the rocky sand, but no one was there. Diamond and Claudine sat down, leaning against a large tree, and watched. When Diamond put their hand down, they felt something ashy, which turned out to be the mangled end of a cigar. They looked around for Ron, but didn't see him or smell his rank body odour nearby. After drinking water and refueling on some snacks, Claudine leaned her head back against the rough bark and closed her eyes.

Diamond guessed about an hour passed before Spence climbed down the back ladder of the boat and swam to the shore, approaching the fire pit. Poking Claudine in the arm to wake her, Diamond gestured to Spence. He seemed to be alone, which was a stroke of luck.

Claudine climbed to the edge of the trees on her hands and knees. "Spence!" she called in a low voice.

Shocked, he turned in her direction. Breathing hard, he came closer. "You scared the shit out of me! What are you doing in there?"

Claudine said, "Hiding from Ron. We found a slimy cigar butt in the woods, so decided to lie low. Diamond is here with me. We walked, from our side of the island, to see if you and Kanda want to come back with us."

Diamond drew near, lifting a hand to wave at Spence. "Where's Ron now?" they asked.

"Inside. So is Kanda."

"Will he be watching you?" Claudine said.

Spence shrugged. Then he smiled, and Diamond thought it totally changed his face. Made him seem dynamic, somehow. Important and authoritative. Like he had once been powerful, which made Diamond wonder again if it was a good idea to invite him over. Kanda was the real mission here. Diamond definitely didn't appreciate the grin Claudine gave him in return.

Diamond asked, "How's Kanda doing now? Is she strong enough to walk back with us? She's the real reason we're here."

"Well, that's not exactly true," Claudine added, frowning at Diamond. "You said you wanted to come with us, so we came back for both of you."

Spence looked over his shoulder, making sure Ron was nowhere in sight. He stepped back to poke at the fire with a stick, his back to the boat. "I've been trying to get her to eat, but she barely leaves her room. I think she may have lost the will to live." He shrugged.

Diamond said, "That's why we came back. I've been worried about her."

"So how do you see this working? Everyone over at your camp wants us to come?"

"Yes," Claudine said with no hesitation. "Not Ron, but you and Kanda are welcome."

Diamond wondered just how long it would take for this lie to bite them in the ass. They said, "And we don't call it a camp. We have a town. With rules and guidelines and log buildings and committees where we vote on all decisions. You and Kanda would have to agree to how we do things, so there's no conflict with the others. But we've spent a lot of time thinking it through so it's fairer and more considerate than the way the world used to be."

Spence nodded at all of this. His expression gave nothing away, but he seemed to be thinking it over.

Claudine inched a little bit closer. "You said you'd leave

the yacht for Ron to stay in. We have shelters to sleep in, both male and female, plus a dining area, cooking hut, rec centre, and a new chapel for praying in or whatever floats your boat for religion. We share everything over there. Maybe we could come back later, with the boat, to get more of your stuff? Right now, we have to travel on foot, and it takes hours. We want to get home before dark. Could you get Kanda and be ready to come with us soon?"

"If I can get Ron out of there for a bit, I can take one of the mattresses and strap some wood to it for a stretcher to carry Kanda. Then I can grab whatever we might need for now and get out of there before he knows we're leaving. Otherwise there'll be a scene."

"We can come back with more of us to get your supplies later, once he's gotten used to the idea," suggested Claudine. Diamond knew she was thinking solely of the satellite radio system.

"Wait here," Spence said. "I'll go see if I can entice him to come out."

Diamond and Claudine watched him walk to the shore, then into the water. When he got to the front of the yacht, treading water, Spence banged three times on the hull with the palm of his hand. After a moment, Ron appeared above him.

"What?" he yelled. Diamond made a face at Claudine. As pleasant as ever, was ol' Ron.

"I swear I just saw a big black bear in the woods!" Spence shouted. "It ran that way!" He pointed to the trees, in the opposite direction of where Claudine and Diamond were.

There were some rustling noises in the boat, then Ron scurried down the ladder into the water with a bow and arrow on his back. He was wearing a torn khaki T-shirt this time, along with the nasty-ass baggy gray boxer briefs. His legs were skinny and long. Ron ran, up the beach and into the trees, trying to fit the bow with an arrow as he moved.

When he was gone, Spence offered a hand, first to Claudine and then to Diamond, to help them to their feet. "Come on. We don't have long."

# fifty-two

## SPENCE

Inside the boat, the three of them hurried to create a makeshift stretcher for Kanda by tying wooden poles under a twin mattress. Spence felt embarrassed by how awful the place looked, and how badly it reeked inside, like sour rotting food and rank B.O. He raced around, throwing a few clothes and critical supplies into a backpack. Diamond went to Kanda's room, trying to rapidly explain what was happening while bundling her scant belongings into a sheet and tying it to the homemade stretcher.

When Spence thought he had what he needed for now, he went looking for Claudine. She was in the captain's seat, scribbling quick notes on a piece of paper about God knows what. "We're ready to go," he said.

Spence peered out one of the huge windows to see if Ron was visible on the beach, but the coast seemed to be clear. That fool would do anything for a bear skin, and the bragging rights that came with it. This was all happening in such a rush. It reminded Spence of his years as a stock trader, the way his adrenaline would spike during a big trade, while he tried desperately to beat someone else to the punch. No time to think, either then or now. Just react, and do the next necessary thing. The worry over what was right or ethical would come much later, in the middle of the night, when you had to wrestle with your conscience.

He carried Kanda like a sack of flour down the back ladder into the water, then set her down on the sand and went back for the stretcher. When all of them were on the beach, Kanda lay down on the mattress and they carried her quickly into the forest, just as Ron burst out of the trees toward the fire pit.

Spence and Claudine traded relieved glances, and he let out the breath he didn't realize he'd been holding. Ron would certainly be pissed to find them gone. He might come searching at some point, and make trouble that no one wanted. But Spence couldn't control everything, and as they moved farther from the yacht, and Ron, he felt the black dog of depression shift and fall from his shoulders. This heavy bleakness had hounded him for a long time, and without the meds he once relied on to control it, he'd come to accept that there was no way out from under this fog.

Until Claudine came. With that face that reminded him so much of Yvonne, his pregnant fiancée. She died the day the power grid failed in downtown Portland. Spence had been a few blocks away from Yvonne, at the bank, when everything went dark. He tried to remove whatever cash he could so they could escape, but instead he learned that his identity had been stolen and he had no access to any of his accounts. He thought that was the worst moment of his life, all that money he'd worked so hard and compromised so much to earn, just vaporized into thin air, until he got home and found Yvonne outside, probably trying to find Spence. Holding her lifeless body in the pouring rain, cradling their unborn son in her round belly—with people panicking, screaming, and looting all around him—was seared forever onto his soul. Like a stamp. There was everything before, and then everything after, when he was alone and had to survive solely by his wits, as he had no family or identification or money or status of any kind.

And now, Spence was here, tramping through mountainous terrain carrying a sick teenager on a stretcher, with two people he'd only just met. He was placing an inordinate amount of trust in both Claudine and Diamond, which might not be wise, but what option did he have? Staying with Ron was untenable, and Diamond had told him they had a doctor of sorts at the other camp. Town, he corrected himself. Apparently, the guy didn't talk, as he was too traumatized or something (welcome to the club, pal), but he had brought one of them back from the dead and Diamond thought of him as a miracle worker. Kanda had been fading for a long time now, and Spence wasn't far behind. He figured this was as good a bet as any.

They walked and walked. No one spoke, unless necessary, to try to conserve energy. They were moving slower and slower now. Spence could feel blisters forming in his skater sneakers, a far cry from the soft leather designer loafers he used to wear on the trading floor. He had found these in a closet in his boss's yacht. They were a size too big, and probably belonged to a kid at some point, but Spence was grateful to have them. He was actually amazed to have anything, to still be drawing breath into his lungs.

It was fascinating to imagine that this whole time, a little town was forming on the other side of the island, and he, Ron, and Kanda never had any clue. They were just limping along, trying to make it through each day, hunting and fishing and avoiding each other as much as possible, while licking their individual wounds. But the way Diamond and Claudine spoke of the other place was almost reverent. A dining hall, bathrooms, and a rec centre? Some type of spiritual chapel to safely contain religious beliefs, keeping them private, so different ideologies didn't erupt between people and unleash hell like they used to? Sharing everything, forming work committees, and making decisions based on thoughtful discussions and a vote? It sounded like some utopian dream, the kind of existence that Spence thought would never be possible in this lifetime. Not after the violence, chaos, division, and loss he'd been trying to survive in America.

Spence decided he had to see it for himself. Maybe there was a way, within this new group of earnest people, to atone for all he had done. The career he had given himself over to, in body and soul, where he knelt every day at the opening bell with his colleagues to worship the money. Always the fucking money, the greed that burned everything and everyone to the ground, leaving Spence with nothing but the taste of ashes in his mouth.

# fifty-three

## KANDA

Kanda relished the feeling of being carried. It was soothing, taking her back to her childhood, when it was just Kanda and her dad against the world. Her mom had left them when Kanda was a toddler, and didn't bother to stay in touch, so other than a few blurry photos around their house in Edmonton, Kanda had no real memories of her. Daddy told her not to be angry with Mommy, but inside Kanda seethed. How do you give birth to a daughter and then simply vanish?

Growing up, Kanda longed to get into politics. Dad would smile and tell people she wanted to change the world, but for many years she mostly wanted to stick it to her absent mother. To show her that Kanda was smart, and worthy of respect. Not a helpless baby, to be abandoned, but a force of change in her own right.

Now, lying on her back and watching the way the sun filtered in uneven patterns through the slits in the leaves, Kanda thought about how she'd never have the chance to prove anything to her mother. She had no idea if she were still alive, or long dead. Kanda had tried to find her dad when the cops had been obliterated by the Men of God, and their own armed militia were taking to the streets. But she'd had to hide away after murdering the men who had attacked her girlfriend Celeste, and by the time Kanda thought it was safe to go to Dad's house, he had vanished. As a Thai man, he had probably already been killed, but Kanda liked to imagine that he made it out of the city in the midst of the chaos, the way she did. One day, they might still reunite. He had been a good father, loving and reliable and smart. He did his best to make up for Kanda's mother leaving her, but Kanda wished she had gone looking for him earlier. But she didn't regret killing those awful, lawless men. It had to be done, and if they were standing in front of her again, she wouldn't hesitate to make exactly the same choice.

It seemed like Diamond, Claudine, and Spence were exhausted. They were moving at a snail's pace, taking turns carrying her. It was easy for Kanda to lose track of time. She slept, then sat up to drink some water, even attempting to walk for a while, before collapsing in the dark loamy soil.

"We're almost there," said Claudine.

Spence grunted, from his position near Kanda's feet where he attempted to balance the stretcher with Diamond at the front. "This Tony guy will be able to treat Kanda, right?"

"Hopefully," Claudine answered. "He doesn't talk, so it might be hard for him to know what's wrong with her, but you can tell him what you know."

Kanda thought, I can tell him myself, but then she wondered how true this was, since she wasn't completely clear on what was wrong with her. Mostly, she couldn't see the point in continuing on. Out here, there were no political ambitions to pursue. No point to prove, to herself or to anyone else. Just a long stretch of open nothingness that called itself the future but didn't offer anything real to hope for. Living with Ron, in that stunning yacht, had drained her spirit like a battery. He talked, ad nauseum, about how women and queers and the poor had ruined North America with their godlessness and greed. When the men had been in charge, for millennia, everyone knew their place and there had been no problems. It was all the rights these fringe groups demanded that began to erode the solid Christian values that had been the bedrock of society. He would drink his foul sour mash concoction and rail on, pointing toward Kanda and Spence for emphasis on certain key points, as if to say that their brown and black skin were solely to blame. He was endlessly proud of his white skin, like he'd done something profound to deserve it.

For every day since she'd been rescued by Spence, Kanda imagined slitting Ron's throat. The satisfaction she'd feel, watching his life drain away, knowing she was the one to take it from him. Listening to Ron was like reliving the MOG nightmare all over again. Feeling so unsafe, and so powerless, while every legal protection was stripped away by Christian men holding guns. While she floated with some dead bodies on a homemade raft at sea, burning under the relentless sun, Kanda expected to feel guilty for the men she'd hunted down and slaughtered. They had felt entitled to Celeste, and to other young women stripped of their defenses, because the Men of God said they could take whatever they wanted. But the guilt never came. If those fucking evil men had left Celeste alone, Kanda wouldn't have killed them. But they deserved to pay for what they'd done. Ron needed to as well, but Kanda couldn't seem to muster up the energy.

She felt the full late afternoon sun on her face, and threw up an arm to block her eyes. The mattress was set down on the ground. There were lots of voices, most of them angry. Diamond was shouting, something about how this young woman was dying, and why didn't Tony care enough to come over and help? She heard Spence, saying he didn't know that they weren't expected. Claudine's voice sounded hoarse, as she yelled about fairness and doing the right thing instead of debating philosophy and coming to no actual decisions.

Kanda decided not to bother opening her eyes. She focused on the word *philosophy* in her mind. It felt safe. She remembered that once it had meant the world to her. Like her dad, and like Celeste.

# fifty-four

## IRIS

ris burned with rage. How dare Claudine and Diamond go against the town like this, acting like a couple of vigilantes when they had all worked so hard to make important decisions together? The tiny slip of a girl on the makeshift stretcher looked like she might already be dead, so why the hell did they bother trekking through the mountain to bring her here? And this barrel-chested young Black guy, who seemed strong enough to snap a neck without thinking twice? He appeared to be extremely pissed off that their arrival was causing so much chaos.

They were all standing near the shelters, where the trees met the beach. Diamond was demanding that Tony take Kanda to the new medical centre and give her something to make her stronger. He had his arms crossed against his body, shaking his head. Good for you, Tony, Iris thought. These two are not in charge here. They don't have the right to demand anything from the four of us. We're not the ones who went against the majority vote. The justice committee would have to get to work finding a suitable punishment for this reckless behaviour.

Jasper and Min stood beside each other, and they both looked as shocked and unhappy as Iris felt.

Iris decided to take action. "This is a serious situation," she said to Claudine and Diamond. "We took several votes on the issue of the people on the other side of the island, and the count stood at three to three. We couldn't reach a majority consensus. So we agreed to wait, until we could discuss it further, and then create a plan that worked for everyone. But now you've taken matters into your own hands, which is unacceptable."

"Oooh, *unacceptable*," Claudine mocked. "All you ever want to do is discuss topics until you're blue in the face. Diamond and I prefer to act, especially when someone's life is on the line."

With tears shining in their eyes, Diamond cried out, "You know what's unacceptable? Saying a Black man and a Thai woman can't come over here to live in our town. You go on and on about being fair and welcoming, but at the end of the day you are as bigoted as Ron, and Claudine and I couldn't take it any longer."

Min stepped forward, looking directly at Spence. "No one said we didn't want a Black man or a Thai woman here. The issue was the older white man, and how to handle inviting two out of three people into our town. We were concerned about making an enemy out of Ron."

"But you voted with us, Min!" protested Claudine. "You wanted to invite all three of them. It's Tony, Jasper, and Iris who held everything up. Let's have one of them explain to Spence, and to poor, sick Kanda, why they aren't allowed in our space."

"Stop this grandstanding, Claudine," Iris hissed through her teeth. "I say the four of us convene an emergency justice committee meeting in the rec centre. Jasper, Min, Tony, and I need to discuss this without any of you present, to see how we want to proceed. That's democratic and fair."

With a shrill note to their voice, Diamond asked, "Are you going to kick us out? And keep all this for the four of you? Is this now four against four, because we thought rescuing these two people from Ron was the right thing to do?"

"No one's getting kicked out," Jasper said, which made Iris bristle. "But Iris is right. We need a bit of time to adjust to this change."

Min drew closer to Diamond, Claudine, and Spence. She looked down at Kanda on the mattress. "You must be exhausted after your long hike. We were very worried about you, when we woke up and saw you were gone. It's a relief to see that you're okay." She smiled, seemingly trying to take some of the tension out of the air. "We'll go have a short meeting, while you show the guests around. Maybe have a swim in the cove. Drink some cold water. Then we'll eat a late dinner together and see where we're at. Would that be okay with you?"

Claudine and Diamond refused to make eye contact with Min, or with anyone. Iris fought the temptation to go to the cooking hut for a wooden spoon and give them both a spanking. They thought they were such brave heroes, when Iris saw them as foolish, impulsive children.

Spence said, "I'm sorry to surprise you like this. I didn't know you weren't expecting us. I understand why you want to talk about this, but I'd just like to say how grateful I am to Claudine and Diamond for coming back for us. It's been hellish, trying to live with Ron, and I really don't think Kanda would've hung on much longer over there." He paused, trying to make eye contact with Tony, Jasper, Min, and Iris. His deep voice got cloudy. "For whatever that's worth."

"It's worth a lot," said Min. "Thank you, Spence. And welcome to both of you."

Iris's patience was at its breaking point. Enough of the

sucking up. They had decisions to make. "Tony, Min, Jasper—let's go to the rec centre. We need to consider the options of the justice committee."

She turned and stalked toward the building she had asked Jasper to build, hoping the other three were following her. As for Claudine, Diamond, and the unwelcome newcomers, Iris felt they were on their own.

# fifty-five

## JASPER

They sat in the dim light of the rec centre, the air stuffy and warm. Tony looked defeated, his skin wan. Iris's face was red, like she was overheated from her own anger. Jasper turned his head to see Min beside him. She smiled at each of them. That was the woman he'd fallen in love with: always eager to get everyone to agree. To keep the peace.

In the quiet, they could hear noise outside on the beach. Splashing sounds, as the newcomers cooled off in the water. A few low voices, carried to them on the wind, the individual words indistinguishable to Jasper's ears. He despised this sense of separation in their group. This was what Jasper feared, every time a vote was called, hands raised to be counted.

It was painful to think about how far they had come, from the shocked early days when no one trusted anyone else and they barely knew how to communicate with one another, to those endless discussions about fairness, and privilege, and what had destroyed the old world not being allowed to continue here on this island, only to end up here, a group split by age and ideals.

Perhaps it had always been foolish to believe any other kind of society was possible. Where there were humans, there was a struggle for power. Division was the common denominator. As an Indigenous man living among mostly white people in the oil sands of Fort McMurray, Jasper knew that better than most.

The ethereal thinness of the young woman on the stretcher had shocked and upset him. Jasper hadn't imagined a person could be so frail. For a brief moment, Kanda reminded him of Min when he first saw her on the beach. He thought then that Min looked like she had only just barely survived a tremendous ordeal, which was of course true for all of them, but Jasper had bobbed for weeks on the open ocean in a fully enclosed float plane. Min had lain under a worn blue tarp on a homemade wooden raft, open to the elements and sea creatures and other horrors he didn't like to consider. And yet she was here, getting stronger and braver with each new day, so why would he begrudge Kanda or Spence the same chance to recover in a supportive and caring environment? If Tony hadn't arrived when he did, Jasper wouldn't be here now, in a rec room he built with his own hands, sitting next to a woman who made him feel like he could do anything at all in this new world they found themselves in.

Jasper found himself flooded by a hot tide of shame. He knew why Iris had called this meeting. She was in charge of the newly formed justice committee, but Jasper understood now that this was a mistake, because Iris couldn't see past her own wounds. Something inside of her itched to punish others for what had been done to her, but Jasper could see that this would simply keep the hatred and the violence in circulation. Once again, Min had been right from the beginning, and, like an idiot, Jasper hadn't listened to her. His own fear of what white men could do had taken hold of him. But somehow, he'd inadvertently become snared up in the middle of the same, age-old problem.

Jasper came to his feet, moving slowly to the square

opening in the log wall that served as a window, where he could see Spence, Claudine, and Diamond in the bathing cove. Kanda was sitting up, supported by Diamond, while Claudine gently washed her face with a cloth. Jasper felt tears come to his eyes. He turned away from the window and looked at Min, Tony, and Iris. Every eye was on him. Min had solved enough of these interpersonal problems. It was Jasper's turn.

"I can see now that I've been wrong," he said. "I was afraid of Ron, and I still am, but how can we think of punishing Diamond and Claudine for what they've done, when what they wanted to do was help two people the way we've all helped each other?"

Iris said, "It's not as simple as that, Jasper. We have rules and procedures, and they clearly broke them—"

"Iris," Jasper interrupted, grief etched into his features, "why don't you come over here and see what I'm seeing? Why don't all of you come?"

Slowly, Min and Tony came to their feet. Tony went to the open doorway, and Min stood by Jasper at the small window. He turned back to gesture to Iris. "Please, Iris. Come and look."

She came. Tony moved aside, so Iris could fit beside him in the doorway. All four of them watched as the three people in the water cared for Kanda.

"We wanted to protect what we'd worked for here," Jasper continued. "I don't think we were wrong, but Claudine and Diamond weren't wrong, either. We did stop them from doing what they thought was right, and now that I've seen Kanda again, and Spence, I feel embarrassed that I said no to them. It would be like turning away any of you when you found us, or Iris and Min telling me I had to get back in my float plane and stay on the water when I was desperate to stand on dry ground again. That feels cruel to me, but I couldn't see that before."

"We all make mistakes," Min said. The woman was more generous than anyone Jasper had ever known. She reached for his hand and squeezed it.

Jasper asked, "Tony? Can they stay? Will we welcome them here?"

Tony drew a deep breath, then looked at Jasper. He nodded.

"What about Ron?" said Iris. "Are you saying we have to invite him too? Even though by all accounts these two people were desperate to get away from him, and that's why they are here?"

"I don't know about Ron. That's a problem for another day. Right now, we're deciding what to do about Spence and Kanda. I say we bring them in, and forget about the justice committee doing anything to Claudine and Diamond. They acted out of kindness, when some of us were too afraid to do anything, and I can see now that doesn't deserve to be punished. As Min said, we all make mistakes. I'm willing to admit mine, and move on."

A silence fell. After a bit, Min asked, "Iris? Can you join us in welcoming Kanda and Spence?"

Her face looked drawn and tired. Iris swallowed hard, glancing at Tony, then Min, and finally Jasper. He was reminded of that first day, when he arrived on the beach, and Iris didn't want him here. So much always rested on Iris, which pissed Jasper off, but that was also a problem for another day.

"I don't think I made a mistake," Iris said. "None of us are going to be safe here as long as Ron is on this island. But I'm exhausted, and don't want to argue about this any longer. If these two new people can live peacefully with us, and this is what the rest of you want, then let's just carry on with the hard business of staying alive."

Min left Jasper's side, crossing the rec centre to give Iris a hug. Jasper and Tony watched. Iris, stiff as a wooden board, eventually melted into Min's embrace, and the men breathed a little easier.

# fifty-six

## BETH

Beth sat up, scratching at the red welts on her arms and torso. They itched worse in the heat of the day, so Beth longed for it to get dark. She felt sweaty and irritable. Her throat was hurting, so she inched her way around on the cracked white leather seats to reach the rain bucket. Lifting the lid, Beth saw how low their water supply was. She decided to wait until the thirst was even more unbearable.

The open deck boat rose and then sank in the wind, the motion of the waves so predictable that Beth barely noticed it. Harpreet was asleep, under the striped frayed canopy. As the water and food ran out, they both slept as much as possible. It was easier to rest at any hour of the day or night now that Anjali was gone. Anjali had cried a lot, when she first got sick with the red spread, but once the fever came and her little body broke out in those awful sores, she hardly made any noise at all. It took Beth a long time to realize Anjali was no longer breathing, because Harpreet had been holding her so close.

And now Beth might have the virus. She thought she would be dead by now, because with Anjali everything seemed to move quickly, but other than the horrible itchiness of her skin, Beth didn't think she felt worse than usual. She didn't have any big fears over dying. Beth was nine, and she'd seen more death than anything else in these last few years: the Men of God taking over, the waves of the pandemic, the forest fires, the weird blue bugs that ate all the leaves and caused the trees to die, the internet going down after people figured out how to fight back against the MOGs, and now the tsunami that destroyed Victoria and the rest of the coastal cities.

Dad was a firefighter, who had died at the beginning of the island forest fires. Mom had tried to get Beth out of Victoria, by boat, but everyone she tried to pay refused to take them. Cash didn't mean much by then, and no payment cards would work as there was no power or no banks. A lot of people walked around with knives and guns—that's what Beth remembered from that time—but Mom was too gentle for that. She kept saying, "It will work out, Bethie, you'll see. I know you're going to live a long, full life." Mom never said that they would both make it. Just her. And she was right.

Beth still heard the single crack of the gunshot sometimes, when there was nothing else out here to listen to, except for the waves, the wind, and some occasional seagulls and dolphins crying. She remembered it, the sharp pop, and the grunting sound Mom made. Beth could still feel the weight of her mom in her arms. They were on a dock, trying to get on a boat before the waves began pounding Victoria, and Beth had thought she would stay with her mom until Beth died, too.

But Harpreet came, running out of the dark with three-year-old Anjali in her arms. She found Beth, pulling her away from her mom, and somehow, they got into this fancy rectangle-shaped deck boat. Harpreet must have started the motor, and they got away. Beth didn't really remember the specifics. Just the sight of her mom's body, slumped on the wooden boards, stained with her blood.

Why did she have to get shot? None of it made any sense at all. She wanted to talk to Harpreet about it, but Harpreet was haunted by Anjali's death, and seemed to have plenty of her own worries, so Beth kept her thoughts to herself.

She scratched again, trying not to break the skin open, but desperate for some relief from the itching. Her long blonde hair was hot on her neck. She ripped another strip from the bottom of her raggedy purple T-shirt and tied it back in a ponytail. The sun was bright, and hot. There was nothing to see in any direction except for more water. Beth had no idea how long they'd been out here. It seemed like forever. At the beginning of the pandemic, people said you could die in less than two days, but for Anjali, it had been a lot longer than that. Beth had gotten the red sores long after Anjali died, and Harpreet seemed fine, so maybe this wasn't the virus that had killed so many people. But it sure did look like it. There was no one to ask. No medicine to take, or doctors to see. No Mom or Dad to soothe her.

Just Harpreet, who had held her dead daughter until Beth convinced her she was really gone, and needed to go overboard, as she was starting to smell. They had a quiet little funeral, but Beth had to be the one to push the tiny body into the water. Harpreet was too out of it to participate. They had no more gas, and were nearly out of food and water. Now all they were doing was waiting. Separately, but together.

Beth went back to her seat and lay down. She sucked her dirty thumb, the way she used to do as a little kid. She saw that Harpreet was still sleeping on the other side of the small boat, her hand resting on her pregnant belly.

One day soon, Beth would close her eyes and not wake up. As she drifted to sleep, she wondered if she would be lucky enough to die before Harpreet did.

# fifty-seven

## HARPREET

Another night fell, making the warm air pleasant instead of sticky and humid the way it felt during the day. Harpreet barely noticed the change in temperature, except now it was dark. Beth was awake, across from her in their stolen open deck boat, likely used during happier days for some rich people to go water-skiing with friends on summer long weekends. She stared out across the blackness of the water. There was nothing to look at, in daylight or at night.

Harpreet's back ached, so she sat up on the white leather bench seat, trying to find a comfortable position. It was not an easy task, with an eight-month pregnant belly. She tried to remember the last time Beth ate something. Harpreet wanted to muster up some concern for this girl, but she wasn't her own child, and she felt disconnected from Beth in some critical fashion. She longed for Anjali, to feel her silky black hair under her hand, to hear her three-year-old giggle. Why had her child died of the virus while Beth, someone else's child, was still alive? That felt wrong to Harpreet. Upside down.

Her throat felt too sore to speak, but Harpreet came unsteadily to her feet, swaying with the motion of the boat on the waves, and searched through their canned goods. She didn't want to think about how few there were. Choosing a can of ravioli, she walked four steps to Beth and held out the can. Beth turned toward her, glanced at the can, and shook her head. She returned to staring out at nothing. Harpreet knew she should be motherly, by insisting that the child eat and drink. She should ask if she wanted to talk about the night her mother was shot, when Harpreet was in the process of stealing the boat, but she didn't have the energy. And what was there to say? Sorry you haven't even been alive for a decade, and you've lost both of your parents, and your home, and the country, along with any sense of safety or security that might have existed once?

Too much to cover, and also too little. It wasn't going to help. There were no real words of comfort anywhere, for any of them. Harpreet replaced the can. She thought about drinking some tepid rainwater but decided not to. She'd save what little remained for Beth. It might not rain again for a while, as this was mid-September (she thought), and hotter than any summer Harpreet could ever remember in Victoria.

She sat back down. The baby stirred inside of her, doing a wild somersault. Harpreet willed herself not to think of Malik, but every time the baby moved, he came to her. She wanted so badly to be free of him. When he first took to the streets, with the angry mobs intent on fighting back against the corrupt MOG government, Harpreet had prayed he wouldn't come home. So many were dying, but Malik did not die. He fought, and evaded capture, coming home blind drunk to Harpreet and Anjali, telling them soon this nightmare would be over, and the world would be a better place.

But instead, everything was destroyed. So many suffered, and then died, in an endless fight for control that never seemed to declare a clear victor. And still, Malik got his way with Harpreet. He took exactly what he wanted, with no concern for her. She'd been a fool to marry him seven years ago, and stay in a marriage that contained her like a prison cell. Before Anjali, she could go to work at the restaurant, enjoying ten-hour shifts without his shadow looming over her. Telling her what to wear, the words to speak, how to please him in the dark. And if she deviated from what Malik wanted, he used his threats, then his fists, and finally the rest of his brute strength to get her back on course. When she found herself pregnant with Anjali, like so many desperate women before her, she hoped he might grow gentler with a baby in the house. But the gambit failed. With this baby, he'd forced himself on her after a successful raid on a prominent bank. Malik came home at midnight, slick with other people's blood, and he'd raped her. Harpreet tried her best to feel nothing, to be ice-cold inside, but being numb turned to fear when her period didn't come. Birth control had been outlawed, but this was not a time to be pregnant, not when everything was burning.

Now, the baby settled down in her stomach. Tears fell onto Harpreet's skin, reminding her that she was still here. Malik, thankfully, was finally dead, washed away from her in the tsunami, as she took to the ocean with Anjali and Beth. She watched him die, from a safe distance, and felt absolutely nothing. She thought she had escaped, with her baby girl, but then she lost her, too. There was nothing left to live for. Beth would have to find her own way. Harpreet would not give birth, in this fucking open-plan leisure boat, and be forced to care for Malik's baby with no food or water for herself. She had suffered enough indignities, and would not suffer through this one.

If only she had a gun. But she didn't. And it wasn't fair to kill herself with Beth here. Harpreet knew that the only reason she was still alive was because of this young girl with her. Beth wasn't Anjali, which broke Harpreet's heart, but she remained alive out of some stubborn sense of responsibility for the care of another woman's child.

She would wait, a little longer, and then when Beth was sleeping, Harpreet would weigh herself down the best she could with supplies that Beth couldn't eat, and slip over the side of the boat into the depths of the ocean. She would drown, the fish would eat her, and that would be the end.

"What's that?" Beth asked, her voice sounding loud in the darkness. "See? That blinking light?"

Harpreet turned her head. Every few seconds, a light flashed. She thought she saw the orange glow of flames, far away, but knew it had to be in her mind.

"I think it's a flashlight!" exclaimed Beth. "And a fire!"

It was nice for Beth to have a flicker of hope out here, in this wretched watery landscape. Harpreet had no optimism left, so she closed her eyes.

# fifty-eight

## TONY

Spence and Kanda had been with them for almost two weeks now, and there had been no trouble from Ron. A few days back, Tony had found a stubbed-out cigar butt near the men's shelter, which was concerning because it didn't belong to any of the townspeople. He buried it in the woods and increased his daily surveillance efforts. Jasper's speech about not refusing Spence and Kanda the kind of welcome everyone else had received had done something to Tony. It brought him back to himself. He felt Pedro's presence especially close to him again these days, and Tony thought this was because he had softened his own heart. When he looked at Jasper's scarred-up leg, Tony recalled that his first instinct upon arriving on this beach had been to rush to his aid. And yet when Kanda came, emaciated and feeble on the homemade stretcher, he had been quick to close his heart off to her. Tony had wanted to stay separate from these newcomers. To not get involved. To protect himself from the sorrow that coursed through his veins when he had failed to save Ainsley. Not every story out here in this wilderness ended with a healed leg and antibiotics that could flush out an infection to bring a man back from the brink of death.

But nearly two weeks ago, after Jasper had brought him back to his own humanity, Tony walked out of the rec room and went to the others at the bathing cove. He pointed to the rebuilt medical centre. Spence carried Kanda out of the water, over the rocks and sand to the little building in the trees. He laid her on the bed. When he turned to leave, Tony reached out to touch his arm. He gestured from Spence over to Kanda. Spence seemed to understand. He began to talk, telling Tony what little he knew about her, outlining that she refused to eat, drank very little water, and appeared to be eager to die. Tony understood this, and did not fault her for it. He examined her, finding nothing beyond dehydration, bug bites, lice, anemia, and rough red patches on her skin that resembled bedsores. With Kanda, Tony longed to talk. To treat her with words, like Ainsley had done for Tony, confessing and sharing and drawing close by sewing up the distance between two people. She had made Tony feel seen, and valuable, something he thought only Pedro could do. He wanted to reach Kanda, before she slipped into a coma, but his words were still frozen inside of him.

So he sat by her, the way Ainsley had refused to leave Jasper's side before Tony arrived. He tried to get her to drink water. He reached for her hand. Tony treated her damaged skin with aloe, and the lice with a mixture of medicines from his kit. He washed her hair. She ate a few small sips of fish broth, then the next day a few more. She said nothing, and Tony did not speak, but like a plant given water and a dose of sunlight, Kanda began to recover. It was slow, and would take a long time, but she was eating and drinking again. For the last few nights, she had come out to the fire to join the group after dinner. Tonight, Kanda offered Tony a shy smile, and he felt a surge of gratitude and delight. He knew Pedro would be proud. He had done what he could for her, and that made it easier for Tony to sleep at night.

Around the fire, he listened while Claudine gave her nightly comms update. She was obsessed with building a radio to try to reach the mainland. Diamond and Claudine had pulled the radios and batteries from Jasper's float plane and Claudine's fishing boat. They really wanted Iris's newer system, but she balked at the request, wanting to keep her boat intact. Tony knew Claudine longed for the communication capabilities of the yacht on the other side of the island, the one they had surrendered to Ron, hoping he would leave them alone if he had that three-story vessel to live in. So far, this ploy had worked. But Claudine wasn't making a lot of progress with the two old radios she was experimenting with. Power was her biggest challenge, and she believed the yacht might have satellite options or old solar batteries that would give her more to work with.

While she talked, Tony looked out over the water. It was dark earlier each evening as autumn approached, so he didn't expect to see anything. But the hair on the back of his neck was raised, which used to happen to Tony a second or two before a siren could be heard. Pedro called it the Tony Warning. He'd felt it here when hunting with Jasper, a handful of times, when a predator drew near. He wished he had sensed the wave coming in time to swim to Ainsley, but he was too late, or too quiet for her to hear him, and he would take that particular regret to the grave with him. He wondered why he should feel the Tony Warning now. Could it be Ron, sneaking up on them? Or a shark or whale, drawing near to their beach?

He stood, moving away from the fire and to the edge of the water. He peered out, summoning all of his senses. There was nothing to see, but Tony felt certain that something or someone was there.

Tony went to the men's shelter and grabbed his small red

battery-operated flashlight. Thanks to Claudine's fishing boat, they had a stack of batteries. Everyone tried to conserve them, using them only in emergencies, but Tony wanted to use his light now.

Back at the shoreline, he used the flashlight to illuminate the simple wooden dock that had recently been constructed to tie up the boats. Iris complained about having to swim out to where her boat was anchored in the cove, so when the other buildings were complete, they prioritized a dock. Tony walked to the very end, with Claudine's boat on his left and Iris's on his right. He held the flashlight up, then blinked it on and off. Jasper and Min soon joined him.

"What do you see, Tony?" she asked.

Tony shook his head, intent on his task. This might be foolish, but what did it matter if he made a fool of himself? He had been willing to let Kanda die, just to avoid the pain of being involved, and that wasn't who Tony was. He had to make up for that now, to be willing to bear his own grief if there was a chance he could help another person. Otherwise, what were any of them even doing here, in this town they had so carefully created together?

He continued flashing the light. Now everyone had left the fire and was standing behind him on the dock. The back of his neck was still tingling. He could hear the others whispering among themselves, wondering what the hell Tony was up to. None of that mattered, not if someone was floating on the water, needing a safe place to land.

When Tony's hand began to cramp, from flipping the plastic slide on the flashlight back and forth, and he was trying to decide when he should stop this madness, an answering light came from out on the water.

One that matched his pattern exactly.

# fifty-nine

## MIN

M in had no idea how Tony had known someone was out there, but the flashing light from the water caused quite a stir in their town. Spence started shouting in the darkness, asking who was there. Iris (being Iris), suggested getting the rifle just in case. Jasper squeezed Min close to him, and as usual, she felt reassured by his solid presence. Diamond, Claudine, and Kanda huddled together, wondering amongst themselves if this person would have news about the flooded Vancouver area. They were fascinated by the idea of making contact with other survivors, and getting off this island to go back to some type of civilization. The three of them seemed to believe the violence and the climate disasters would be over by now, and that anyone who made it through would be willing to participate in the type of peaceful community they had formed here, but on a bigger, more sustainable scale. These young people wanted the resources of the mainland, the chance to reclaim all they'd been forced to leave behind. They felt it was their right. Min couldn't help but marvel at their enthusiasm and optimism, but then again, they were young. They still believed their future was ahead of them, which wasn't a luxury Jasper, Min, or Tony had, in their forties and fifties.

When the open deck boat drew close enough to see,

Min could feel Iris's palpable relief that there were no men on board. It seemed to contain a woman, and a kid who appeared in the dim light to be female. A child was not something Min ever expected to see out here. It was impossible not to think of Chul when Min looked at the little one. She couldn't help but remember Ainsley's children as well, even though they were much younger than this girl. And Spence's girlfriend had died while carrying their unborn child. It was difficult to read Spence's expression, but Min imagined he was thinking about Yvonne as well. So many deaths, too many to make any sense out of. How had this woman and this child made it this far, so long after the collapse of everything on the coast?

"Hello there!" Jasper called.

Tony aimed his flashlight at the boat, but its weak beam didn't illuminate much.

Spence pushed to the front of the group on the dock. "Do you have a rope?" he asked.

The woman in the boat seemed to be crying. And shaking. The child came to the V-shaped bow. "There's a rope here," she said.

"Throw it to me, okay? Then I can tie up your boat so you can come ashore."

With Tony's light shining on the little girl's face, Min thought she saw red sores on her pale white forehead and cheeks. "Jasper, look," said Min, pulling on his arm.

The child tossed the rope to Spence, then began to cough—a violent, sputtering sound. Everyone on the beach took a step back. Diamond threw an arm up over their mouth.

Spence dropped the rope. He moved quickly away from the boat.

Iris shouted, "You can't come into our town if you are

sick! Stay where you are!"

When the girl finished coughing, she said, "It's not the virus! Or it is but I've been sick for a while now, but I haven't gotten worse." She turned in the boat and pointed to the woman with her, who hadn't said anything. "Harpreet's daughter, Anjali, died of the red spread, and then I got these spots, but it's not the virus, or I'd already be dead."

"What's your name?" asked Min.

"Beth," she answered. "I'm nine. Please let us stay! We've been out here for so long and we don't have much food or water left. Please." Her voice went up on the last word, pleading with them.

Tony leaned over the edge of the dock and picked up the rope. He held it tight, pulling the boat closer. The eight of them huddled as a group on the dock.

"It's too dangerous," said Iris. "We can't risk getting infected."

"We all had plenty of exposures before we came here, and none of us got it. We must have some kind of immunity." Claudine had voiced this theory before, but no one knew how true or scientific it was.

Spence said, "Are we supposed to pretend we didn't see them? Tell them, 'Sorry, you have to stay on the water because we're scared of you?' It's a woman and a little kid, for Christ's sake!"

"How about they quarantine away from us for a few days, until we know it's not the virus and must be something else?" Jasper made this suggestion while attempting to make eye contact with everyone around the circle in the inky darkness.

Diamond nodded. "I like that idea. But where?"

Min thought of the rec room, but knew Iris would never go for it, as she saw that as her building. "The medical centre?" Min offered. "And we give them a chamber pot? And bring food to the door but don't go in?"

Iris said, "But what if any of us need the medical centre while they are in there?"

Kanda reached out a hand to touch Tony's arm. Her voice was quiet, and deep. It was the first time anyone had heard her speak. "Tony? What do you think?"

Min watched Tony turn his head to look at Kanda. Not for the first time, Min wished she knew what he was thinking. He had worked a miracle with Jasper, and also with Kanda, but he seemed to blame himself for Ainsley's death. Maybe there were no more medical miracles to be had.

With the flashlight in one hand, and the rope in the other one, Tony turned from the group and back to the boat.

Iris called, "Be careful, Tony!"

In the dim light, Min could see that the child, Beth, was crying. The woman (Min had already forgotten her name), rose and came over to the girl. Both of them stood there, side by side, unsteady in the current, staring out at the group on the land. Min gasped when she realized that the woman was pregnant. Everyone else seemed to notice around the same time, and a jolt of shocked energy went through the small crowd.

Tony turned and handed the rope to Jasper, who went to tie it up.

Lifting his arms, Tony gestured for Beth to come to him. She grabbed for the pregnant woman, unsure.

"I'm Tony," he said, his voice raspy and wavering.

Min held her breath, stunned that he was speaking to the child.

"I'm a paramedic, and I'll stay with both of you until you feel better. It's okay. You're safe now."

# sixty

## RON

Ron hid in the forest, watching this group of people who didn't want him to join them. His anger felt hot and dangerous inside of him, bubbling up until he could taste bile in the back of his throat. He spat onto a tree, as quietly as possible. Ron had come this far without being detected by anyone, and tonight was the night for him to get even.

He was here the night the pregnant Indian came with the little girl who was sick. What a shame the virus had to target a kid, even way out here, and one of his kind at that. His people had been vilified, blamed by the minorities for every manner of evil in society, before the Men of God had finally seized power in order to fight back and return the country to its Godly values. Ron and Cindy had been members of their Regina Pentecostal church for more than fifty years. He had served as a church elder and board member, and yet that didn't seem to count for anything when people started rioting against the stable government the Men of God provided for Canada.

Why was it the white child who had the virus and not all these ethnics, living it up on this side of the island? Nothing made any sense to Ron any longer. He used to be so certain about everything, so in control of his faith, his family, his farming, and his church. People came to Ron for answers. Cindy listened to him, deferring to what he wanted because that's what a Christ-like wife did. When Patsy and Paul went off the rails as teenagers, backsliding from their faith and experimenting with drugs, alcohol, and sex, with Ron's son committing the ultimate abomination of lying with another man, Ron did the right thing as a Godly man and father. He cut off all ties with both of them, comforting Cindy and their obedient daughter, Louise, when they wept for the lost family members, but Ron knew he had done what God wanted him to do. The pain of losing two of his children was better than losing the respect of the church.

Now that the Black man and that weak Chinese girl left him all alone, Ron had been mourning for his lost kids in a new way. He wanted them to feel ashamed of their worldly ways and come back into the fold, repentant and humble, ready to submit to Ron's leadership and solid Christian standards once again. But they didn't return to him. And when the backlash came against the Men of God, and Ron felt threatened enough to flee Regina, he failed to save his wife and daughter. Ron worried that he was being punished by the God he'd worked so hard to serve. Being abandoned and alone filled Ron with rage. He wanted these people to pay.

It took Ron a while to find this camp. It was hours away on foot, through a dense and thick jungle of trees, roots, and animals. But he finally stumbled on it, hiding out where no one could see him. Ron counted their numbers (eight, including the two traitors who left him), and then two more when the pregnant lady and the white kid arrived. He couldn't believe the structures they had built out of logs and tree boughs and leaves here. They seemed to have predictable daily rhythms, from what Ron had seen, so after his second visit he went back to his boat and started making plans.

He considered a lot of different options: setting their camp on fire, finding their rifle and shooting them one by one like a sniper, contaminating their food, stealing their supplies, taking someone hostage and then using that person to negotiate for a better deal, so Ron wasn't isolated while they all lived it up in some happy clappy summer camp nonsense, without a care in the world. Considering these were the type of people who had destroyed the old world, their arrogance and superiority here on this island really got under Ron's skin. How dare they invite Spence and that weak dying girl over here and completely ignore Ron? The disrespect enraged him to the point where he couldn't think clearly at all.

In the end, he didn't think he could manage too big of a plan on his own. Ron was sluggish and tired, not eating enough since Spence stopped hunting and cooking for them, and he didn't want to get caught in the middle of some elaborate scheme, with a number of complicated steps to follow. He preferred to strike them where it would hurt, under the cover of darkness, and then vanish before anyone saw him.

He waited under the protection of the trees, until they finished their fireside blather. One by one, they drifted off to the bathroom, or to wash a few dishes in the water, and to lock any food up in their cooking shed. Finally, they all went to bed. Ron had been careful to notice on his other reconnaissance missions where everyone slept. After the Indian and the child arrived, they stayed in a small building with the swarthy South American–looking guy with the long hair, probably because the rest of them were worried about the virus spreading, but now they were all back together on the beach. Just one big happy family (minus Ron, of course). No one seemed to be staying in the boats or the float plane.

Ron's legs started to cramp up, from crouching in the dark. He figured he'd waited long enough, and he was desperate for a smoke. He stood and stretched his tight muscles, arching his back like their white barn cat, Morris, used to do. It was a cloudy night, with a refreshingly cool wind, which helped Ron because the moon and stars weren't as visible as they were in a clear sky. His feet bare, Ron crept onto the rocks and the sand, checking over his shoulder periodically to make sure no one was awake and moving around.

When he got to the dock, he slowly reached for his knife, hanging around his waist, and removed the blade from its sheath. Ron had spent most of the day sharpening the steel. He could untie the knots, but he was concerned that would take too long as the ropes were thick and knotted securely to their posts. He walked to the end of the dock and chose the fanciest cabin cruiser line first, sawing carefully at the rope until it split with a satisfying snap. Then he started in on the line to the fishing boat with the blue sail, and the open deck speed boat, and finally the float plane. He wasn't going to bother with the homemade raft, but it was easy to untie that and set it free, as Ron figured it might have sentimental value to someone here. It was high tide, and by Ron's calculations it wouldn't take long for the boats to drift from the cove and back out to sea. He saved the rowboat for last, as he thought it might be a useful thing to take with him back to his side of the island. Ron's hands and wrists were aching after all the cutting, so he sat back to take a break, enjoying the beautiful sight of their transportation vessels floating away under the blanket of darkness. That would show them. Where was the Christian generosity for someone alone and in need like Ron?

The noise of someone moving behind him startled Ron. He did not want to be caught here. His heart pounding with fear, he replaced his knife, then ran back off the dock toward the trees. Ron grabbed his sandals, with his celebratory cigar tucked inside, and headed for the forest, but stopped dead when he saw the beautiful blonde woman step out of a log shanty marked with a "W" on the door. She held a small camping lantern in her hand. Her face froze in shock at the sight of him. She gasped, the sound echoing around the trees. Ron reached for his knife, the blade glinting in the pale yellowy lamplight. The woman's eyes fluttered shut and she fell to the ground at his feet, the lantern rolling away from her.

Ron's breathing sounded loud in his own ears. He should probably leave her and run, in case she woke up the others, but she'd seen him now. In a split second, he decided to bring her with him, and to steal the rowboat. Ron tried to lift the woman, wanting to throw her over his shoulder, but she was too heavy for him. So he dragged her, by the ankles, over the rocky beach. Ron had no idea why she fainted, but he could use her as a bargaining chip when they inevitably came for him after they discovered that he'd set their boats free.

He was trying to lift her body into the rowboat, grunting softly to himself, when Ron heard a thunking sound behind him. He dropped the woman into the water, attempting to unsheathe his knife, when he felt the skin of his back tearing. Ron turned, before he felt any real pain, to see an axe raised in the air.

The second blow came at his face, and the crunching sound his bones made was the last thing Ron heard.

# sixty-one

## KANDA

Kanda didn't realize she was screaming until she heard her name being called, over and over. She was in a chopping rhythm, which seemed meditative to her. Swinging the rusty axe, feeling the reverberation when it connected with its target. This was muscle memory, like with the men who had attacked Celeste.

"Kanda, stop! Please, Kanda—let us come get Iris! Kanda!" She heard the voices, but they were blurry, strained through a fog or a net. She felt the hot blood on her skin, spraying up at her, and could not seem to stop the repetitive cadence of her arms. Kanda was determined to stop him before he could hurt Iris. She would not let this happen again.

As she raised her arms above her head for another strike, Kanda saw Spence in front of her, around the other side of the rowboat, standing in the water. His mouth was moving, but she couldn't hear any words. Only the pounding of her own heart, which pumped in time with her anger. The axe went down with a thud, landing not in Ron's flesh but in the wooden lip of the boat. Kanda tugged at it, hard, but Spence used the pause to rush toward her, placing his strong hands over her arms.

"It's okay, Kanda," Spence said. He sounded far away, but over her panting breath she could hear him now. And then other sounds: the waves slapping against the rowboat, hushed voices behind her, an owl hooting in the forest, a shout about cut ropes.

Then Diamond was there, beside Spence. "Kanda," they said, their voice low and warm. "You did it. You stopped him. You can let go of the axe now."

Kanda swallowed a few times, trying to come back to herself. She was vaguely aware of people in the water, trying to get to Iris, pulling her limp body out onto the sand.

"He was going to attack her," said Kanda, her voice panicked. "She fell over, and he took her in the boat. I had to stop him. It had to be me, so the rest of you didn't have blood on your hands. I've done it before, for Celeste. I had to. They had hurt her so badly…"

Diamond pulled Kanda close, soothing her. "I know, it's alright, you saved her. He didn't hurt Iris because of you. She's safe, Kanda. You are so fierce, a real badass."

Kanda could feel her fingers being pried off the handle of the axe. Diamond gripped Kanda, holding her tight, and she let herself go. The tears came, hot and tight in her throat. She wondered what the others would think of her now, this nineteen-year-old with a pipe dream of being prime minister one day. Kanda wanted to fix what was so obviously broken in their political system in Canada. To stop white men from holding all the power and status, and to fight for women, her queer friends, and people of colour like herself who had been forced to the bottom of society for far too long. She knew that it was someone else's turn to lead, and Kanda believed that person was her. So had her dad, telling her from the day she was born that she would be a leader who would change the country. But here, in this fucked-up after world, she was a murderer instead.

Diamond slowly led her to the bathing cove, splashing cold water onto Kanda's boiling skin. In the firelight, Kanda saw the blood on her arms, watched it stain the water pink. Diamond sang to her as they cleaned Kanda's body, an old folk song about nurturing women who cared for the hurting. God, they had a stunning voice. It sounded like hope and promise and youth. The melody, sung with such tenderness and love, transported Kanda from this place and time to someplace better. Where men no longer took whatever they wanted, or violated the bodies and souls that didn't belong to them. Kanda couldn't tolerate the cost of what these men had done. She felt it in her very bones, as though she'd been the one attacked, ravaged, devastated.

Later, Diamond led Kanda out of the water and toward the women's shelter. She tried not to look at the carnage on the beach, but everyone was awake, moving around in the darkness, talking softly, dragging Ron's corpse, and cleaning the axe.

Kanda turned her head to Diamond. "I didn't know what to do," she said, but even as the words left her mouth, she knew they were a lie. Kanda knew exactly what to do, because she'd done it before, just not in enough time to save the woman she loved. This time, she acted faster, and without concerning herself about the ethics of the situation, because the man hauling Iris to the town's boat didn't seem to consider whether or not his actions were right. So Kanda didn't either.

Diamond led her back to bed. They settled Kanda in place, fussing with a thin pink sheet, then lay down beside her, moulding their gorgeous shape to Kanda's. Diamond stroked Kanda's neck, whispering reassurances to her. Kanda listened, straining for every nuance in Diamond's voice, picturing Celeste's face in her mind. She was smiling, and looked to be at peace, and for now, it was enough.

# sixty-two

## IRIS

When Iris woke up, she was on the beach, with her head in Min's lap. It felt so much like when she first arrived, and had collapsed by the fire, waking up to hear Min speaking Korean to her in a soft, comforting manner. She remembered then feeling like a child, with her mother, but this time she was numb. Anesthetized. Unable to feel a single thing. Not relief, or contentment, just blank. Like a clear canvas, devoid of colour or vibrancy, mercifully wiped clean of pain.

Min was talking, something about safety and Kanda and not worrying because it was all taken care of now, but these words meant nothing to Iris. She may as well have still been speaking in Korean. Where Iris's brain should have been, there was only an empty white space, like her office walls. How had Iris listened to people talk about themselves, hour after hour, day after day, year after year, without losing her mind? She had been good at her job, or at least she sensed she had been competent, but it was difficult to imagine ever giving a shit about what happened to her clients. Expending that type of energy on empathy was as far from her now as her favourite bottle of Moët, the fizzy anticipation she used to feel when the cork would slide out and the golden wine would pour into her crystal flute.

Slowly, she became aware that activity was occurring around her, but every time Iris tried to move her head, Min held it tight between her hands. "You don't want to look," Min said. "Better not to see this. But Kanda took care of Ron. He won't be a problem for us anymore. And you are safe."

The word *safe* bounced around the emptiness of Iris's sterile mind. It seemed like gibberish. Nonsensical prattle. A word with no meaning whatsoever. For so long, since her house had burned to the ground, Iris had been in search of safety. She thought for a while that her handgun would make her safe, but it didn't. Then she believed other people would give her security, but that hadn't been true either. Everyone had radically opposed ideas about how to run this settlement, this town. Like in the before world, no one could agree, and somewhere in Iris's addled mind she knew that agreement was where safety lived. Without it, Iris was afraid. Now, she felt like there was no way out. Maybe she should've burned to death in her own home. There had to be some poetic beauty in that. Or perhaps she was already dead, living here with these people as a ghost, where a man could still attack you with a knife in the middle of the night, and this was Iris's penance for not caring enough for others in her previous existence.

Iris looked up to see Jasper's face, hovering above her, next to Min's. "He's in the woods, a little ways up the mountain," he said quietly. "A gift to the animals." Jasper smiled, his eyes tinged with sadness. "Would you like to go back to bed, Iris? Or I can add to the fire and we can sit up with you a little longer?"

She gazed at him, unable to comprehend the words. Min shifted on the ground, allowing Iris to move to a sitting position.

Min said, "A fire would be nice. Let's stay together."

Jasper helped Iris to her feet. She swayed, unsure if she had the strength to stand. He held her elbow. Automatically, Iris glanced to her left, to check on her boat. It wasn't there. Nothing was there but the dock and the rowboat. She started to breathe quickly, short desperate pants. Her head felt light, unattached to her body. Min came close, turning Iris toward the fire pit.

"Let's go sit down, Iris. You've had a shock tonight, and you're not yourself."

Those words made more sense to Iris. As she walked, supported by Min, she remembered in jagged flashes. The bathroom, the darkness, the old man's craggy face, the knife glinting in the dim lantern glow. After that, nothing. Iris didn't know what happened to her boat and she didn't want to know. Nothing was making sense, and maybe this feeling of oblivion was what she'd been searching for all along.

Min settled her on a log by the fire. Jasper added more sticks of wood. Iris breathed, in and out, but wouldn't allow a single thought to form in her brain. She was aware that Min and Jasper were talking, but she couldn't hear them. Or she didn't want to. It amounted to the same thing. Other people were moving around this strange place, murmuring and whispering, even shouting (the young Black woman was always so loud).

Iris let it flow around her, like the water, and remained isolated inside of herself.

# sixty-three

## HARPREET

Something seemed dangerously broken in Iris, the white therapist. Claudine never had anything kind to say about her, and Harpreet certainly found her chilly in the short time she'd known her, but whatever happened here tonight had caused Iris to develop a faraway look in her eyes that Harpreet recognized. It was how she imagined her face appeared when Malik would start in on her. A person had to maintain the pretense of protection by escaping somewhere else when you were terrified out of your mind.

They were all sitting around the fire, this motley group of survivors whom Harpreet knew but also didn't know at all. Everyone but Kanda and Diamond, who were together in the women's shelter. It was the middle of the night.

Harpreet had heard the screaming and the sound of the axe biting into flesh and bones, but Tony told her to stay in the shelter with Beth, so she did. Later, when Tony, Spence, and Jasper came back from disposing the man's body somewhere up the mountain, Tony pulled Harpreet aside and told her that this Ron, whom everyone feared, had tried to take Iris in the town's rowboat. Kanda had killed him, with the axe they used to chop wood every single day.

Now, Iris sat between Min and Jasper, staring dully into the flames. Claudine and Spence whispered to one another, gesturing at the empty space where the boats used to be.

They were no doubt trying to plan ahead for what this would mean for the town. Harpreet felt no sense of loss about her missing deck boat, but she knew that Iris had been deeply attached to her cabin cruiser. In the firelight, Jasper's face was lined and weary. He had also loved his float plane. The senselessness of this vandalism baffled Harpreet. What was the point? What the fuck was the point of any of it?

Beth was sitting next to Tony, her favourite person out here, and she leaned against his arm. She looked drowsy, the way Anjali used to look sometimes at the dinner table, about to fall fast asleep with her face on her favourite monkey plate. Harpreet wanted to mother this young girl, who remarkably didn't die after her strange brush with the pandemic virus that had killed Anjali. But she couldn't seem to do it. Caring for another child felt like too much emotional work. Harpreet knew this was ironic, and tragic, because in a month or so she'd be giving birth to her own baby, one that she didn't want and couldn't imagine caring for out here in this wilderness.

Min got up and came over to the empty chair by Harpreet, where Diamond usually sat. "How are you doing?" she asked.

"Oh, you know, just another murder." Harpreet heard the words and knew they sounded terribly callous, but what words made sense in this situation?

Thankfully, Min laughed. "It's crazy, but you'd think we'd come to expect that by now."

"Did you ever meet this guy? This Ron?"

She shook her head. "No, but Jasper did, when he went over there with Diamond and Claudine. He said he was awful, the type to support the Men of God and be shocked by anyone who didn't." Min paused here, deep in thought.

"Before you got here, we had lots of discussions and votes about whether or not to invite Ron to live with us. We couldn't come to an agreement, so we did nothing. He seemed to represent an obvious danger to our town. But then Claudine and Diamond went to get Spence and Kanda, which I can see now was the right thing to do, but obviously Ron wanted to hurt us for it." Her voice trailed off.

"So he cut the lines to our boats," said Harpreet. "As payback."

Min sighed. "That seems to be the case. I was sound asleep, so I didn't hear him, but from what I can gather, Iris was awake and in the bathroom. Ron had a knife, and well, Iris had been attacked by a group of men in her home. Before. They held a knife to her throat and violated her, then burned her house down and made her watch."

Harpreet stared at Iris. She thought about the chain of events that had led each one of them here, and the horrors that were just below the surface of their skin. No one here knew about Malik and his drunken rages. Or about Anjali. And the conflicted feelings Harpreet had about this baby that had been inflicted upon her, without her consent. But now Harpreet knew that Iris had been forced as well. How many others here had a story like this? She knew she couldn't talk about it yet, as she felt too raw, too exposed.

A noise came out of Harpreet's throat, a strangled type of gurgle she'd never heard before. Her breath was coming too fast, like a panic attack. She felt dizzy, the faces around the fire swimming in and out of focus. Min placed a warm hand on Harpreet's knee. Her eyes were gentle and inviting.

"I'm here, you know," Min said. "We're all here. Any time you want to talk. We've known each other a bit longer, but that doesn't mean we don't care about what happened to you. We're in this together, otherwise there's no point at all to any of us being here."

Min continued to pat Harpreet's knee. She focused on the sensation of being touched, and how pleasant it was not to be afraid of being touched. Harpreet saw that Jasper was smiling at both of them. It was hard not to be jealous of their relationship. He was so protective of Min, and she was the obvious leader out here. It must be wonderful to be loved and cherished. Harpreet focused on that, so she didn't have to think about Iris, or Malik, or her own sweet Anjali. Thinking about others only brought pain, and Harpreet thought she couldn't handle another drop of it, or she might drown.

# sixty-four

## BETH

Beth could feel herself falling asleep, but she didn't want to get up. It was cozy here by the fire. She liked the feel of Tony's sturdy body beside her. His shoulder was comforting to lean against. Her eyes kept drifting closed, then she'd force them back open. Beth listened to the sound of Min and Harpreet's soft voices, and the popping from the logs in the fire. She could sense Tony breathing, her head moving up and down with the rhythm of his inhales and exhales.

The grown-ups all seemed shocked, which reminded Beth of how her mom and dad had behaved in the months and years before they died. She remembered a lot of late-night whispering between them when they thought the kids were sleeping. The house felt tense and strained. Beth was the oldest, and she worried right along with her parents, but she hated never being told what was going on. It was scarier to see people shooting guns in the streets, breaking the glass in stores, and setting fires all over the place and not get any answers to your questions. The words *Men of God* didn't mean much to Beth. Or *Martial Law.* She heard that a lot, when there were no more police to call, but Mom and Dad told her not to worry about it. They said they would take care of her and her brothers. But they couldn't, and now Beth was on her own.

She yawned, unable to stop herself, and Tony stirred beside her. "Time for bed, little one," he said. Beth loved his dry, gentle voice. Min told her that he hadn't spoken a single word from the time he arrived here. She said Tony needed Beth to come and unlock his ability to talk, that Beth had been the key. That made her feel important somehow. And even though Beth had a fever and a cough and horrible red scabs all over her skin when she got here, Tony had stayed with her and Harpreet in his medical centre. He could've caught the virus from her, but he didn't care. That made him someone Beth trusted, and would do anything for.

Beth stretched her back and stood up. She wasn't sure she wanted to go back to the shelter, not after Iris had been attacked by some mean guy. Kanda had killed him, which Beth was happy about, but she didn't like sleeping in the women's shelter away from Tony. When her spots had cleared up and the fever had gone away, Tony had set her blankets up near Harpreet, who almost never talked to Beth or even looked at her. Beth had begged to stay with Tony, Jasper, and Spence, but Iris said that was a bad idea. "Women protect their own," Iris said, but at night Beth missed Tony with an acute pain. She'd been thinking of ways to get sick again, or burn her arm in the fire, just to get back into the medical centre at night with Tony.

"Night night, Beth," Min said. Jasper reached out a hand to touch her lightly on the head as she walked by him, but no one else acknowledged her. Tony took her hand, leading Beth toward the washroom.

"Don't forget to brush your teeth. I'll wait right outside here until you are done."

Beth opened the leaf-covered door, hearing it close behind her with a thunk. She peed, then found her toothbrush and rubbed it all over her gums and teeth. Jasper had made them for everyone, carving wooden handles and weaving in grasses for the bristles. It tasted gross, and it was strange not to have toothpaste, but Beth hadn't brushed her teeth for more than a year, so this made bedtime seem a little more normal. She placed her toothbrush back on the shelf by her name, then opened the door.

Tony's face, turned away from her toward the water, appeared strained in the dim moonlight. He seemed like he might be afraid, which caused a chill to run up Beth's spine. If Tony was scared or worried, what chance did Beth have?

When he moved his head and saw her, his face relaxed and he looked more like himself. "Ready?" he asked.

Beth felt frozen in place, standing in the raised doorway of the women's bathroom. She could feel her head shaking back and forth, because no, she wasn't ready. Not for bed, not for being here on this island away from her parents and her brothers, not for the world to have ended. Beth wanted everything and everyone back.

He reached for her, and Beth shoved past him and ran. Where, she had no idea, but she thought maybe if she got far enough away from this place, she'd be able to make some sense of what was happening. Panicked, she ran until her lungs screamed and her head pounded, faster than she'd run in a long time, straight into the water.

She kept going, until the cold water was up to her chest, and then Tony caught her. She felt his arms come around her. He lifted her up, then turned her, pulling her into his chest. Beth flung her arms and legs around him, burying her face in his neck. Her body convulsed with sobs. She shivered from the night wind on her wet skin.

Beth knew there was nowhere else to go. This was it, all

they had, but Tony had followed her when she ran. He hadn't left her when she was sick, and now he held her like he might never let her go.

# sixty-five

## TONY

Tony brought Beth back to the fire. He had to get her dried off and warm before she could go to sleep, but he sensed that she was too raw and upset to have everyone's eyes on her. He pulled Jasper aside and asked if the group could go to bed so he could be alone with Beth. Jasper said, "Of course," then quickly rounded everyone up. Tony sat with Beth on his lap, her weeping slowing to a few hiccupy whimpers. She clung to his wet T-shirt with her small fists, like he was her life preserver at sea.

Spence banked up the fire, then offered Tony a shy smile before leaving. Min returned with two faded yellow towels, then went in the direction of the sleeping shelters. Tony nodded his thanks, then started on the challenging task of trying to dry Beth and himself while she was still glued to him. When he thought he'd done what he could do, Tony leaned over and dropped the two damp towels on an empty log chair. He put both of his arms around Beth, squeezing her tight, breathing in her briny smell.

When she spoke, it was muffled, competing with the rustling sound from the fire. Her cheek was against Tony's heart.

"What do you think happens when people die?"

He stroked the child's hair, taking his time, not wanting to rush such an important answer. He thought of the many conversations he and Pedro had had on this topic. Once, out on a walk in Banff National Park, Pedro had stopped, looked up into the tall maple, aspen, and willow trees, and said, "When I'm gone, think of me as the leaves on these trees. I'll still be there, giving you shelter, so you'll know where to find me."

Tony's eyes filled with tears. "I don't know for sure, little one, but I like to think we become part of nature, so we're never actually gone. I hope our essence, our souls, live on, but we'll get to be limitless, not in a physical body, so we can be all around. In the air, the trees, the soil, the water, the wind. Still here."

"So my mom and dad might be here? And Granny? And my brothers, Jake and Wyatt?"

"Would you like that?" Tony asked.

He felt her nod against his chest.

"My husband, Pedro, told me he'd be the leaves on the trees. Giving me shelter. Not leaving me."

Beth sat up, leaning back so she could see Tony's face in the firelight. She kept hold of the back of his shirt with one hand, but with the other one she wiped the tears from his face. He and Pedro had longed to be parents, before they had to separate from each other to try to stay alive. Tony often wondered what kind of parent he would be. He knew Pedro would be the fun one, who thought up all the wild family adventures. Tony thought he would be the steady and reliable one, who was around to pick up the pieces when their kids had their hearts broken.

Beth said, "I don't want you to leave me."

He tipped his head forward, softly, so his forehead was touching hers. "Oh Beth, I don't want to leave you either. But there's so much we can't control any more. I don't know if we ever could control anything, but I thought we could.

Can I tell you I'll do my best? And you can count on me, for as long as I'm alive, to run after you whenever you need me." He paused, then smiled, his eyes watery and red. "I think I might need you, too."

Beth smiled back. "Good."

She put her arms around his neck again and tucked in close, like a duckling to its mother.

"Tony?" she asked.

"Yes?"

"After what happened to Iris tonight, do you think she'll be mad if I sleep in the men's shelter with you?"

Tony grinned to himself. "I don't think she'll be mad. And even if she is, who cares? I think you should sleep wherever you want to."

"I want to be wherever you are."

"Okay, little one, let's stick together. You and me."

He could feel her body relax. Tony leaned back, in the chair, stretching his feet out closer to the flames. Beth's warm weight was comforting. She felt like a blanket. He looked up to the stars, infinite in the sky, a kaleidoscope of light. Behind them were the trees, their leaves offering up shelter to the townspeople, waving tenderly in the wind.

# sixty-six

## DIAMOND

In the morning, Diamond woke up just before sunrise. Their right arm was asleep, from Kanda lying on it. Diamond eased their arm out from under Kanda's head, riding out the stinging pins and needles from having the blood supply cut off. Just looking at Kanda's face made Diamond feel stirred up again, remembering her with the axe, chopping at Ron's body without mercy or regret. It was as if she had done this kind of thing before. Diamond wanted to know so much more about Kanda—who she was and what she had done to survive. Now wasn't the time to push her, Diamond knew this instinctively, but they were determined to get the full story at some point. It was impossible to know how any other person really felt, but Diamond thought they might have a chance at a real relationship with Kanda, to go deeper than the sex they'd enjoyed with Claudine.

Stealthily, Diamond crawled over to where Claudine slept. Diamond touched her hair, leaned down to whisper in Claudine's ear. "Hey, wake up." Her eyes flew open, startled, to focus on Diamond's face. Diamond put a finger up to their lips, to ask Claudine for silence. Then they indicated that Claudine should follow Diamond out of the shelter onto the beach.

When they were both by the fire pit, Claudine said,

"What the hell, Diamond? I hardly got any sleep last night. What's so fucking urgent?"

Diamond knew Claudine wasn't great in the morning. She needed a bit of time to wake up in order to be civil. In trying to impress her, Diamond had spent a lot of time and energy tiptoeing around Claudine's moods. They weren't interested in doing that anymore. The thought of not caring so much what Claudine thought was liberating. It gave Diamond a surge of well-being, the way they felt on Christmas Eve as a little kid.

"I want to talk to you," said Diamond. "Before everyone else is around."

"I'm not going all the way to the stream. Forget it. Not after what just happened with Ron and Kanda and everything. God, Diamond, not everything is about sex."

"I know that. I just want to talk. Let's go up to Cat Point and watch the sunrise."

Claudine sighed, like Diamond was asking her to do something incredibly arduous and unfair. Diamond breathed in deeply, trying to keep their cool. They were tempted to sweeten the deal by saying the discussion would be about Claudine's dream to rebuild the internet, and her interest in Spence, and how badly she wanted to find out if there were other reasonable people inhabiting the damaged cities again. But as Diamond watched Claudine's sour expression, in the milky pre-dawn light, they realized that somewhere along the line, Diamond had become far too focused on what everyone else might need. Their mom had warned about this when Diamond started coordinating marches, lobbying politicians (when democratically elected ones were still a thing), recording protest videos, and getting mildly internet famous. She would look at Diamond with concern in her eyes, and say, "Easy, baby.

You can't fix everything."

So Diamond said nothing. Having their father turn away from Diamond when they no longer identified as female had imprinted some serious abandonment fears on Diamond's soul. On a one-to-one relationship level, Diamond needed others to feel okay before they could be okay. But maybe now was a good time to work on this. Maybe Claudine was there for Diamond to practice on.

"Fine." Claudine had already started walking east, toward the bluff overlooking the bathing cove. "But let's be quick about it. I've got things to do today."

They climbed the hill quickly, as the sky began to lighten. From the bluff, it was hard not to think about Ainsley, who had died, swept up in the monstrous wave just below this spot. Claudine and Diamond sat down, under the shrub that looked vaguely like a cat's head, both glancing over to where the boats should've been alongside the dock. The rowboat had a lot of blood on it, the rough wood stained red, and several chunks had been cut out of it by the axe last night.

Claudine seemed to be waking up now, her anger coming back online. Diamond could feel her body vibrating. "Can you believe what that fucking asshole has done? Spying on us? Cutting the ropes to the boats? Trying to kidnap Iris? If Kanda hadn't been there, who knows what else he might have done. I should've shot him with the rifle when I first saw him."

She shook her head, irritated by the missed opportunity. Diamond wondered if Claudine had killed anyone before, but they didn't bother asking. What did it matter, anyway? Diamond would ask Kanda that question, when the timing was right, as she had all but confessed to killing last night, but right now Diamond wanted to close off a few loose ends.

"Thanks for coming up here with me, Claudine. Sorry it was so early, but I thought we should try to figure out a few things. Like how I feel about Kanda, and how you feel about Spence. I want to make sure we are both clear about everything."

Exasperated, Claudine said, "Look, Diamond, you are a lot younger than I am. I told you we were just messing around. It was a bit of fun, a way of blowing off steam. We weren't making a lifelong commitment, for Christ's sake."

Diamond looked away from Claudine, over the water, where the sun was emerging from the horizon. The sky was pink, but also tinged with yellow and purple. It was still mesmerizing, a sunrise, but that could be because there wasn't much else for entertainment options out here.

Softly, Diamond said, "You were my first. And I'll always be glad that it was you. But I've seen the way you are with Spence, how you seem to come alive when he's around. I was jealous at first, but now I'm not, because I'm starting to feel that way with Kanda. I have no idea if she feels the same, but I'm hoping to find out. I guess what I'm saying is, I think we should hit the pause button on the sex. You were right that it makes everything more complicated, and it seems like we both want different people now anyway."

Diamond ran out of words. They waited. After a moment, Claudine slid over, until her side pressed against Diamond's. She put her arm around their shoulder, then leaned her head against Diamond's. Together they watched nature showing off. It felt like they were the only two people in the entire world.

When the sun was above the water line, and the colours stopped being so magnificent, Claudine shifted to face Diamond, lifting their chin so they made eye contact.

"Thanks for saying all that. I agree with you. But it was fun while it lasted, and I think you're such a cool person. I often forget that you're only seventeen. I'm twenty-four and I feel ancient. I hope Kanda can see how fabulous you are, and you're right that I feel something happening with Spence that I've never experienced before. I'm glad you're not jealous, because I'm going to want you to come with me, when I build a radio that lets us communicate with other people. My plan is to get off this island, Diamond, and bring you and Spence with me. And Kanda, if she wants to come. The old folks can stay here, playing house until they die, but we're all young, and have big plans for rebuilding the world. I need your dynamic energy, and your vision for the future. And your fame, too." Claudine grinned, showing her dimples. "It's going to happen, D, I can feel it. We're going to get out of here, and start again. I really hope you'll come with me."

Diamond smiled. They felt like the very air around them got bigger, wider, more expansive. It was hard to believe that Claudine could actually build a radio that might work, but even imagining it was possible was better than having no hope left. Maybe the four of them—Claudine, Diamond, Kanda, and Spence—were exactly what the world was waiting for. People of colour, nonbinary, lesbian, women. It was their time to lead. This was only fair and right, after the old white men had failed so spectacularly. Here, they had learned as a group how to share resources and complete daily tasks, and talk openly about what divided them and what made them feel safe. They voted on every major decision after a lot of discussion so everyone felt listened to without any one person or ideology in charge. Why not see how this type of grassroots community might function on a bigger scale?

They bit their lip, thinking through the infinite prospects Claudine had proposed. She nodded at Diamond, then leaned forward to brush their lips with hers. This kiss was tender and caring, without asking for anything in return. Diamond was amazed by how many different types of kisses there were, and how much there still was to learn about each one.

# sixty-seven

## SPENCE

Spence and Claudine were in the rowboat, on their way to Ron's side of the island. Now that he was dead, Claudine was itching for the satellite capabilities of the yacht. Thankfully, she had removed most of the working parts of the radios in Jasper's plane and Claudine's fishing boat, before they were set adrift, but she was obsessed with the yacht and didn't want to waste another day without it.

Spence rowed for the first hour, and then they switched positions. It had started to rain, which made conversation challenging, so Spence sat in the front of the boat, sodden and chilled, wondering if Claudine's dream to build a radio was inspired or insane. He really couldn't tell.

His feelings for Claudine were complicated. She ran hot and then cold, which was familiar to him, as he'd struggled with various levels of depression during his high-pressure career as a stock trader. When his meds ran out while he was at sea, Spence felt panicked that the darkness would sneak back in and take him under. But he was okay, at least while he was alone. It was only when Ron came aboard that Spence began to struggle. And now he was dead, his head cleaved almost in half by tiny Kanda, who had been nearly dead herself from starvation a few weeks back.

It was so much to process. The added complication of Claudine's blatant interest in Spence was causing him stress. He had given himself so completely over to Yvonne, knowing that in her he had found his true soulmate, so anyone else seemed like second-best. She knew Spence, the realest version of himself. Not the one he showed at work, with the bluster and bravado, and not the iteration his parents knew, where he was meek and studious. With Yvonne, Spence felt like he could say anything to her and she would understand. When they were dating, before they'd even slept together, they had stayed up all night in downtown Portland, moving from diner to diner, talking non-stop while comparing the quality of the pancakes and vanilla milkshakes. He told her how guilty he felt about the obscene money he made, and how he worried about his direct contribution to the capitalist machine that had been oppressing his people. She listened, and she seemed to understand, until the choice to work as a stock trader was taken from him by the growing U.S. war on inequality. Spence had to hide out, and then his identity was stolen, along with the dirty money he'd worked those insane hours to accrue, followed by the power grid failure. And at the end of it all, Yvonne and their unborn baby were killed in the street, and Spence was alone.

"There's no chance he got rid of the yacht, right?" Claudine was shouting over the sound of the rain, interrupting Spence's morbid thoughts.

He turned his head. "No chance. He would've needed it to live in." Spence didn't know for sure that this was true, but it was the answer Claudine wanted.

"And you think our sail will work?"

Spence nodded. "We'll give it our best shot."

When Claudine had come to Spence, just before breakfast, she asked him how they could possibly bring the yacht back over here. The town now had only one seaworthy vessel, and it was this small rowboat. Spence suggested they jury-rig a sail, using one of the tarps, the way Claudine had turned her ancient fishing boat into a sailboat. Then they could try to tie the yacht to the rowboat and tow it. The process would be arduous, and exhausting, but attempting to steer the yacht with no fuel to power it seemed far too risky. It was a miracle that Spence, Ron, and Kanda had ever anchored the thing by this island in the first place. This madcap plan felt like a fool's errand, but Claudine really wanted this boat on their beach, especially since they now had nothing else to possibly escape in. Spence was willing to go along and try, just to keep the peace. With Claudine, it was always easier to say yes than no.

The heavy downpour eased to a sprinkle. Spence felt Claudine pause in her rowing to tap him on the shoulder. "Hey," she said. "Can you turn around?"

He did, moving slowly, trying to conserve every ounce of energy for the physical task ahead, provided his boss's yacht was still there.

"What do you think will happen with Iris? She seems like she's in a coma, like the lights are on but no one is home." Claudine started rowing again, but clearly wasn't done on this subject. "God knows I've never liked the woman, but Ainsley told me she was one hell of a therapist. She suggested I should go talk to Iris about what happened to me, and my family, but I just laughed. I couldn't see myself opening up to her, you know?"

Spence didn't know what to say to this. He could see that Iris was locked in her own mind. Shut down. Checked out. He hoped she would come out of it, because she wasn't likely to last long out here with no will to live, as he had seen with Kanda, but it was hard for Spence to summon too much compassion for her. Iris really hadn't wanted Spence in their town at first, and even after he'd proved himself to be valuable and non-threatening, she looked at him with suspicion, like so many white women in the before world. He knew she must've been terrified when Ron came at her with a knife, and Spence did feel sorry for Iris, but if she acted like a benign nursing home patient maybe the rest of them would all breathe easier, and feel safer.

He still couldn't manage a reply, so Claudine continued. "Shouldn't a therapist have the skills to be able to heal themselves? It seems like that's how it should work, but Iris failed at that, too."

Spence thought, can any of us heal ourselves? But he didn't say it out loud because he knew there was no good answer to that question. Each person out here was trying, in whatever way they could, to make it through each day without collapsing into a dust pile of grief. The anguish was ever present, just under the skin, infiltrating the bones and the marrow and the blood, but healing seemed like a luxury to Spence. He suspected that his feelings of guilt would nip at his heels until he drew his last breath.

He saw some of the coastline that looked familiar now. "This is it. I recognize this. Our beach should be just around this bend."

Spence felt his heart pounding. Claudine increased the speed at which she was rowing. Her breath was loud between them.

The rain stopped, creating a misty fog that dampened the skin. The rowboat sailed forward, skimming lightly over the water, and when they made the turn, they both saw the yacht at the same second. It was there, anchored and shining in the cove.

Spence grinned at Claudine, and she leaned over to kiss him.

# sixty-eight

## KANDA

When Spence blew the whistle, three short blasts, everyone came running. That was the signal for success, and all hands would be needed to wrangle the yacht carefully to the dock. But when Kanda came out from the cooking hut, where she'd been working side by side with Harpreet to prepare a racoon and duck stew for dinner, she felt rooted in place by the sight of the ship. People moved around her, exclaiming at the yacht's size and splendour, with its three storeys, but Kanda couldn't seem to move.

She hated this boat. It reminded her of Ron, and the feeling of being powerless. More than anything else, Kanda despised spinelessness. She understood why Claudine wanted the yacht, and knew it could be useful for the town without Ron around to challenge them, but the craft itself gave Kanda a shivery, frightened feeling.

Kanda sensed more than saw Diamond. They brushed up against Kanda's side. "Let them handle this," Diamond said. "You don't have to do anything."

She shook her head, wanting to explain to Diamond what she had no words for. But Diamond seemed to understand. They were perceptive, like Celeste used to be. Kanda needed that sensitivity around her, because she didn't possess it for herself. What Kanda had was pure adrenaline-fueled action. She was a woman who wanted to do whatever it was that needed to be done. No brooding or debating. Just jumping in and getting her hands dirty. But to balance that, someone else had to be Kanda's support system, or she had no tether to what might be right or wrong, or to know when caution should be employed. Kanda remembered suddenly that Diamond's stunning face had appeared in her cabin when Kanda was at her lowest point, and that their name had seemed like the answer to a question.

Now, she turned to look into Diamond's hazel eyes. "I never thanked you, for saving me on that boat. For coming to find me, and then coming back for me, when no one here wanted you to do that. And with Ron, the other night, you were there. You took care of me. Why did you do that?"

Diamond stepped even closer. "Because I think you're the strongest, most decisive person I've ever met. I'm in awe of you."

They looked at each other, studiously ignoring the frenzied activity of the others in and around the long dock as the yacht was secured. Suddenly, Kanda felt the urge to confess what she had done. To test out the response from another person she admired. Kanda wanted to be able to reconcile the leader she longed to become with the crimes she'd committed. She wanted to know if Diamond would hate what she'd done, or if they would admire it.

"My girlfriend Celeste was violently raped after the MOGs took power and there were no more laws protecting women. She died from her injuries, and I wasn't there to stop them. But I knew who the men were, and I hunted them down, one by one, and I slaughtered them for what they did to her. And then with Ron, I didn't even stop to think. I saw him carrying Iris, and he was holding a knife, and I went for the axe. I didn't feel anything at all, watching him die, except for relief."

Kanda waited, noticing that she still felt nothing. No remorse or guilt. Simply a resigned sense that she had completed a necessary task. But she did care about what Diamond's response would be.

Smiling, Diamond said, "I think we all felt relief when you killed Ron. Don't waste time worrying about him. Or those other men. They sound like bastards. That kind of power-crazed man has always done whatever it takes to survive, and now we're doing the same thing. Fair is fair. But I'll tell you one thing: when shit goes down, I want you by my side, holding a weapon. That's fierce as hell, not to mention fucking sexy."

Kanda's insides turned to liquid. She felt reprieved, absolved, exonerated. In her first university philosophy class, the students had debated the ethics of murder. It was only an idea then. A theory. Out here, where Kanda had to act quickly, she didn't have the luxury of wondering what her actions said about her. Her childhood dream was to be the prime minister of Canada. Lying on a damp mattress in that yacht, Kanda did her best to surrender that ambition, believing that a murderer could never do that job. But that was a rule from the before world. This was a new frontier. A place where a Thai lesbian woman who wasn't even out of her teens could fix the problems that needed solutions, and still be capable of leading. She could hold her head up high. *Fierce as hell.*

Kanda said, "Fair is fair."

Diamond laughed, and to Kanda it sounded like a bell being struck, the key perfect and pleasing to the ear. She reached for Diamond's hand. It felt warm and solid against Kanda's palm.

They stood there together, looking at the yacht and the rest of the townspeople climbing up into it. Kanda could feel the excitement of the others in the air, but she had no desire to move from this place. Maybe later, she'd want to go back in there and see what could be salvaged. She knew Diamond would go with her if she asked. But for now, there was no rush at all. Kanda wanted to stand here for a little longer, feeling her strength returning, swirling inside of her like a gathering storm.

# sixty-nine

## CLAUDINE

Claudine's enthusiasm grew as she worked in the bridge of the yacht. She tried to tune out all the other voices, as everyone prowled around exclaiming how huge the rooms were, that the chandelier must've looked incredible lit up at night, why was there so much garbage in here, what the hell is that smell and other banal observances. These people didn't seem to understand how valuable the communication system was. Claudine knew if she could get it working, she'd be able to make contact with the outside world, which meant information on how the recovery attempts were going on the mainland or on Vancouver Island. There had to be a civilization re-forming somewhere, made up of those who had learned the hard way that the old systems didn't work. Real change was coming, on a big scale. Claudine believed it in her very bones. And she meant to be part of it.

Thankfully, no one was bothering her. She knew they thought she was obsessed with this radio idea, but Claudine didn't give a shit. For as long as she could remember, she wanted to build a free and non-capitalist internet. A tool that would not be used to make people money, or to spread alarmist conspiracy theories, or cause women to compare their faces or thigh gaps with starving actors and models. Claudine's vision was for pure connection possibilities.

She longed for simplicity, ease, and most of all, equality. A system for all the voices to be heard and amplified. A place where hatred, bigotry, misogyny, xenophobia, and other similar horrors were outlawed. Claudine wanted what the original internet was designed to do, before it failed so thoroughly. This would be her legacy. Claudine knew she was the person to do it.

When she found a satellite phone, behind a locked door, she held her breath when pushing the power button. Claudine hoped that a small charge would remain in the battery, but the phone was dead. She thought she could create a trickle charge system, enough to power the radio she was building for short periods of time, but she wanted everything this yacht offered to put it all together. Solar panels would've been fabulous, but in the last gasp for oil and gas before the world imploded, most solar and wind products were ignored in favour of old-fashioned fuel.

Spence stuck his head in, holding an armful of flattened cardboard and empty metal food cans. He smiled. Claudine felt her heart turn over in her chest. God, he was sexy when he smiled. "How's it going in here? Find anything useful?"

Claudine grinned. "Oh yeah. There's a satellite phone with a dead battery, and a sophisticated GPS. If I can find something in here to generate enough wind power to trickle charge the batteries, I can power a transceiver for two-way radio comms."

"What kind of wind power?" Spence asked.

"A wheel would work best. I'd take the steering wheel off, but I don't want to disable the rudder system in case we need this to get back to the mainland. Or I'm going to try to build something at the fresh water source, for hydro power."

"Would a bicycle wheel work?"

"Why? Do you have one hidden away somewhere that you haven't shared with us? Do you go for long secret bike rides around the island?" Claudine tried to make it into a joke, but even to her own ears she could hear it falling flat. She wished she didn't feel so hyped up around Spence, so eager for him to like her.

"Beth found one in a closet in the hallway. Both tires are flat, but she was hoping we could patch them for her to ride on the beach."

Claudine's eyes lit up. A bicycle was just what she needed. She got up, squeezing past Spence, noticing how strong his arms felt against her skin. She wanted to feel them around her body. Claudine wasn't a patient person. She knew that soon she would be pushing the issue that lay between them. The attraction was there, in the air, but he seemed resistant to pursue it. But Yvonne was gone. Claudine was here, standing right in front of him, and when she'd kissed him in the rowboat he hadn't pulled away. She wanted a future, away from this remote place, and with everything that had already happened, Claudine didn't want to wait too long to see if Spence felt the same way. If she could get this radio working, and hear a voice on the other end that would be able to help them get off this island, she planned for Spence to be her lover. Now it was a matter of finding the right time, and not scaring him off.

She took a few steps into the sitting room, which reeked of urine and sweat (goddamn nasty MOG asshole Ron!), then backtracked toward the bridge, back to Spence. Fuck waiting. Claudine couldn't see the point. If anyone was going to make a move here, it would have to be her. She drew near to Spence, pressing as close as his armful of trash would allow her, and she looked up into his dark brown eyes.

"Spence," Claudine said firmly, "I want you. I know you lost Yvonne, and your baby, and I know you loved her. I've never loved anyone, at least not properly, but I think I might love you. Or I will eventually. And if my radio works, and there are people out there, in an actual city, we can leave here, together, and start over somewhere else." She paused, to draw a breath, then decided to keep going. "Later on, I might want to have a baby of my own, in a show of faith that the world will be safer and better for my kids than it was for me. Or for you. And I'll rebuild the internet, and you can do whatever it is you want to do, but I'm hoping we can try doing it together. What do you think?"

She had placed all her cards on the table. Her breath came in short bursts as she studied Spence's face for a clue to what he might be thinking. His eyes got cloudy, but he didn't cry. Behind them, somewhere in the boat, a woman shrieked and then a man laughed.

"I'm not sure I want to feel that kind of pain again, if I lose you like I lost them," he said.

"But it's all pain," Claudine answered. "I don't think we can avoid it."

"Are you willing to go slow? So I can sort of get used to the idea?"

Claudine shook her head. "Slow isn't my style. We don't have time for slow." She gestured behind her. "And now we have all this. Cabins with doors that lock. We can be alone, finally, and I can help you forget. And make you feel good again. I think we deserve that."

She could see the conflict written on his face. Claudine took the garbage out of his hands, one piece at a time, dropping it at their feet. "I can't promise you anything," she said. "But I want to try and see if we can still make something beautiful. Just you and me."

When his hands were empty, Claudine took his wrists and wrapped them around her waist. She melted into him, lifting her mouth to his. This time, he participated in the kiss, which felt like progress to Claudine. He tasted like dried halibut, and smelled like wood smoke. His body was strong and solid next to hers. Claudine wouldn't rush this moment, as she was getting exactly what she wanted here with Spence, but still her mind raced ahead. With the bicycle wheels, she could create a wind power turbine that would charge the batteries enough to make outside contact. If she could reach other people, everyone in their little town would have fresh choices, and Claudine would be the one to provide them with those options.

# seventy

## HARPREET

Harpreet watched as Jasper took his turn pressing the button on the black radio Claudine had built.

"Hello?" he said. "Is anyone there?"

Static. He shook his head, putting the handpiece down on the rec room table. Min continued riding the bike with the flat tires, which Jasper had propped up on a stand and Claudine had rigged to one of the large batteries from the yacht.

"It's probably the rain, interfering with the signal," said Spence. He'd been saying this kind of thing more and more, to make Claudine feel better that so far her communication system had failed to make any contact. Claudine smiled at him, then reached out for his hand. She looked at Spence like there was no one else in the room, which gave Harpreet another stab of envy, like the one she felt watching Min and Jasper. These couples made her think of the beginning, with Malik, when she still believed a happily-ever-after ending was possible. Before they had reached their first wedding anniversary, Harpreet had to ice down her swollen jaw and her first split lip. She had bought a dress he thought was too revealing. That first punch hurt more than all the other ones to come, because it meant her romantic dreams had vaporized, and Harpreet was left with nothing to believe in.

She didn't realize she was shivering until Tony got up from

his spot by Beth and came over to Harpreet. He held out his blanket, made of furs loosely stitched together. Harpreet shook her head, but Tony settled it around her shoulders anyway. She knew he was worried about her. About the baby, which could come any time now. Harpreet's back ached, along with her feet. She had muscle pain in her abdomen that could be early contractions, but she forced herself not to think about it. Maybe Iris had the right idea after all. Harpreet longed to simply check out mentally as Iris had done, but the baby performing gymnastics inside her body kept her uncomfortably anchored to the present. She knew she could die in childbirth, or the baby could, or both of them at the same time. So many things could go wrong. Hoping for a smooth birth was ludicrous, on an island with no hospital or doctors or surgical suites. Just Tony, and his white plastic medical case.

Tony walked back over to Beth. Harpreet tugged at the furs. She could still feel Tony's eyes on her. Min got down off the bike and approached Harpreet. The rain sounded loud on the leaves and boughs that covered their roof. Fall was here, and winter wouldn't be far away. It was exhausting being wet and cold. The rain made hunting harder, and food scarcer, and the daily chores took longer and were more frustrating to complete. She sighed. A surge of pain gripped Harpreet's side, and she shifted on the log bench to try to find a more comfortable position.

Min sat beside her. "Can I help?" she asked. "What can I do, Harpreet?"

Harpreet shook her head. "There's nothing anyone can do." Since she'd landed on this beach, Harpreet thought of suicide every single day. When she cooked, Harpreet cradled the knife in her right hand, imagining where she would cut into her left wrist, and how the blood would drip down to pool into the ground. When she bathed, she looked up at the cliff above her head, fantasizing about stepping off it in the middle of the night, crushing the baby on the rocks below. When she went to the creek to get her cooking water, she thought about the nearby game trails, and how it might feel to be ripped limb from limb by a black bear or a wolf. But somehow the weeks had slipped by, and she hadn't done it. Lately someone always shadowed her: either Min or Jasper or Tony or even Beth, her bright blue eyes peering at Harpreet from a distance. It was as if they all knew she was in danger, but as her belly strained against her skin, this fact was obvious to everyone.

Claudine kept saying she would make contact with the mainland, and they would be rescued in time for Harpreet to have her baby in more civilized conditions. Now the radio was supposedly working, but whenever they tried it, at all hours of the day or night, no one had answered. Harpreet knew it was entirely possible no one else was out there. And she wasn't sure she would want to go back, even if she could. Was it better to stay here, with these mostly kind and resourceful people, and wait to die knowing you weren't alone? Or should she spare them the pain of her death, and make it someone else's problem?

Harpreet turned her head to look at Min. She never stopped trying to help. Her heart was so good, so transparently pure. "Do you think I should go back to the mainland, if Claudine's radio works and someone answers us? Would you go, if you were the one having a baby?"

Min considered the question. Harpreet liked watching her think, with her brow furrowed in concentration. There were other conversations happening in the rec room, muffled by the sound of the rain, but Harpreet focused only on Min's lined and intelligent face. Suddenly, whatever she had to say seemed crucially vital and important.

When she spoke, Min's voice was gentle, her expression sad. "Everything's a risk. Staying here, having a baby in these primitive conditions, with only Tony for medical help, has got to be very scary for you. But even if you could go home to Victoria, or to Vancouver if it's dried out and livable again, it doesn't mean that's any safer. There might be lots of Rons, who want everything to go back to the way it was before the collapse, which could be worse for women like you and me. At least here, we can make our own society, and try our very best to make it fair for everyone, or certainly better than the one we came out of."

This was the longest speech Harpreet had ever heard her make. In her gut, Harpreet felt that Min was right. Out there didn't hold the promise for Harpreet that it seemed to extend for Claudine, Spence, Diamond, and Kanda. It was as if the four of them had smoothed down the rough edges of the previous world, believing from their months here that they had more power and influence now than they did before. They seemed to believe that they could step into some kind of leadership role that wasn't open to them earlier, but would be this time. Harpreet knew that power didn't work like that. Those who had it once always craved it again, and were never willing to share it. The men who had been at the top would do anything to get there again. Spilling more blood would be meaningless to them. They'd done it before, and they would do it again.

Harpreet looked around the circle, at the other nine faces. Now Diamond rode the bike, singing a cowboy song while pretending to ride a bull. Claudine was clustered around her precious radio, with Spence and Kanda nearby. Tony and Beth had their heads close together, whispering, his mouth turned up in a grin. Harpreet could hear Beth giggle at whatever he had to say. Iris sat alone near the door, a patchwork quilt on her knees, that familiar vacant emptiness behind her eyes. She had been losing weight, not eating much at their group meals, and Harpreet knew it would just be a matter of time until she slipped away. Once the will to live had been lost, the body began to shut down.

Jasper sat across the room, watching Min. His face was bright with love. Min was a lucky woman, and Harpreet wished her well. Min wrapped her arm around Harpreet, pulling her close, like she could sense that Harpreet needed to be brought back into this physical space, to feel loved and cared for. Harpreet laid her head on Min's soft shoulder. No matter what happened to her, if Harpreet's baby survived, the child would be taken care of. Min would make sure of that. The thought warmed Harpreet up, pushing the shards of fear further away, offering her a temporary reprieve.

# seventy-one

## JASPER

The weather was getting colder, and wetter, and still Claudine's radio didn't find anyone on the other end of it. Jasper had mixed feelings about this. On one hand, he felt disappointed for the young folks, who had placed so much faith in this lifeline to a bigger society, but on the other, he was relieved. Jasper didn't want to go anywhere. He had everything he had ever wanted right here.

When they were cleaning out the yacht, searching in every nook and cranny of the three-storey vessel for anything and everything they could use to survive, Kanda had broken open a locked compartment to reveal a stack of American cash. Under it (and much more valuable out here), was a bundle of seed packets. She called out to Min, who had been scrubbing the galley kitchen with a bright yellow sponge, and Min took off at a run to the little desk where Kanda stood. Jasper had been collecting sheets and blankets from the cabins. He knew he'd never forget the look of wonder on Min's face as she sorted through the envelopes. Seeds for sunflowers, daisies, and marigolds, but more importantly, stacks of envelopes containing vegetable seeds. Carrots, peas, cauliflower, beans, onions, potatoes. This discovery changed everything for the town. Now they could grow food in the spring, which gave them significant and exciting long-term nutrition possibilities. Jasper held

Min close as she cried from joy, the faded packets clutched in her hands.

She and Jasper found a suitable patch of forest soil, not far from the bathing cove, and they spent a lot of time there getting the land ready to plant. Many days, they were both soaked to the skin from the chilly autumn rain, but still they worked, clearing the undergrowth, chopping down trees to give the soil more sunlight, and tilling the black soil to get it ready for seeds.

Jasper loved working side by side with Min. They had a shorthand between them, where no words needed to be said but they both seemed to understand what the other person was thinking. It felt like magic. He would get lost, watching her capable hands in the soil, knowing she was dreaming of eating their harvest one day. And now that Harpreet had joined the town, they had a chef in their midst who not only knew how to cook, but actually enjoyed doing it. He knew it wasn't a good idea to plan too far ahead out here. Jasper did his level best to take things day by day, but when he looked at Min, his attraction to her flared, and he longed to be even closer to her.

He knew she was afraid to be intimate with him. At first, Jasper thought this was due to her exhaustion out here, and her ongoing digestive issues, which he put down to stress because Min felt responsible for everyone. For a little while, he worried that her hesitancy to go beyond kissing and sleeping next to each other in the shelter was due to him, some physical flaw that was obvious to her, but Jasper was unaware of in himself. He had done his best to wait until she might be ready, biding his time like he used to in the before world, when he had willingly handed over his agency to others. His ex-wife. His grown daughters. His white bosses. Until he landed on this island, Jasper had spent his whole existence apologizing for his Indigeneity. When he started to fall in love with Min and saw that she also had feelings for him, he thought all of that insecurity was behind him. But now, he felt a searing shame in the core of his being that she didn't want to have sex with him.

"Is something wrong, my darling?" Min asked.

Jasper looked up, from his spot on the other side of the newly tilled vegetable patch, to where Min had paused in her work to study his face. He wondered if his expression was as strained as he felt inside. Jasper couldn't begin to imagine how to answer her question. The love he had for her was like a fountain, bubbling up in the core of his body, but even with Min, he still felt different. Like he might not belong, and could, at any moment, be cast aside.

He hung his head, hoping she wouldn't see the tears stinging his eyes. Quickly, she was there, by his side, wiping her dirty hands on her baggy jeans, then cupping his face with her hands. "Jasper." When she said his name, it sounded like music. The tenderness of the word never failed to move him. "Please tell me. Whatever it is, I want to hear it."

The tears didn't stop, and the words were all jumbled up in Jasper's mind. How could he possibly say that he was afraid she would never care for him enough to have sex with him? That he was good enough for now, but not for her to give her whole self to him? He wanted to accept that whatever she could give him was enough, but watching Diamond and Kanda head off to the yacht, hand in hand in the middle of the afternoon, or waking in the night to hear Claudine and Spence in the throes of passion, made Jasper painfully aware of his own inadequacies with Min.

"Are you thinking of leaving with the young ones if someone answers on the radio? Is that what's upsetting you? Because I would like to stay here, but only if it's with you. If you want to leave, I'll go, too. I love you, so I won't be able to be apart from you." Now she was crying along with him.

Jasper cleared his throat. He shook his head. "No, I don't want to leave. I love living here. I love being with you. I love you."

"But something is wrong."

He smiled, wanting to refute it, to stay on safe ground, but he felt his body stirring, betraying him.

Min glanced down. Jasper tried to turn away, but she put her hands on his arms and looked up into his face. Gently, Min said, "Oh, Jasper, it's Harpreet, you see. Her baby. I'm still bleeding, even though I'm fifty, and however unlikely it may be, the thought of getting pregnant out here terrifies me. It's too big of a risk. When we searched high and low in that yacht, I was desperately hoping to find condoms so we could be together. It's not you, my love. I'm sorry I didn't say this to you earlier."

Relief flooded him like the tide. He gazed into her flushed, yet beautiful face, then kissed her. Slowly, with all the passion he couldn't contain in his body.

"But Min, my heart, after my three daughters were born, I had a vasectomy. If you are with me, there will be no babies. Just us. You and me."

He watched the surprise, and then the dawning joy steal across her face. Min laughed, the sound of pure hope and possibility, then lay down in the middle of their dark, rich, moist soil and pulled Jasper to her.

# seventy-two

## MIN

They took a vote, and decided to eat tonight's dinner outside, by the fire. The driving rain cleared up in the late afternoon, making life easier all around for everyone. After so many days of being sodden and wet, to be dry for a few hours felt like a miracle.

Min was setting a stack of plates on the small table Jasper had built. He was tending to the fire, adding wood that Spence had chopped earlier in the day, and he looked up and grinned at Min. She felt her face turn red, thinking of what they had been doing together in the vegetable patch, and Min hoped no one else was looking at her. She sat down on her log, the first place she'd ever sat on this beach, when it seemed like she might be the only person alive in the entire world. But of course she wasn't. Iris came next, and then her sweet Jasper, followed by Claudine and Ainsley. After that was Diamond, with Tony, who had saved Jasper's life, so Min felt she owed him everything. Min thought of them as the key components of the town, because Spence and Kanda talked so early on with Claudine and Diamond about leaving this place. But it was impossible to think about Tony now without imagining Beth, for she hardly ever left his side. And there was also Harpreet, but for Min she remained a question mark, with the upcoming birth of her baby casting a shadow of anxiety over everyone.

Spence and Claudine had brought the bike and the batteries outside, setting it up on the far side of the bonfire. Kanda was riding it now, with Diamond pressing the radio buttons and calling for help every few minutes. Their energy for this project was boundless. Min wished all four of them well. They could visualize a future for themselves back in some form of civilization. Each one of them, in their own way, wanted a chance to lead. To grow into themselves. Min had no idea if it would be possible, or if the after world would function just like the before world did. She herself had no interest in finding out.

Beth and Tony were throwing a football they had found in the yacht. "Not too close to the fire, little one," Tony cautioned, as they moved farther down the beach. Min thought about all the dangers out here. The ones they had seen, and the ones they had yet to see. A rogue wave had already washed their camp out once, taking beautiful Ainsley back out to sea with it, forcing the town to rebuild. Animals were harder to come by these days, as the weather changed from hot and dry to cool and rainy, so they might be in for a lean winter. But in the spring, they would grow vegetables. And flowers. The very idea made Min feel happy.

Min looked at Iris, who sat on the ground by the bathing cove. She was alone, lost in her thoughts, cut off and adrift from the rest of them. Min had been taking care of Iris, the best she could, but Jasper kept reminding her to hold loosely. For so much of Min's life, she had fought to control the outcome, to make circumstances bend to her own will. But she was learning that you couldn't do that out here and expect to stay sane. It was too hard, too painful, too exhausting. Min was trying to preserve her own strength. Out here, you could give to others, but only after you made sure you had what you needed to survive. It had felt selfish to Min at first, but now she knew it was the key to making it. You had to snatch little moments of joy wherever you could find them, and not plan too far into the future. She was learning that this moment was all she had, and she wanted to stay present and anchored in it.

Harpreet brought out the fried fish, and a small amount of squirrel stew. Spence left Claudine, where she was fiddling with the boat batteries, and took the frying pan and the bowl from Harpreet. She smiled her thanks at him. Min watched as he carried it over to the table. They had made quite a little family for themselves. They fought occasionally, and no one saw eye to eye on any one thing, but the level of care, from one stranger to another, often moved Min to the brink of tears. She wished Dae and Chul could've lived to see this. What would they have thought of Min here, in this rugged and wild environment, where they were establishing new rules and patterns as a town? She knew she'd never know, but Min couldn't help wondering from time to time.

Jasper walked over to rub Min lightly on the back. He still limped, with his scarred-up right leg a visual reminder of the wounds they had all sustained in trying to get here. But he stood tall, not hunched over like when he first arrived, and Min thought he looked strong and sure of himself. She raised her left arm, crossing it over her body to touch his hand. Soon, they would fill their plates and go sit by the fire, but there was no rush. No one had anywhere else to be.

Kanda was still pedaling the bike, the wheels going nowhere but generating enough electricity to slowly charge the batteries to run the radio. Diamond passed the handset over to Claudine, who cradled it in her hand like a newborn. She believed so badly that someone would answer her call, and make it possible to live another kind of life; one much bigger than this mysterious island could offer them.

Spence called out, "Dinner time!" Beth caught Tony's last throw of the football, and they made their way over to the table, stopping to help Iris to her feet first. Min stood, turning around to kiss Jasper, savouring the comfort she felt in his solid presence. Kanda, Claudine, and Diamond stayed by the radio, unable to quit just yet, even for the promise of hot food. Over and over again, Claudine said, "Hello? Is anyone there? Can anyone hear me?"

As Min ladled her stew, she watched the waves rolling into their beach, grateful that she was no longer out on the water. The yacht bobbed in the current, with the little rowboat on the opposite side of the dock. Birds sang in the trees. The sun was low in the sky. The fire crackled and spat, promising warmth for Min's cold skin. She remembered how stunned she felt when she first saw these trees from her raft. The leaves so green and full, offering a respite from the punishing heat of the summer. Min didn't know then that she would find new love here. And friendship. A fresh beginning, for a woman who had almost surrendered completely to her grief. But she was still here. All ten of them were.

When everyone but the comms crew had dished up, they sat around the fire pit, on the chairs and logs that Jasper and Tony had built together. The conversation flowed, about nothing and everything, at the exact same time, and Min was content to simply listen. Harpreet smiled at Min, a fork halfway to her lips, and Min smiled back. Beth pretended to feed Tony, and he behaved like a toddler having a tantrum, stamping his feet and clamping his mouth shut, which made Beth laugh. Spence offered Iris a spoonful of stew, which she refused by turning her face toward the water, so he ate it instead. Jasper leaned his shoulder against Min, letting her know without words that he was there. Diamond stood behind Kanda, wrapping their arms around her waist as she rode the bike.

Claudine pressed the black button. "Hello? Anyone there? We really want to reach someone. Please answer if you're there."

Min nodded at Claudine, trying to encourage her across the dancing flames, when the static faded, then disappeared. Min held her breath, along with everyone else in the town.

After a few seconds of silence, they heard a buzzy crackling sound, and then a man's voice, clear and bold, like he could be standing in the next room.

"Hello from Vancouver."

## author's note

The idea for this novel came out of my frustration during the fever dream that was the Trump presidency. First, I felt angry at how far we still needed to go to create an equal and fair society, and then I became despondent that it might not even be possible to achieve egalitarianism under the hierarchical structures of patriarchy and capitalism. So I decided to destroy it all—through climate disasters, civil war, cyberterrorism, pandemics, and other horrors—and start over with a handful of survivors, to see if they could build something better.

Writers are steadfastly advised not to write from the perspective of characters where they have no lived experience. I think this is good advice, designed to encourage writers to tell stories from a place of authentic knowledge, but this story demanded that I break this rule. I wrote with great care and concern, asking for help from a lot of different people who knew more than I did in a variety of areas, but I fully acknowledge that some mistakes have likely been made. For these errors, I take full responsibility, and where I missed the mark or may have caused offense, I am truly sorry.

I felt a lot of fear while writing this. I tried to imagine losing everyone I love and everything I count on for safety and security. I leaned into my subconscious while I wrote, learning to trust that my intuition knew the way. And as the town began to grow and flourish in this fictional after world, I found myself feeling genuine hope. For a long time now, I've wanted to believe that a fair and equal world was possible, but I couldn't begin to describe how it would look or feel or function. *Post Civ* is my attempt to imagine this possibility. I hope you find the story as healing to read as I found to write it.

# acknowledgements

I dreamed up these twelve characters and the overall storyline for *Post Civ* toward the end of my BA program at Kwantlen Polytechnic University in my Writers Studio class. Big thanks to Ross Laird for his help and enthusiasm as I created a TV series-style bible for this project in his class.

This manuscript was my thesis project for my Master of Fine Arts in Creative Writing degree at the University of British Columbia. I had the best possible thesis advisor for this work—the brilliant and kind Taylor Brown-Evans—who told me to write the book I longed to write. I did exactly that, under his expert guidance, and I'm so grateful to him for his belief in me and his steadfast support through several rounds of revisions.

I also want to thank my MFA friends from my Spec Fic class with Nalo Hopkinson (who served as my thesis committee second reader) for reading the opening chapters and giving such helpful and warm feedback to me. You really boosted my confidence to keep going with this story.

Indie publishing is hard work, but it's made lighter and easier by partnering with fun and talented people. I want to thank Karen Ydenberg White for her editing prowess; Dani Compton for another incredibly beautiful cover design (plus her guidance on all things boats); Jan Westendorp of Kato Design and Photo for the ebook and general tech assistance; Gage Rodelander and the book department at Digital Direct Printing for the interior design and the paperback book; and Jessica Bondy of Bondy Books for keeping Ruby Finch Books in tip-top shape on the financial side. I couldn't do this without my kick-ass team.

I'm grateful to each one of you for your encouragement, knowledge, and support.

Gratitude goes to Lauren Abramo and Anthony Oliveira for permission to use the epigraph, which served as a key inspiration for the story.

Thank you to Liz for her medical advice, Justin Schultz for the cover images, and my son William for my author photo.

I can't write an acknowledgements section without thanking Toby Welch, my long-time writing mentor/ Mucho Burrito buddy, or Kari Steenhart, my nurturing pal who can achieve miracles with my hair. Every girl should have friends of this calibre who get excited about every word I write. Thank you so much for all of your cheerleading. I need it and I love it.

To my family: Jason, Ava, William, and Teddy. You are my world. I love you forever and always. Extra thanks to Jason for early reading and for your knowledge about building radios and powering them.

Thank you to each one of my creative writing students. I learn as much from you as I hope you learn from me.

A huge thanks to public libraries for ordering my books and inviting me to teach writing classes in your meeting rooms. Librarians and library patrons are truly the best people.

And to the reader, thank you for picking up this book and giving it a try. I'm so grateful to you. May the dream of a kinder, better, fairer world be possible for each and every one of us.

## questions for discussion

1. Which character do you identify with the most? Why do they resonate for you?

2. Why do you think some people flourish in this after world and some people struggle?

3. How might you function on this mysterious island if you lost everyone you love and were forced to give up every comfort you've enjoyed in our modern world?

4. Which aspect of our current civilization would you miss the most in this after world?

5. Do you share many of the fears for our current world that are explored here in this novel? What concerns you the most?

6. Would you choose to stay on the island or leave to re-join others on the mainland? Why?

7. What do you imagine happens to these characters after they make radio contact with the mainland?

## about the author

*Photo by William Harvey*

Julianne Harvey is an author, educator, and nurturer. She is the author of six books and holds an MFA and a BA in Creative Writing, along with a Certificate in Counselling Skills. Julianne works with teachers, librarians, writers, and readers on creative practices, writing, and wellness. She lives in Vancouver, BC with her family and one unruly, badly behaved cat.

julianneharvey.com | rubyfinchbooks.com